HUGE GAMES

A FAKE-DATING FRIENDS-TO-LOVERS REVERSE HAREM ROMANCE

STEPHANIE BROTHER

HUGE GAMES Copyright © 2024
STEPHANIE BROTHER

All Rights Reserved. This book or any portion thereof may not be reproduced or used in any manner whatsoever without the express permission of the publisher except for the use of brief quotations in a book review.

This book is a work of fiction. Any resemblance to persons, living or dead, or places, events or locations is purely coincidental. The characters are all productions of the author's imagination.

Please note that this work is intended only for adults over the age of 18 and all characters represented as 18 or over.

Chapter divider by Vecteezy.com

ISBN: 9798876386052

1

CELINE

"Eddie is the biggest rodent in the northern hemisphere." Gabriella rests her hand on my arm and reaches for a tissue from the box on my dresser, handing it to me before I ruin my makeup.

I dab under my eyes, and grimace. I hate crying in front of people. I'm not usually this broken and pathetic, but I invested a lot of time in the relationship I had with the cheating bastard who has now become my ex, and that wasted time makes me mad as hell.

I didn't want to get serious with him. From the very beginning, I told him I wanted to be free at college, not shackled to the first guy I met freshman year. But he wouldn't let me break up with him. Any time I tried to pull back so we could branch out and see other people, he'd find a way to pull me back in. The man had the sex drive of three average men, and I feel like I've spent most of the last couple of years beneath him in one way or another.

Don't get me wrong, he wasn't bad in bed. The asshole could fuck. But pleasure from fucking, and emotional satisfaction are two very different things. I just didn't feel connected to him, and other than wanting to be up inside my body every half an hour, I didn't feel like he really saw the important parts of me.

Then he cheated, and all our time together suddenly seemed so futile.

I'm mad at him, but I'm mostly mad at myself. I want to erase him from my memory and go back to seize all the months I wasted, but life doesn't come with a do-over, no matter how much we wish it did.

I sniff and wipe my nose. My eyes are bloodshot but still passably made-up. "He might be there tonight."

Ellie, who's sitting on my bed with her legs crossed and one foot shaking, meets my eyes in the mirror.

"What are you going to do if he is?"

She's asking the question because we're not just going out for a good time tonight. We're celebrating Dalton getting a place at catering school and it's an occasion I don't want to add any drama to.

"I don't know." It's the truth. My rage is a volcano of trapped lava, a pyroclastic cloud ready to erupt and wipe out all in its path. "Maybe just drink cocktails."

"Cocktails and chocolate are the best when it comes to breakups." Gabriella snaps off a square of the giant bar of Hershey's she brought me today to help with the heartache.

"Cocktails and chocolate are great, but you know what's better?" Ellie's perfectly arched eyebrow raises in question, and she shifts, leaning forward and grinning like she's about to share the most excellent gossip. Her dark hair falls over her shoulder and her tongue darts out to wet the bottom of her lip.

"What?" I swivel on my stool and ball up the damp tissue in my fist.

"Rebound sex." With a slight shrug, she makes her suggestion seem entirely innocent.

Gabriella snickers. "Ellie!"

"What? It's not like Celine hasn't wanted to experience other guys. Eddie smothered her for way too long. It's time for her to spread her wings."

"You mean my legs," I mutter.

I tip my head at an awkward angle to hear Gabriella's response. She gestures openly with her hands. "I mean, good alternative sex can be freeing…like wiping the slate clean. But it can also be messy." Ellie snorts and Gabriella rolls her blue eyes, crossing her arms across her chest. "You know me… I'm not a one-night-with-a-stranger kind of girl. When I was hungry for sex, I went next door, and Ellie just crossed the hall."

We all laugh at the strange truth of that statement. Gabriella's in a relationship with three of her neighbors who are brothers, and her brother's best friends. Ellie's shacked up with her triplet stepbrothers and she has a little boy called Noah. They might be lazy about where they found their men, but with three each, that's where the laziness ends!

"Yes," Ellie gasps. "Get-over-the-asshole-ex-sex needs to be safe and satisfying."

Shaking my head, I rise on weary legs to find my shoes at the bottom of my closet. Going out tonight and painting on a smile feels as appealing as entering hell through flaming gates, whilst being pelted by crap, but I'll do it for my friend.

"So, you're saying cocktails and cock are the solutions to my current misery?"

I slide my feet into uncomfortable sandals, adding three inches to my average height and making me feel more powerful as a result.

Ellie and Gabriella look at each other and then turn to me.

"Nothing makes what you're going through easier

except time and perspective," Ellie says. "You're on a new path now. One that Eddie isn't steering anymore. So you do whatever you like. It's your time."

I blink, staring between my friends.

My time.

No time has felt like my time since Mom and Dad called it quits on their marriage. Now, all I do is worry about whether Mom is lonely or if Dad will ever call me or come to visit again.

I don't want to be in this swirly vortex of other people's emotions and demands. I want to call the shots for a change.

"My time. I like that."

Gabriella stares pertinently at Ellie as though she's worried her comment has unleashed a monster. The tears that have burned against the front of my throat for weeks lessen with a swallow and a deep breath.

I smooth my hands over my dress and fluff my hair, glancing into the mirror to check my mass of red curls. They look like they usually do: wild and crazy.

"I guess it's time to go."

At the bar, the music is pumping, and the lights are flashing, casting the moving crowd in rainbow colors. We head over to the back, where our group has already gathered. Colby, one of Ellie's triplet boyfriends, pulls her against him and kisses her forehead possessively. She's passed to Sebastian and Micky and given the same princess treatment. Gabriella immediately seeks out Dalton, Kain, and Blake, her own harem of men, wrapping her arms around them in turn for a long embrace. I stand behind like a spare part, scanning the crowd for someone who can make me feel like I belong even a little. Dornan is leaning against the wall, talking to Gabriella's brother, Travis, and I make a beeline to my friend.

I know Dornan well. We've been friends, through Ellie, since freshman year. His size makes him an overwhelming presence but as soon as he speaks, his face softens and his eyes light up, and all the menace that makes him an invaluable member of the football team, slips away.

"Hey." I touch Dornan's arm, interrupting what sounded like a conversation about sport. His sky-blue eyes find mine and crinkle at the corners.

"There she is." He throws his massive arm around my shoulder and tugs me against his solid chest with vigorous affection. I half-grin, half-grimace at Travis as I'm squashed like a beetle. Dornan doesn't seem to be conscious of his immense strength.

"Hi," I squeak.

"Hi, Celine." Travis uses his hand to brush over his neatly trimmed, light brown beard as he studies me. I didn't think he'd remember my name. We've only met a couple of times, and he generally keeps to himself.

"Hi, Travis." His eyes are a deeper shade of blue than Dornan's, like dark sapphires, and they sparkle beneath his fair brows and lashes. It's weird looking at him because he seems more familiar than he should, probably because of how much he looks like his younger sister, Gabriella.

"You guys took your time. I swear Gab left to go get you three hours ago."

"A girl needs time to look her best," I say, but my eyes are already roving for Eddie. If he's here, I want to find him so that I can avoid him. I need to know where he is before he spots me.

Travis turns, glancing over his shoulder, and his light blue shirt pulls over the very nice muscles of his chest and arms. I haven't ever told my bestie that I think her brother is a hottie, mainly because of Eddie and because it feels a little weird to lust over your friend's older brother.

I haven't told Ellie that I think Dornan's sexy, either. Well, maybe sexy is the wrong word for a man who's more wall than human. He's got the kind of masculine presence that feels safe, like a hug but as solid as granite. The funny thing is, he's a big softy underneath all the brawn.

"He's over there." Dornan indicates the far corner with a jerk of his head, where a large group of the football team and their cheerleader-type girlfriends are gathered around a table. Eddie isn't visible from where I'm standing, but I guess Dornan saw him arrive.

"Who?" Travis turns, completely unaware.

"My ex." Blood spreads heat over my fair skin.

"Oh. An ex you want to avoid?"

"At all costs."

Travis nods, and Dornan gives me a reassuring squeeze. "The douche cheated on my girl. Can you believe he'd have the audacity?"

One of Eddie's friends laughs raucously and almost falls off the tiny stool he's sitting on, and I shiver. Travis's expression turns grim, his strong jaw ticking like a heartbeat.

"Fuck people who cheat." It's said with so much venom that my head jerks back in surprise.

"Yeah. Fuck them," Dornan agrees.

If I could kiss them both right now without it being weird, I would. I swear, the number of dudes I know who have cheated on their girlfriends is obscenely high. I don't know why I thought I'd experience anything different. Men have a problem, otherwise known as a dick, and they can't help themselves. I think there is something very wrong with Eddie because we'd fuck twice a day, most days, and he still found the time and the urge to wander.

"I need a drink."

The bar is way over the other side of the dance floor, which seems like ten miles away in my ridiculous shoes, and moving from where I am, sheltered between Dornan and Travis, feels risky. Maybe sensing my unease, Dornan steers me so his body shields me. "I'll come with you."

"Me, too." Travis leads the way and clears the dancing throngs like Moses parting the Red Sea.

At the bar, I order two of my favorite peachy cocktails and drink them both so fast, I gasp from the immense brain freeze.

"Easy, tiger." Travis orders me another and pays before either Dornan or I can offer. Dornan tips his beer at Travis gratefully, and I sneak a sideways glance at Travis's profile, watching his throat move as he swallows down his drink. Damn, there's something really masculine about him. Maybe the extra years he has are enough to set him apart. He has that strong jaw and brow thing about him that's seriously sexy, and his biceps are more than lickable.

"So, what's the plan?" Dornan leans against the bar, still using his body to shield me from Eddie. "Are you going to hide out over here all night because that cocksucker is marking his territory over there?"

"You think he's there on purpose?" Travis asks, resting his beer on the wet bar top.

"He knows Celine is hanging out tonight. I caught him listening while I was talking about it with Ellie in the coffee shop earlier. There are plenty of other places he could have chosen to go with his friends, but he happens to pick this place where he can intimidate Celine."

"I'm not intimidated." Without thinking about it, I draw myself taller and push my shoulders back.

"Down girl." Dornan touches my arm, his big, rough hand warm against my skin. "Maybe intimidated is too strong. Where he can make his presence felt."

"I'm done with him. I don't care where he is."

"So, let's get back over there."

For all my bravado, I'm not eager to face Eddie, especially in front of everyone. But Dornan is looking at me expectantly, and I don't want to lose face in front of Travis. Ellie's words are still simmering in my alcohol-loosened mind. Rebound sex seems mercenary, but maybe a little fun could help take my mind off things and show Eddie how unbothered I am by his infidelity.

As I follow Dornan back across the room, sipping on my peach cocktail with Travis at my side, the alcohol makes me wobble. Yowzah! I'm going too fast, or maybe it's my mood combined with the drink that has me spinning out of control.

Ellie grins at me from where she's resting with her back against Colby's front. Her stepbrother-boyfriend has his arm across her chest, protectively holding her in place and sending the 'mine' signal to anyone looking. A pang of envy shoots through me. Eddie was never like that with me. He'd be sexual in front of other people, grabbing my ass or groping beneath my shirt, and I'd swat him away, but there was never any protectiveness in the way he treated me in public.

Dornan stops to talk to Colby, and Travis slides into a booth. I crane to look in the direction of Eddie's table, and my head spins. My feet seem to get tangled, and suddenly, I'm stumbling right into a huge, rock-hard chest. Big beefy arms close around me, and I scramble to stabilize myself, grabbing handfuls of soft, warm shirt.

When I look up to see who's holding me like a log, I find Elias staring down at me with one dark eyebrow cocked.

Elias. Fuck.

A flash of him hefting me against him with just one hand and then pinning me against the wall momentarily blinds me. The furious way he fucked me knocked the breath from my lungs then, and the memory of it does the same.

"You're drunk."

"I'm fine." I try to push away as his onyx eyes bore into me, deciding something different, but he lifts me like a sack of potatoes and tosses me into the booth next to Travis. I brace my hands on the cool table before me, my mouth hanging open. Angry, indignant words catch in my throat, but Elias grins as he slides in next to me as though he intends to use his big, strong, unbelievably muscular, sexy body to block me from leaving the booth.

Idiot.

The picture of Eddie cheating flashes into my mind. He was in a booth like this with his tongue rammed down another girl's throat and his hand up her shirt.

Distantly, Travis asks me if I'm okay. I blink as his familiar blue eyes, filled with concern, trail over me. If Eddie can do it, so can I.

Without seriously considering the impact of my actions, I shift closer to Travis and press my lips against his. We both have our eyes open so I can see his surprise, but then he moves his mouth over mine in a sensual, slow, spine-tingling kiss, pushing his hand into my long hair and pulling me closer.

My head spins, but this time, it isn't from the cocktails. It's all Travis.

The scruff on his chin scratches my face in an arousing way, and when his tongue slides against mine, my pussy clenches between my thighs.

Jeez. Gabriella's brother has skills.

"Come on, Celine. You don't need to be doing that..." Elias's huge hand scoops me around my middle, and he hauls me off Travis. I blink, woozy in too many ways, turning to rail against the interrupter of my fun. Except, when I do, I find Elias's expression is quizzical rather than aggressive or judgmental. He has a smile playing at the corner of his mouth and eyes that seem to light with amusement.

"Celine." The way he says my name is like melted chocolate, and I'm immediately transported back to his dorm, where he moaned it loudly as he came inside me. It was a one-time thing when Eddie and I were on a break, a one-time thing that shattered every preconception I had about Elias. In daylight hours, he's a bear with a sore head with enough snark to cut through steel, but by night, he's a man of determined passion.

Those lips did things to me I can't think about without messing my panties.

I kiss him before the ramifications of my actions have time to register. The familiarity in how he kisses me back is like slipping into a warm bath with a glass of wine.

Jeez. Elias kisses me like he's searching for my soul in the rubble of my mind. His hand clasps my hip, and in a flash, I'm on his lap, straddling his big, solid body, pawing at him like we're alone and naked rather than in a bar, surrounded by our nearest and dearest.

A hand rests on my shoulder, pulling me back, and Dornan's voice cuts through the passion. "Hey, Celine..." I blink up at him, finding soft, concerned eyes. His blond hair flops as he tries to help me stand. "It's okay. You're okay." He's always the one looking after everyone. As soon as I'm on my feet, I grab the back of his neck, rising on my tiptoes to kiss him, too.

It's stupid. He's my friend. We've been through a lot together, and he's shown himself to be a good and reliable person. I don't need to mess with good relationships because a bad one turned sour.

But instead of shoving me away and telling me to stop, Dornan kisses me back, and it's good. So good.

I moan as he pulls me closer, his huge hand on my ass.

But before I have a chance to enjoy the experience fully, a familiar voice cuts through the bliss. "Come on, you guys. Pack it in." Ellie pries us apart with surprisingly strong hands.

Dornan blinks as though he's emerging from the depths of hell into the midday sunshine, and I sway as a broad smile breaks out across my face. I turn to my friend, suddenly feeling lighter than I have all evening.

"What's wrong, Ellie? I'm just gathering my own harem."

She grimaces, and pity widens her eyes and makes her shoulder rise in a dismissive shrug. "I don't think that's how it works, sweetie." When she pats me on the shoulder, words that would cut slash through my mind. Somehow, even though I'm drunk, I manage to keep a handle on them.

"You know, those drinks have gone right to my head." I laugh, and it sounds a little unhinged, then I laugh some more because it's funny as shit.

"I think you need some water, honey."

As I follow Ellie into an empty booth and, as she tells Seb to get us a bottle, a different idea about what I need forms into a plan.

2

DORNAN

"I don't know what to do with her," Ellie says, waving her arm in Celine's direction. "She's a mess."

"She's okay. Just hurting. All it will take is a little time."

"A little time while she kisses her way, or worse, around campus?"

"She's just getting back on the horse." I fold in my lips, remembering how Celine's mouth felt against mine. The passion in her kiss. The way I felt it from the roots of my hair to the tip of my dick. The way it felt so completely right.

Jeez.

Ellie doesn't know, but I've been crushing on Celine since I first laid my eyes on her. She was draped over Eddie's lap, and he had his hand up her shirt, so she wasn't exactly available, but that didn't matter. She was pretty and fiery and funny as hell. She flicked all my switches and more.

But for some crazy reason, she stayed with that idiot, going back to him over and over despite the fact he was a terrible person. Everybody could see it except Celine.

When we suggested that maybe she'd be better off without him, she seemed to double down and stay with him longer. She didn't want to face up to the fact that she chose wrong or admit it to anyone else.

And now here she is, wasted and floundering, her vulnerability peeking out from behind a mask.

"I can take her home."

Ellie touches my arm in a gentle thank you. "I would, but I need to get back to Noah, and Gabriella needs to stay for Dalton."

"It's no problem."

As I kiss Ellie goodbye, Elias moves to the booth Celine is currently sleeping in, touching her arm to bring her around. Over my dead body is he going near Celine when she's in this state.

"Hey," I say, covering the ground between us in four long strides.

"What?" Elias turns as Celine cracks one eye open, looking around like she can't focus on anything.

"I'm taking Celine home."

"Like fuck you are."

"What's that supposed to mean?"

"She's wasted. I'm going to take her home."

"So you can finish what you started?"

Elias straightens, drawing himself up to his full height, which is equal to mine. Eye to eye, we both bristle with underlying tension. He's not my favorite person, and even though we play on the same team, I've always felt he's an adversary rather than an ally.

"I hope you're not insinuating what I think you're insinuating because that is fucking sick, Dornan." His eyes are dark and furious, and I immediately feel bad. He might be a moody, prickly asshole, but insinuating he'd violate a drunk woman is a step too far.

"I just want to make sure she gets back safely."

Travis approaches, looking down at Celine, who seems to have fallen asleep again, her red hair tangled around her face and shoulders, making her look like a mermaid washed up on a godforsaken shore.

"She's out for the count," he says.

"And I told Elias I'm going to take her home."

"And I told Dornan I'm going to take her home."

Travis looks between us like an umpire at a table tennis game. "So, who's taking her home?"

"ME!" we both say in unison.

He snorts and shakes his head. "How about we all take her home, and that way, she'll be safe, and you guys won't end up killing each other in the process?"

"That isn't necessary." Elias narrows his eyes. I don't know why he's suddenly so possessive of Celine, but I don't like it.

"I think it's a good idea."

Travis nods. "Now, help me get her up so we can get her to my car."

"You drove?"

"Yeah. I wasn't in the mood to get drunk."

"I'll pick her up," Elias barks, reaching out to get his arms under Celine's body. He lifts her like she weighs nothing and holds her against him like a bride he's carrying over the threshold. I shake my head, frustrated that I'm not getting to be the man who keeps Celine safe. She's my friend, after all.

"This way." Travis heads to the door, kissing his sister goodbye and shaking hands as he goes. Eyes follow us as Elias makes his way through the crowd. I spot Eddie looking on with a smirk on his face. He thinks Celine drank herself into a coma because of him—the smug asshole.

When the cool night air hits, Celine wakes with a long, loud inhale of breath and begins to struggle against Elias's hold. "Hey," he says. "Keep still, or you'll fall."

"What are you doing? Where are you taking me?"

"Home. We're taking you home."

Celine twists to look at me, then spots Travis opening the rear door of his vehicle. "All of you?"

"Yep. You hit the jackpot. Three knights in shining armor."

"My harem." She flings her right arm out expansively and laughs.

Travis cocks a brow, and Elias makes a choking sound. "Right now, we're just a glorified rescue crew."

When Elias lowers Celine to her feet, she shakes her head. "I'm disappointed in you guys. This has the potential to be a seriously hot situation."

"You're drunk." Elias urges her into the car and slides in next to her.

Oh, hell no. I'm not leaving him in the backseat with her while I'm confined to the front. I round the car and slide in on the other side, nudging Celine into the middle.

"Dornan," she squeals. It's not a large car, and Celine is pressed between us like ham between two wedges of bread.

Travis starts the car, turning his head to look at us with an amused smile. "Where to, Celine?"

She recalls her address despite her inebriated state, and Travis puts the car into drive. Music begins to play, and Celine sings along in an adorable but tuneless way. I catch Elias smiling, which is an expression he doesn't make very often, and I'm suddenly hit with the possibility that he might also like Celine in more than a friendly way.

Hell. There's no way I'm letting her go from Eddie's arms into Elias's bed. That's like jumping from the frying pan into the fire.

"This is a tune!" Celine sings at the top of her voice, and I wince as Ellias laughs.

"Has anyone ever told you to audition for America's Got Talent?"

"There's no talent here. Just a whole lot of enthusiasm." She throws her arms wide in a showgirl-style way and nearly clips me and Elias in the face.

"Enthusiasm goes a long way," Travis says, making Elias snort. I guess he agrees.

"I had a great night," Celine half-sings. "Except these stupid shoes hurt my feet, but you guys are all great kissers."

"Thanks." Travis seems genuinely pleased.

I would be, too, if I thought she could remember any of it.

"You're drunk, Celine." Elias folds his arms across his chest, making his biceps bulge in a way Celine notices and appreciates.

"I might be drunk, but I'm not dead."

We all laugh because Celine's pretty funny when she's slurring and abrupt.

We're at her dorm in no time, and Travis throws the car into a spot close to the entrance.

We all exit the vehicle like three bodyguards protecting a celebrity, which Celine seems to like. She links arms with me and then Elias. Travis walks slightly to the side, his expression mostly bland with a side of amusement.

At the door, Celine fumbles around in her purse, then fumbles some more. Her hand grows increasingly erratic as she rummages and doesn't come up with the keys.

"They're not in there," she gasps.

"Give it here." Elias takes her purse and shakes it. The contents make a dull thudding sound, and there is no telltale jangle of keys within it.

"You lost your keys?"

"They were in there. At least, I thought they were."

She tips her face to look up at the window of her room as though she's contemplating doing a Spiderman-style climb up the fascia of the building.

"Well, we're not getting a locksmith out at this hour." Travis looks at his watch to confirm.

"You can stay with me," Elias offers, handing the purse back.

"You can stay with me, Celine." I step forward, placing my hand on her elbow.

"This again, guys. What am I? The mediator?" Travis twists his mouth to the side, considering. "I suggest we get a motel room for Celine."

"Okay," Elias says. "How about Molly's?"

"Sounds good."

Celine seems confused and sways in her ridiculous sandals. As she stumbles into the car's back seat, she starts to laugh. "You know Molly's is where Ellie and Gabriella did the nasty with their boyfriends?"

"Please don't talk about my sister doing the nasty." Travis meets my eyes in the mirror and grimaces.

"Yeah. I'd rather not be reminded that Ellie conceived Noah at Molly's."

"Did she?" Elias finds that amusing enough to crack another smile. I swear, the dude has smiled more tonight than in the past six months.

"Molly's is a dive," I say.

"Yeah, but it's cheap and local." As Travis is paying, and it's already the middle of the night, I don't object.

Celine's head drops to my shoulder on the journey, and she snores gently, making all of us quietly laugh so as not to wake her.

When we pull into Molly's, she's fast asleep. "Shall I carry her?" I ask Elias.

Surprisingly, he agrees, and we work together to get her safely out of the car.

Travis heads to reception to get the key, and we follow slowly, waiting outside so the receptionist doesn't see Celine and fear anything untoward is going on. From an outsider's perspective, three men hiring a room for an unconscious woman is the very definition of red-flag creepy.

"Room one-one-one-nine," Travis says, emerging with the key dangling from his index finger.

He leads the way, and we lumber after him, watching as he unlocks a battered green door and opens a far-from luxurious room.

"She's out for the count." Celine's head rests against my chest, and her face is peaceful.

"I don't think we should leave her," Elias says. "At least one of us should stay."

Travis puts his hands up, palms out, grimacing at the prospect of me and Elias bickering again. "I think we all need to stay. That way, Celine will be in safe hands, and we will have each other as witnesses to what does and does not happen in this room. Plus, I'm dog tired."

"Good point."

Elias steps in to tug down the comforter, and I gently lay Celine on the mattress, arranging her beautiful red hair in a fiery bundle behind her head and covering her gently so I don't disturb her. We stand around, looking down on her like she's Sleeping Beauty, and we're about to duel over who will be the one to wake her. There are only two huge beds in the room and a weird chair that looks like it might fall apart at any second. The carpet has seen better days. I don't know how we're going to all stay here.

I can see Elias and Travis thinking the same thing.

"So, we need to leave Celine to sleep alone."

"Yes," they both reply.

"So, two of us can share the other bed and one of us on the floor?"

"Didn't know you cared." Elias shoots me an amused look, shoving his hands into the pockets of his black jeans.

"Very funny."

"I'll take the floor. You guys know each other better." Travis is already pulling a spare blanket from the closet.

"That doesn't make this better." Elias flops into the chair as though he imagines he'll sleep in it. His bulk makes the chair appear the size of a child's.

Travis wrinkles his nose and sniffs the dark brown fluffy bundle. "I don't think I want to know what people have done on this blanket."

"Take your shirt off, fold it up, and use it as a pillow." It's a surprisingly useful suggestion from Elias.

I flop onto the bed, find my phone, and set an alarm. "I'll sleep for a couple of hours, and then you can have the bed."

Elias nods and rests his head against the wall, closing his eyes.

Travis flicks off the light, and we all settle in the darkness. When I'm just about to fall asleep, Elias says, "She's a good kisser, isn't she?"

"Yeah." Travis's voice sounds like a distant whisper.

"Her ex is such a fucking loser."

"We can agree on that." I turn, trying to make out my teammate's shape in the darkness.

"She deserves so much more."

Again, the creep of jealousy fills me. Celine makes a small sighing sound, and I focus on the curve of her hip and dip of her waist in the darkness. "She does."

"She's going to go off the rails. Last time she broke up with Eddie, she ended up in my bed."

"She what?" I bolt into a seated position because Celine never mentioned anything about spending the night with Elias.

"Yeah. She wanted sex. She was sober. I'm a man. I didn't say no."

"Well, you should have." My anger makes my voice a harsh, low spit.

"If she'd come to you, you would have done the same. And don't try to deny it."

"I would have done the same," Travis admits.

It's hard to face up to the reality that I would have, too. "She's vulnerable. She doesn't need another asshole taking advantage of her like Eddie."

The room goes silent, and after a few more minutes of focusing on Celine's breathing, I fall asleep with the imagined image of her spread out beneath me.

3

CELINE

A loud beeping noise behind me cuts into my sleep like a dagger. I cup my ear with my hand to muffle the sound and open my eyes a crack, finding shadowy shapes I don't recognize in my line of sight.

Despite my pounding head and the fact that my tongue has fastened itself to my palette, I fling myself into a seated position and search the darkness.

"Celine," a husky voice whispers from the shadows. "It's okay. You're okay."

"Celine," another husky voice whispers from my left where I can make out another bed. "It's okay. We took you to a motel. Me, Elias, and Travis."

"A motel." Instinct drives my hands between my legs, but I don't feel any post-fuck soreness or wetness. I'm still fully clothed.

"You lost your keys. Don't you remember?" Elias's voice comes from the end of the bed where I can make out his shadowy shape sitting in a chair.

"I have no idea what you're talking about. Where is Travis?"

"I'm down here," a gruff voice mumbles from the floor. I glance down to find him stretched out on what looks like a bearskin rug, shirtless, with his jeans unbuttoned.

Lordy.

That is one fine stretch of man-torso right there. It's a shame I was too drunk to appreciate the opportunity that surrounds me on all sides.

Elias stands from the chair I can make out at the end of my bed, stretching his huge, muscular arms over his shoulders. He's still wearing his shirt, which is a shame, but even in the darkness and through a layer of gray fabric, I can make out his dinner-plate-size pecs and the tightness of his abs. His athletic physique is still scorched onto my brain from our previous shared night of torrid pleasure.

Dornan rises from the bed and swaps places with Elias.

"You set an alarm so you can switch?" I ask.

"Yep. We've got practice tomorrow. We need at least some sleep."

"So why didn't someone share the bed with me?" There's a beat of silence before I comprehend what gentlemen they've been while I've been in a drunken coma. "Dornan, get over here. You can't sleep in that chair."

"Why Dornan?" Elias, who has already made himself comfortable in the adjacent bed, props himself up on his elbow and fixes his devil-black eyes on me. Even in the dark, they have a strangely opaque reflective quality that sends a shiver up my spine. Those eyes stared into mine as he made me come, and it felt like he turned me inside out emotionally as well as physically.

"Because he's the one in the chair."

"Damn," Elias mutters, flopping onto his back and folding his arms behind his head. "I knew I should have stayed in the chair."

"Stop fighting over Celine." The sound of rustling

follows Travis as he moves to his side.

"Maybe Travis should share with me, and you guys should bunk down together?"

Dornan is already spread out beside me and nudges my arm with his elbow. He's mirrored Elias's posture, and it amuses me how much they are alike, even through their obvious differences.

Elias is all sharp edges with his razor tongue, dark piercing gaze, brows that are like slashes across his forehead, and a sweep of black hair as dark as ink. Dornan is all lightness with his broad smile, blue eyes, and blond hair, which are an angelic contrast to his bulk and height.

They're so different and yet sexy in their own right. More so tonight because I can still remember what it felt like to kiss each of the men sharing the room with me. Their kisses rest like butterflies on my lips.

"I'm sorry about tonight," I say softly.

"What for?" Dornan's fingers brush mine, the contact forming a lump in my throat, which presses up, threatening tears. I don't want to cry in front of them. I don't even want to cry in front of myself.

"For kissing you all like a rabid animal."

"I didn't get rabid animal vibes." Dornan twists to grin at me in the dark.

"Yeah. It brought back nothing but good memories for me." Elias turns, too, and shoots me the wicked smile that seduced me in the first place.

"No complaints." When I lean over the edge of the bed, Travis is grinning. He presses two fingers to his lips and holds them in the air like he captured my kiss on their tips.

Jeez.

Not what I was expecting.

"I guess…what Eddie did was so fucking humiliating. I

just want to prove to him that I don't give a shit. No loss…and all that." I wave my hand dismissively, even though they'll struggle to see the gesture in the darkness.

"You don't need to prove anything to that douchebag," Elias says fiercely. "Seriously, if he didn't value what he had, then he's an idiot."

"Yeah." Dornan turns toward me a little before I have a chance to swoon at Elias's compliment.

An engine rumbles to life in the parking lot, and a ripple of female laughter cuts through, reminding me of where we are. Molly's for flip's sake.

"Once a cheater, always a cheater." The bitterness in Travis's tone makes me wonder if he's experienced his own cheating heartbreak.

"I wish I could find a way to get even."

"What about a fake relationship?" Elias has now moved to a sitting position, the conversation taking all his attention. My head is still fogged from sleep, and I'm probably still drunk, so his comment takes a while to settle.

"A fake relationship?"

"Yeah. I mean, I can stand in to make Eddie jealous. Seeing you with me would make him crazy, especially because rumors circulated the last time we hooked up, and I know he heard them."

"Rumors?"

"Someone saw us leave together, that's all."

"So you didn't go bragging all over the locker room?"

"Hell no." He sounds offended, but I'm not sure why he would be. I've heard him talk shit about girls before. Elias Mazur isn't exactly what you'd call a gentleman or even a good guy. In fact, I've always seen him as a bad boy, through and through.

Dornan makes a grumbling sound in the back of his throat as though the idea of me even fake dating Elias doesn't sit well with him. "I can stand in."

"I'd be up for it," Travis says. "Eddie doesn't know me and me being older might make a fake date even more effective."

"We could all do it," Dornan suggests, and my mouth drops open. Is he serious?

"Three fake boyfriends?" As I say the words, the idea becomes real and interesting. Eddie would hit the roof if I dated Elias, but he'd be apoplectic if I was dating three men.

Ellie's idea for me to get over my feelings was rebound sex. Rebound fake dating doesn't quite have the same ring to it, but maybe it could be a little of both. Fake relationship, real smoking-hot sex. And not just with one man. With three!

I'd get to see how my two best friends live every day and dust the Eddie cobwebs away.

I don't tell them my embellished ideas. That part can come in time. "Three fake boyfriends. Now that's what I call a proposal."

Seemingly satisfied by my decision, the room quietens, and I settle back against the pillows. It's strange to sleep in the same bed as Dornan. We're close, but this is a big step into new territory. He doesn't encroach on my space, which under the circumstances is a relief, but as he closes his eyes and falls asleep, I can't help but imagine what it would feel like if he did at some point in the future. If all of them did.

Saturdays always feel like a drag. Ellie's busy with family life, and Gabriella tends to stay in bed for at least half the day. I hate my weekends becoming focused on chores. When I was dating Eddie, we'd also hang out in bed, go for brunch, and then return to bed. I spent a lot of horizontal time with my ex. And vertical against the wall.

Ugh.

I don't want to think about sex with Eddie.

I want those images burned from my brain. Most of all, I don't want to feel like the same stupid girl I was. I need to be someone new to mark a line in the sand.

This Saturday morning started out a little different. Waking in a motel room with three half-naked, gorgeous men. Awkward goodbyes and a walk of shame when Travis dropped me home, and Dornan stayed with me while I retrieved a spare key.

Their proposal is like a little light shining, but not enough to drag me from my dark mood, so I do what I always do when I'm feeling down. I hit the shops with my dad's credit card in hand and no idea about what I'm going to buy. I start off in my favorite shop, grabbing some jeans and a pretty brown silky blouse to try on. In the mirror, the same me stares back. Flaming red hair and bright green eyes, the same style of clothes I've been wearing since I was a teen.

I twist my hair into a bun at my nape and study myself again. I cover my hair with my hands, wanting to see what my face looks like without the distinctive hair. Maybe that's what I should do. A big change. Dye my hair so it's dark and dramatic. Chocolate brown, maybe, with some caramel highlights.

I hang the clothes back up and return them to the sales advisor, then stride out of the shop and into a boutique I've never entered before. It's filled with darker, more dramatic clothing that would wash my red hair right out but would probably look amazing with a tumble of dark curls.

I trawl the racks, searching for black jeans and tops in a range of colors I usually avoid like the plague. I find three knockout dresses more like something Ellie would usually wear as an option for my fake dates. The total bill is wildly extravagant, but I don't feel guilty. It's been over a month since my dad called me. Since the divorce and his escape overseas, he's proven that he has very little interest in me or my life. The only way I can connect with him is with money. Spending money on his credit card stupidly fills me with a little hope that he's thinking about me somewhere and has my best interests at heart.

There's a hair salon in the shopping mall, which is my next stop. When I tell the hairdresser what I want, she practically weeps in front of me. "You can't cover up all this beautiful color," she moans, waving her hands around on both sides of my head. "It's perfect as it is."

"I want to be a new me," I say. "I just need a change. A big change."

"I can't do it," she says, but when I tell her about Eddie, she rests her hand on my upper arm, sympathy raising her brows. "We've all been through it, sweetie. You do what you need to do."

It's so weird to see her painting my hair from root to tip with gray-looking cream. The smell is acrid, and my scalp is weirdly cold. I flick through the messages from Ellie and Gab with photos of last night attached, zooming in on Dornan, Elias, and Travis.

The hairdresser leans over my shoulder. "Now, those are the kinds of men I would go for if I was a few years younger."

"But they're all so different," I say.

"They're real men, though. Look at those muscles and those determined jaws. Is one of them your ex?"

I tell her about what happened last night, including the afterparty at Molly's and the slightly awkward goodbyes in the morning. When I explain their proposal, she whistles. "You're going to go on dates with them all."

"I guess."

"Who are you going to pick to go first?"

"I don't know. Dornan's a good friend, so he'd be the safest option. Travis is my friend's hot older brother, and his sexy, mature vibe would make Eddie intrigued. But Elias is Eddie's true nemesis. He hates him with a passion. And Elias won't get bogged down with feelings. He didn't last time." Plus, he's the most likely date to lead to the sex I desperately want. I don't tell the hairdresser that part, though.

"Him." I enlarge Elias's photo, and the hairdresser whistles again.

"Lucky you, darlin'. Lucky you."

I leave the salon an eon later with a cascade of soft chocolate brown curls and feeling like a different person.

And with three fake dates on the horizon, I'm starting to feel more in control of my life, too.

4

ELIAS

The wind gusts up the road, causing the trash in the gutter to spin and roll. I push my hands into my favorite dark jeans, shivering against the cold. I should have brought a jacket, but I spilled beer on it last night and didn't have time to wash it. Having only one jacket makes me feel like a loser. My friends have closets filled with clothes, and moms who send them care packages and buy them pricey gifts for special occasions. I get the privilege of struggling for myself.

I glance in both directions, searching for Celine. I did offer to pick her up, but she told me she'd meet me at the bar instead. This arrangement doesn't sit well with me, but I'm not her boyfriend, and arguing about her lack of concern for her safety isn't my place.

In the distance, a petite girl with long dark hair strides towards the bar. I ignore her, glancing at my watch and registering that I've been waiting for fifteen minutes. Celine's late, which I guess is a female prerogative. It doesn't take me longer than fifteen minutes to shower and dress and run some product through my hair. With all that beautiful, long red hair, it must take Celine hours to get ready.

"Elias." The voice sounds like Celine's and when I whip around, I find a girl with a face like Celine's, but everything else about her is different.

Dark hair spreads around her shoulders in soft waves, and the dress she's wearing is bright red and so tight, it's like a second skin. Her green eyes are ringed with black shadow, and her lips are painted to match her outfit.

She's a bombshell but not the real Celine.

"Wow." I don't know what to say. If I tell her she looks amazing, will she think I didn't like the way she looked before? If I tell her I prefer her natural hair and her more subtle way of dressing, will she feel bad about the changes she's made?

This situation is as treacherous as a minefield.

"You like?" Celine pivots on one very shiny black stiletto shoe, revealing all her slim curves that I remember so well.

"I like it," I say. "Do you like it?"

She beams. "I feel different, which is good. I like this new version of me."

"I like both," I say, treading a careful line.

"I didn't think diplomacy would come so easy to you?" She steps closer, hooking her hand around the back of my neck to press a soft kiss to my cheek. She smells good in a feminine way that sends heat flooding low, tightening my balls. Moving closer to my ear, she whispers, "You always seem to say what's on your mind." She's right. I usually do. But for some reason, protecting Celine's feelings has modified that tendency.

When she draws back, she swipes my cheek to wipe away the lipstick she left behind. "Thanks for suggesting this. It's good to be out rather than sitting at home."

"I've seen a lot of people we know go inside," I tell her.

"Not Eddie yet, but plenty of people who will mention it to him."

She nods, smiling at the prospect. There's something wicked about her desire to rile Eddie up. Something vindictive that I enjoy. Revenge is a base emotion, but it sure feels good when you give in to the desire.

I take her hand in mine and lead her to the entrance, nodding to the doormen who know me well. "Have a good night," one of them says as we pass.

Inside, the bar is only half full. It's still early, and I prefer not to be crushed amongst too many people. Being big and bulky has its advantages, but it also makes pushing through crowds a challenge if you don't want to be an asshole and knock people off their feet. I smile at the thought of knocking a pathway through the current crowd, separating everyone like pins at a bowling alley.

When I was a kid, I dreamed of being a man as big as my dad, who wouldn't ever have to worry about getting hurt again. I love my bulk and have cultivated my menacing stare. Since I turned eighteen, not a single man has tried to take me on.

At the bar, Celine stands on tiptoes and struggles backward onto a stool. She's so much smaller than me; it's almost humorous. "What's your pleasure?"

She grins, her perfectly shaped brows rising suggestively. "I think you know."

Damn. My cock thickens against my zipper, but I resist the urge to adjust myself. "Oh, I know. But I'm talking about a drink."

"Spoilsport." Her eyelashes flutter. "How about a Cosmo?"

I wave at the barman to get his attention and order one cosmopolitan and a bottle of beer. The drinks are ridiculously expensive, but I pay anyway, thinking through where I can tighten my budget later in the month.

Celine makes easy work of the drink, but I savor my beer, scanning the bar to see who's around. Eddie's best friend is in the corner, speaking to a girl. When he raises his head, our eyes meet, and he tips his head in greeting. Then he notices Celine, and his eyes widen.

"We've been noticed." I lean close to Celine's ear, brushing my lips over the sweet shell and relishing the shiver my touch elicits. There's something about our connection, a different level of awareness between us that I haven't found with anyone else. It's what prompted me to suggest this fake date. I want a chance to get in between Celine's legs again and find out if a second night with her will be as explosive as the first. She's the only girl I've wanted more of after a one-night stand. "Want to put on a good show?"

"Yes." Her agreement is a breathy whisper, and her hand on my chest is gentle encouragement. I dip my head and press my lips to hers, savoring the softness of her lips and the slide of her tongue. As I move deeper, she grips my shirt, wrapping her lean, toned, and very bare legs around my waist. I press hard against her pussy, using a hand to urge her hips closer to mine.

With no care for who's around us, she grinds up against me, moaning softly.

"Get a room," a deep voice says from behind us, but I don't stop. It's too good, and the memories of how much better it gets when I'm up inside her spur me on.

It's Celine who pushes against my chest, bringing the kiss to an end. My mouth separates from hers, wet and bruised. My cock is thick and hard, a bar against my boxer briefs. Her mesmerizing green eyes blink; dazed and confused. I feel the same.

"Remembering how good it was?" I tip my head to the side and fold my lips into my mouth, tasting her again. I shoot her with my most smoldering look, sure that my arrogance is part of what turns her on. It's what all girls seem to like. Treat them well, and they run a mile. Dangle them from strings so they don't know whether you like them or not, and they want to marry you.

"Yep." It's said with no pretense, which catches me off guard.

"I know this is a fake date, but we could make it a real one-night stand?"

Celine stifles a smile. "You're a real Romeo, you know that?"

"Didn't Romeo fall in love with an underage girl, have a three-day relationship, and then kill himself?"

Celine snorts, frowning in confusion. "That's a pretty dark summary of an amazingly romantic play."

"It's not a romance. It's a tragedy, and that doesn't answer my question."

She narrows her eyes and then glances around the bar to see who's noticed us. I keep my eyes on her, not caring about the observers. All I want to know is whether she's coming home with me tonight.

"Eddie's friend is on the phone."

"Oh, really. Want to give him something else to tell his asshole cheating friend?"

I lean in again, and she holds me back. "You're seriously going to tell me you never cheated?"

With my nose brushing against the tip of hers, I tell her the truth. "I don't date, so cheating isn't a thing."

"You mean you don't commit?"

"Exactly."

She kisses my lips again as though she's assumed this isn't going anywhere apart from the fake date arrangement and is happy about it. She's probably right. Relationships are bullshit. People just latch onto each other and then spend the rest of their lives trying to tear each other apart. It's better to just enjoy what there is to enjoy: a few stolen moments, some shared passion, and a little surface-level connection. Then part with happy memories we'll both smile about in a few years.

God, I want this girl in my bed.

I pull back, gripping her mane of chestnut hair in my hand, tipping her face up to mine. "Do you think we've made enough waves here?"

She nods, and then her eyes flick to the left. "Can I get a picture before we go for socials?"

I grit my teeth because social media is my pet peeve. It's just a load of fake people faking their happiness or empathy to make everyone else feel bad about their lives or about themselves. I don't like people taking photos of me, either. I like to move through the world living in the moment. Looking back is for people who've had childhoods filled with blissful memories, and that isn't me.

But Celine is all wide, pleading eyes, and for some reason, with her, I don't want to say no.

She pulls her phone from her purse and holds it over our heads the way influencers do to reduce their jowls. I don't look at the camera but rest my forehead against the side of her head so that only a portion of my side profile is visible. Celine seems content with the image because she quickly uploads it to Insta while I finish my beer. I don't have an account to check who's responding to it, though.

"Let's go," she says eventually. Making a big show about sliding off the stool in a sexy way, Celine plumps her new curls and pivots in her new dress, cocking her hip and showing off her perfect legs. If people weren't looking before, they sure are looking now. Taking her by the hand, I walk her to the door, enjoying the glances we receive as we cross through the crowd. Outside, Celine drops my hand and stretches her arms into the air, making a high-pitched, happy sound. "That was good, Elias. Really good." She focuses on me with a big, bright smile, sending something warm that wraps around my heart. "If that doesn't make him scream, I don't know what will."

"Forget making Eddie scream. How about I make you scream?"

Even in the darkness, I can see her pupils swell with arousal. When I take a step closer, looming over her, she holds her ground.

With a husky whisper, she says, "I thought you'd never ask."

We don't even make it through the door to my dorm room before grasping at each other in desperation. I shove down the thin straps of her dress, baring her perfect breasts cupped in a bra that almost reveals her nipples. My mouth is on her neck, her clavicle, and lower until I'm latched onto one tight little nipple and sucking hard enough to make her gasp. Celine pulls my shirt, and I tear it from my body in one rough motion that has the stitches breaking.

"Damn," she says, trailing my body with lazy eyes. "Your body is insane."

"Nothing insane about it. Just hard work and dedication."

I push my shoulders back and make my pecs jump one at a time and laugh when I make her giggle.

"Well, I, for one, am very happy to appreciate the results of your intense focus." She trails a hand down the middle of my chest, reading the bumps of my abs with slow precision. When she gets to my belt, she stops.

"Show me what I've been missing."

She doesn't need to ask twice. I remove my belt with one hand, tearing the leather from the loops fast and hard. Her mouth drops open at the whip-crack of the sound it makes.

Interesting.

I toe off my shoes and lose the socks—there's nothing less sexy than a dude standing around naked in footwear—then drop my jeans.

Celine's focus zeros in on my cock, which is a very obvious bar in my tight black boxer briefs. "I've had dreams about that night." Her hand trails gently over the outline, sending a shiver of sensation up my spine and over my scalp. This girl is going to kill me.

I don't admit that I've thought about that night a lot as well. Mostly alone with my left hand working. "Celine. Fuck." I grab her beneath the ass with one hand, pulling her high against my body. Her legs wrap around my waist, clinging on as she gasps. Our mouths find each other, and we slide into a kiss that feels like mayhem. I can't breathe; I want to get inside her so much.

When her back hits the wall, it knocks the breath from both our lungs. Celine throws her head back, baring her throat, and I run my tongue over her pulse until I'm close to her ear. "Shall I fuck you now, Celine? Tell me what you want."

"Hard. Fast. Jesus, Mazur. Just give me your dick already."

With a heart that feels like it's beating hard enough to punch its way out of my chest, I release my cock, pushing her panties aside, and thrust deep in one slick motion that makes Celine scream and forces me up on my toes.

Oh god. It feels so good. So right. I can't even breathe.

I grind up inside her, pressing my hips against her sweet little pussy, relishing the wetness between her thighs like sweet pudding. Each thrust is a violent punctuation of my craving for her. I'm out of my mind, kissing her so deeply my jaw aches, shoving down her bra until her breasts are bare, and leaving hickeys all over her skin.

I'm deep, but I want deeper.

I yank her away from the wall, striding across my room with her clinging to me like a koala. I lower her onto the bed, still embedded deep, resting her legs over my shoulders before I fold her in two. That's it. That's it. Fuck.

"Oh god," she cries out. "Oh...oh... don't stop."

"Fucking come for me," I growl, keeping the unyielding tempo but adding more force to each slam of my hips. Celine's eyes roll, and her pussy clamps down so hard, I see stars. Her body jerks, spasming under my weight. I rest a hand over her heart and feel the explosive race as she orgasms violently.

I keep going, focusing on her pretty, parted lips. I lean back, looking between us at the sweet patch of red curls at the apex of her thighs. She's dyed her hair, but this part of her is still as I remember it. I close my eyes as heat licks over my balls until my cock swells and everything tense inside me for weeks and weeks spills between Celine's thighs.

Oh fuck. It feels so damned good.

So damned good. "Mmmm," I groan. Sweat trickles down my back as I pump slowly into her, easing my cum deeper and deeper, watching my cock disappear into her sweet little pussy.

She trembles, and her legs shake. I like knowing that I wrecked her. If I want more, which I do, she has to know she can't get better anywhere else.

I don't want to pull out. She feels so good. So perfect beneath me. Celine blinks up at me, her pupils still blown so wide, her eyes are almost as black as mine.

"Fuck, Elias. That was..."

I rest a finger over her lips. "It was." There's no point in either of us sliding into something emotional after sex.

Yes, fucking Celine is the best sex I've ever had. Yes, she makes me smile with her sassy humor and fiery character. She's not afraid to bite back or to go for what she wants. I respect that. But that's it. That's as far as it goes, for both our sakes. I don't date, and even if I did, Celine's rebounding hard, which is not a foundation for building anything new.

But that doesn't mean I won't enjoy this for what it is.

I roll onto my back and pull Celine against my chest, staring up at the ceiling I face every night.

"Girl, you rock my world," I tell her.

"You smash mine into a million tiny pieces."

We stare at each other, and I take in the tiny freckles that dust her nose and cheeks like glitter and the pout of her bottom lip. I've kissed all the makeup from her face, but that's okay. I like her better this way.

I let my hand roam her hip and ass, and then I slick my finger between her legs. She's dripping what I shot inside her, and the sensation that I've claimed her makes my balls tighten again. Instinct drives me to push what's leaking out back up inside her.

"We didn't use protection," I say. "You were on birth control last time."

"I still am. I got tested, too, in case Eddie passed me something nasty. I'm all good."

"I'm good, too." I don't elaborate that she's the only girl I've ever gone bareback with.

I let my thumb play with the short curls between her thighs, and she moans enough to make my cock thicken. She shifts like she's already hungry for more. Like last time, we're a match just waiting to ignite. "I know you wanted a change," I find myself saying as I focus on a lock of her hair between my thumb and forefinger. "But you looked good before, Celine. Don't be afraid to go back."

Her throat clicks when she swallows, focusing on the wall I've covered with posters of my favorite footballers and some bikini-clad women. She doesn't answer, but when her hand snakes around my cock, making it hard all over again, and she shifts until she takes it into her mouth, I forget everything I was thinking in an instant.

5

CELINE

Dornan arrives at my door at seven pm, dressed smartly in a light blue button-down shirt, dark blue jeans, and brown leather boots. His hair, which is usually floppy, is styled more formally and pushed back from his rugged face. He smells good, too, like a forest during a thunderstorm.

The way his expression changes when he sees me is hilarious. "What did you do to your hair?"

"I'm a new me." I twirl in my dark green dress, tossing my hair over my shoulder.

"Wow. You look good. It's just a shock."

"Yeah. You're kind of having the same reaction as Elias, except he did a better job of covering it up."

Dornan holds out his hands with the palms facing forward. "I'm sorry. You look good...I just wasn't expecting it."

"Yeah. Elias was happy the curtains didn't match the drapes."

It takes Dornan a couple of seconds to work out what I mean, and when he does, his eyes drop to my crotch before he forces them back up. The splash of color beneath both of his eyes is so cute. "Did you have a good time?" He raises his right hand before I can answer. "You know what? Probably best you don't answer that."

"We had a good time." I rest my hand on Dornan's upper arm, appreciating the firmness. I can't resist giving it a little squeeze. "And I'm sure we're going to have a good time tonight, too."

Wow. That came out stronger than I intended, and Dornan seems slightly winded by the idea that we might share more than just cocktails. I get why. We're buddies. We don't share bodily fluids, or at least, we didn't until I kissed him the other night. It was a frivolous thing that I did while I was drunk, but it stirred something inside me that I haven't been able to forget.

Fake dating is weird. Three men have offered to help me exact my revenge against Eddie, but none of these dates will be the same. I know Elias best physically, Dornan best emotionally, and Travis hardly at all.

Dornan is staring, so I jangle my keys to jolt him out of the daze that mentioning possible sex has put him in. Jeez. Dudes can be weird about women being sexually confident. It's like they want us to cover our faces with a veil and lower our eyelashes while coyly staring at the floor. Those days are long gone, and I won't apologize for going for what I want when I want it. I spent too much time doing what Eddie wanted. I'm not going back there again, ever.

"Let's go." I follow Dornan, jumping into his old but very shiny, silver car. Fastening my belt, I watch him gently shut my door and attempt to fold himself into the driver's seat. Seriously, the dude is massive, and this car isn't sized for a football player's bulk.

"You sure you don't want to trade this in for an SUV?"

"I love this car."

He cranks it into drive, and we head to the same bar

Elias and I went to last night. It's probably weird to go to the same bar two nights in a row with two different men, but it's the most popular place to be, which means I have a greater chance of seeing people who know Eddie.

"What do Gab and Ellie think about this fake dating scheme?" Dornan asks.

I turn to face his profile, taking in his strong, bristly jaw and straight nose. He holds the steering wheel with just one powerful arm, and I enjoy his relaxed control. I don't need to second guess anything when I'm with Dornan. It's comfortable and I can relax because I trust him to handle everything and take care of me. "I haven't told them about it," I admit.

His blond brows shoot up. "Are you serious? You guys tell each other everything."

"I haven't seen them." The truth is that I know they'll be disapproving, not in an unkind way but because they'll worry about me and the effect these dates might have on our group dynamics. It's easier to avoid conversations than deal with the possible fall out.

He cuts me a glance. "You know, there are these things called phones, and all you have to do is push a few buttons, and suddenly you get to talk to your friends?"

"Funny." I play with the handle of my purse, flexing the soft leather. "I've cried on their shoulders too much recently. I think they need a break from The Life and Dramas of Celine Lauder."

"No true friend needs a break from their buddy's life. That's not how friendship works. We carry each other through the hard times. No questions asked."

I rest my hand on his huge thigh and squeeze it. "You're a good friend, Dornan. You always go over and above."

"Ellie would probably disagree in this situation."

I cock an eyebrow, surprised. "Why?"

"Because I should be talking you down from going ahead with these revenge games. I should be encouraging you to see it as a waste of your time and energy and get you to focus on moving on."

"I am moving on." I fold my arms across my chest, resentful of imaginary Ellie for her negative assessment of my decision-making. "This is an excellent way of moving on. Elias helped me so much."

As soon as the last part is out of my mouth, I regret it. I don't want to sound manipulative. Whether Dornan intends to go as far as Elias did with me is up to him. I'm not pressuring anyone to have sex with me if they're not crazily up for it.

"Elias is out for himself."

"Dornan, that's not very nice."

He shakes his head, and his nostrils flare. Down, boy. "You know Elias. He never has anything good to say about anyone."

"He had lots of nice things to say about me."

"Because he wants to get his dick wet."

I bristle because, even though that might be true to a certain extent, I think Dornan is being tougher on Elias than is justified. "He has a big brooding bear thing going on, but I've never heard about him being a dick."

"He was a dick about Ellie when it got around about her fooling around in the closet with the Townsend Triplets."

"He was?"

Dornan nods. "He was asking them about it in the locker room."

"Asking them?"

His shoulders stiffen. "Yeah. Poking his nose in where it doesn't belong."

"So, he was curious? Did he call her names?"

"No."

"Did he make bad insinuations about her?"

"He started talking about stepsister porn."

"Sounds like he was trying to be funny."

As we pull up a little down the road from the bar, Dornan unsnaps his seatbelt. "He was trying to get under their skin. I don't like that shit."

I pull the sunshade down to check my face in the little mirror. My make-up is still perfect. Ready for the second phase of this operation.

"Well, he's been supportive of me. Maybe he's turned over a new leaf."

We step out of the car, and our eyes meet over the roof. "He'd have to turn over a new forest to make up for his past assholery."

I slam the door shut, watching another couple head down the road to the bar with their arms wrapped tightly around each other. I look back and find Dornan watching them, too. "It's not like you to be vindictive."

His eyelids lower a little, then he shakes his head. "I just don't want to see you hurt."

When he rounds the car, I glance around to make sure no one's looking. Then I hitch up my dress. "You see these. These are big girl panties, Dornan."

His eyes almost bug out of his head at the sight of my black lace thong, but I think I've made my point. Before he has a chance to fix his shattered brain, I drop the fabric and link my arm through his. "Let's get some drinks, shall we?"

It's weird hanging out with Dornan without the rest of the crew. Weird and easy. We never seem to run out of conversation, maybe because we know so many of the same people and have shared a lot of time together because of his friendship with Ellie. In contrast to Elias,

Dornan keeps a respectful distance while we sit across from each other at the bar. Some of Eddie's crew are seated in a booth across the dance floor, and I've already noticed them looking our way. Being out with Dornan is good, but it's not good enough. I need to be seen with his hands on me if Eddie's going to believe that this is anything more than two friends catching up over beer and cocktails.

When we've finished dissecting Dalton's party where we first kissed, and I've finished two deliciously different cocktails, I notice one of Eddie's friends moving closer. I rest my hand on Dornan's knee. "I'm going to kiss you now, okay?"

With wide blue eyes the color of a cerulean sky, he blinks. Then his head bobs in almost imperceptible agreement. The distance between us is too great, so I slide off my stool, stand between Dornan's beefy legs, and rest my hands against his slab-of-granite chest. He breathes in so deeply that it's a wonder he doesn't get a head rush.

It feels strange to slide my hand around the back of his neck and to feel his palms encircling my waist. Strange but also fluttery and exciting. He's so big and brawny, exuding a level of protectiveness that settles the uncertainty lurking inside me like a dark weight under my ribs.

I lean in closer, leaving it until the last minute to drop my eyelids. When our lips meet, it's a brush of contact that sends shivers up my arms.

Unlike Elias, Dornan is gentle and tentative at first, only becoming demanding when we've learned the way each other moves, and I get lost in the teasing way he sucks my bottom lip between his. Dornan's hands go from gentle to greedy, pulling me closer until I'm clamped between his strong legs. It's good because my knees are the consistency of Cool Whip, and my mind has chosen this exact moment to exit my body.

When Dornan makes a low rumbling growl in his

throat, and his hands slide up my sides so that his thumbs are resting just beneath my breasts, I draw back so that I can look into his eyes.

For the first time, I get to witness his pupils spread with arousal, darkening them to the color of the sky just before darkness falls. The flashing lights reflect into them, and he stares at me like I'm something new and shiny and fascinating.

"Was that okay?" he asks.

"More than okay," I find myself replying with a husky, breathless voice.

"Did they see?"

I don't look around to check who's watching us. I'm too caught up in the moment.

"Can I take a selfie of us?" I swallow, trying to fuse my splintered mind again. This is Dornan Walsh, not a Hollywood A-lister. I need to get myself together.

"Sure. Of course."

I turn in the circle of his arms and pull out my phone, holding it high and resting my face against Dornan's. On camera, we look like a sweet couple. My dark hair contrasts with his, but our features seem well matched.

"Where are you going to post it?"

I open Instagram and show him my page. The last photo I posted was with Elias. It hasn't had as many likes as I hoped it would get. I upload the picture I just took, studying the images side by side. There's a remoteness to the image of Elias and a *presentness* to the image of Dornan.

I glance around, trying to find anyone who might tell Eddie about this fake date, but I don't see a single person. Playing games without an audience is a waste of my precious time. Time that could be spent doing other things.

If Dornan is happy to play more games.

"You wanna get out of here?" I ask in a blasé way even though my heart makes a funny squeezing thud in my chest at the thought of taking him back to my dorm and riding the fuck out of him.

What will Ellie think? It's weird to contemplate sharing this with her. We've been open about our sex lives, but that was when the men involved weren't mutual friends. Dornan has been Ellie's best buddy since kindergarten. Would sharing a night of sexual exploration with him be like treading on her toes?

And there's Elias.

What we had last night was casual, but that doesn't mean he won't have thoughts about me fucking Dornan.

"Whatever you want to do," he replies.

The words *my time* sing through my mind. What do I want? It's such a novel question to ask myself. I want no strings affection that doesn't blast our relationship skyward. Can I have that with Dornan? I think so.

I touch his cheek, and grin with all the wickedness that comes with being selfish and focusing on my needs. "Take me home, Mr. Walsh."

The car journey is relatively quiet. The kiss has settled between us like a curtain of uncertainty. I can practically hear the cogs cranking in Dornan's mind and all the questions he wants to ask me but is holding onto tightly in his mouth.

I stare out of the window, thinking about my sister, Marie. She's never experienced relationship issues. She met her husband in high school, and they settled down so quickly, it made my head spin. Now I have the cutest niece, and Marie seems blissfully happy. By contrast, I've never found a man who really sees me or who's prepared to do the work to see more than what's on the surface. I know I put up high barriers because letting people get close always ends up with me getting hurt. As a result, trusting is hard, and I pick men like Eddie and Elias because they keep me at arm's length where there's no chance of getting burned.

Except there is. Infidelity and rejection hurt whether you're in love or not.

Dornan isn't like that.

He doesn't have hang-ups that make his corners sharp. The way he thinks and moves isn't clouded by past experiences. He's in the moment, secure in himself and who he is. He doesn't doubt that the world will bring him good things. I know this because he expects good things to come to everyone around him.

It's easy to be with Elias because my jagged edges slot into his, but with Dornan, every time I get close, I feel like I have to smooth over everything that's sharp about me.

I catch him glancing at me out of the corner of my eye as though he worries I'm going to throw open the car door and bolt. He doesn't realize that inviting him in so that he can make me feel less broken is all I can think about.

Always the gentleman, Dornan walks me to my door. When I've unlocked it, he takes a step back, expecting to say goodbye. Instead, I take his big, capable hand in mine and drag him inside.

Before he has a chance to ask any questions about whether I'm sure or whether it's a good idea, I kiss him and push my hands beneath his shirt.

What I find is rippling solid muscle and warm, soft skin. His mouth devours mine like he's been thinking about doing this with me for longer than just a few days. His hunger sends a squeezing wave of need between my thighs. I'm the one who urges him to tear his top over his head. I'm the one who scrambles to untie the strings keeping my wrap dress together. In my stilettos and underwear, I feel sexy and powerful, and Dornan stares wide-eyed, his gaze slipping down my body, lower and lower, with a burning heat that licks against my skin.

"Fuck, Celine."

"Yeah, Dornan. It's time to fuck Celine."

Pushing him back with a hand in the middle of his chest, his legs meet the edge of my mattress. He sits, and I place a leg on either side of his thick thighs, urging him back on my soft comforter. Unfastening my bra is quick and easy, and his hands react with swift reflexes to cup my breasts. I grind against the hard ridge of his cock, tipping back my head, letting my body feel the way. With breathtaking speed, he rolls me to my back and looms over me, his wavy hair losing its formal style and flopping messily over his forehead.

"You're rushing, Celine."

Oh, he wants to take his time.

But taking his time means I have time to think, and I don't want to do that. I want harsh and mindless fucking. I want Dornan to be okay with treating me like Eddie used to so I can get off and then get on with my life. Anything else will seep into my bones and make me *feel*, and I can't cope with that. I don't have the strength not to crack open and weep.

"I'm ready, Dornan. I don't need warming up. Just give it to me."

"Jesus…" His eyes roam my face as though he can't quite get to grips with this really happening between us.

I fumble with his jeans, my fingers feeling as coordinated as sausages. He finds a condom in his pocket, and I don't object. More talk at this moment only has the potential to destroy it.

When I've succeeded in wrapping my fingers around his cock, I groan in satisfaction. Dornan's big, and his cock matches in every perfect way. He's thick and long and my fingertips don't meet as I give it three testing strokes.

"Fuck..." He grits his teeth like he's raging, not enjoying himself. Then his hands become frenzied, shoving down my panties until there's nothing between us. I tug his hips, urging him forward as he sucks each of my nipples into hardened points. His cock is so broad that I have to drop my legs wide to accommodate just the tip, and when he pushes inside me an inch, he groans with deep satisfaction.

This is what I need. To be filled to the brim. To be owned by greedy hands and an even greedier mouth. To forget everything that came before.

"Celine." Dornan groans into my neck. His hips grind into me, deep and then deeper. I cling to his broad shoulders, breathing in his scent and tasting his salty skin.

"Dornan." His name on my tongue tastes strange because we're friends, not lovers. But now we're something in between.

He pushes me up the bed, the power in his thrusts knocking the breath from my lungs. He fucks like he plays ball, with dedicated precision and the power of two men, staring down at me like he realized he's lost in the wilderness and needs to find a way out.

I feel the same way.

"Please," I whisper as my neck arches and my whole body draws tight. "Please."

Dornan grunts as he gives me everything he has, and I come and come and come, shattered, and spent, seeing stars in the pulsing blackness behind my eyelids.

He releases with an almighty groan that will probably wake my neighbors, but I don't care. He's glorious. Disheveled and beautiful. Like an angel dropped to earth only to be corrupted by me.

I touch his face, and his skin is burning. He turns his

face into my palm and kisses the center, and it's tender and sweet, just like his smile.

"That was…"

"It was," I agree. Perfect. Ecstatic. Glorious. So many words to describe what Dornan just did to me.

But now it's over, and we need to disengage. It's time to go back to the way we were before.

Friends.

Friends who do each other favors.

Friends who've seen each other naked.

Friends who've been joined in the most intimate of ways.

We can do that, can't we?

6

TRAVIS

When Celine's message pops up on my phone screen, I frown. It's been three days since the weird night at Molly's motel, and I was sure she'd forgotten about our strange agreement.

Hey Travis. Can we hook up later for our 'fake date'?

I place my phone back onto my desk without answering, return to the email I received from a recruiter, and attach my resume. I need to get a job, and messing about with fake dates with a girl immature enough to think that seeking revenge on a cheating ex is a good idea should be the lowest thing on my priority list.

However, as I try to focus on scanning through companies who are currently recruiting for roles I'm qualified for, my eyes keep straying back to the phone and Celine's message.

I agreed to help her out. I could explain it as a moment of weakness by blaming my exhaustion and the pressure of two other men agreeing to the same thing, but that isn't the whole story.

Celine might be doing something crazy, but I get her motivation. When a person you think you can trust cheats on you, a part of you changes forever. The trust you give easily becomes something you place in a cage. The simple act of allowing feelings to develop becomes a road of jagged hot coals and exploding mines.

You want revenge, but nothing can make it any better.

Revenge wastes emotions, but I don't know Celine well enough to tell her to just leave it alone. Looking back at a burned-out relationship won't make her happy. Facing the truth that she trusted wrongly and wasted a load of time on that douchebag, Eddie, isn't something she's ready for.

I feel so far beyond this emotional immaturity. I walked away with my head held high when I faced the same situation. It's what Celine should do, but only a friend can deliver that advice, and we're not friends.

But I do like her, and I do feel sorry for her. My sister Gabriella would expect me to do whatever it takes to help a friend.

It's the way our momma taught us to live our lives.

Picking up my phone, I tap out a quick response. **Tonight's fine. Where?**

She responds almost immediately with the name of a club. Shit. I don't want to go to that kind of place with an almost stranger. The music's too loud, making it impossible to talk. I can already feel the awkward silence stretching between us, or worse, having to dance.

I'm not a dancer. At least, I don't enjoy doing it in public. I have rhythm, so that isn't the problem. It's more that I find the whole ritual of strangers moving around in the dark weird.

I type out three messages suggesting other places, deleting them repeatedly. She obviously has a good reason for suggesting the bar she has. In the end, I agree to collect her from her dorm at ten pm and then rest back in my chair, stretching my back and dreading the night already.

A girl is waiting outside Celine's dorm as I approach, dressed in a gorgeous dark blue dress and strappy silver heels. With long dark hair set into loose curls, she's a knockout. I dial Celine's number as the girl approaches my car, placing her hand on the handle and pulling the door open. I'm about to tell her she's got the wrong car when I realize that it's Celine.

"Your hair," I gasp. She looks so frickin' different that I'm staring with my mouth open.

She slides into the passenger seat, closes the door, and fastens her seatbelt. "You like it?"

"It's…"

"You don't like it?" She frowns as I try to find the right words. This is some thin ice I'm skating on.

"You look good both ways. It's just a radical change."

"Radical changes are good for the soul."

I get that. I left Germany because I needed that kind of radical change. If dying her hair is what Celine needs to feel good, then all power to her. I just liked her red curls. They made her unique. Now she looks like half the girls out there.

I put the car into drive and flip it around so we're heading in the right direction.

"You're listening to The Eagles."

"Yeah. You know them?"

"Of course. Man, I love this song."

Celine starts to sing along with a voice that's way too sweet for the strumming guitar and gritty lyrics, but she knows all the words.

Glancing at her out of the corner of my eye, I can't help but smile as she presses her hands against her heart and throws everything she has into the song. She's so enthusiastic that I find myself joining in, and we spend the whole journey to the club trying to outdo each other with perfect renditions of the seventies rock classics we both seem to love so much.

The club is only half full when we arrive, but that's okay. I get us drinks, and Celine leads the way to a booth in the upper section that I didn't know existed. The music is loud and pumping and not the kind of thing I enjoy listening to, and I can't drink because I'm driving. But Celine beams at me and touches my arm.

"I know we don't know each other very well, so I appreciate you doing this for me."

"Any friend of my sister's is a friend of mine."

Celine smiles at that. "Gabriella is a really good friend."

"She's a good person."

"And what about you? Are you a good person?"

I let my attention drift to the bar where a blonde bar waitress stacks drinks onto a large tray. Am I a good person? I like to think so, but we all have thoughts and feelings that rest uncomfortably under our skin. I've been having more of those than I'd like recently.

"I try to be," I answer. "I guess that's all we can do."

Celine focuses on her drink, sucking half of it through the straw. "What I'm doing isn't good, is it?"

"Trying to make Eddie jealous?"

"I don't want him to be jealous," she says quickly. "That isn't what this is about. I don't want him back. I wouldn't touch that man with a ten-foot pole. This is about me showing him what he's going to be missing for the rest of his goddamned life. And me washing away all the horrible feelings I have with some new, more enjoyable experiences."

"And how's it working out?"

"Good, so far." Celine tucks her hair behind her ear and rests back in the booth.

"Have you been on dates with Dornan and Elias?"

"Yeah." Her answer doesn't give anything away, but the blush on her cheeks and avoiding eye contact does.

"And did Eddie see you?"

"His friends did."

I nod, understanding that this is about more than Eddie witnessing her moving on. It's about his friends all seeing and realizing how much Eddie screwed up.

"And does that make you feel better?"

Her pretty green eyes meet mine, and the sadness in their depths wraps around my heart and squeezes. But her response is markedly different. "Absolutely." She blinks and plasters a fake smile across her face, but I saw the truth. These bullshit games aren't making her feel better. Not really. They're just something to take her mind off her true feelings. The trouble is, we can bury our hurt beneath layers and layers of distractions, but it still lingers and needs to be dealt with.

"Can I take a selfie of us to post on Instagram?" she asks, already fiddling with her phone and fluffing her hair.

I hate social media, but I get that Celine wants to extend the reach of her games beyond the four walls of this nightclub. Throwing my arm around her shoulder, I focus on the image of us framed on her phone. We're a total contrast now. Light and dark. She smiles broadly, and I focus on looking mean and moody. If Eddie sees this image, I want him to realize that I'm not some simpering college dude he can fuck with. I left all this behind a long time ago.

I watch as she posts the image with some hashtags. When she's done, she places her phone on the table.

"We should dance," she says. "Make sure we get seen by as many people as possible."

"We could sit at the bar," I say. "Would that work?"

Her shoulders slump, but she nods. "Sure."

I take Celine's almost empty glass and mine and find a center spot at the bar with two free stools. Celine glances around for any familiar faces. "I thought it would be busier tonight," she says.

"Do you see Eddie or any of his friends?"

"Only one, and they're not close."

Celine perches on the edge of the stool and nibbles on the side of her finger. Her posture is tight, her shoulders curled forward. The confident woman who asked me to take her out has gone, and in her place is a girl who seems defeated.

It breaks my heart. "Let's give that asshole something to rage about," I say.

Celine seems confused, but I pass her phone. "Another selfie," I say.

When the screen is on camera mode, and she holds it high, I take her pretty face in my hands and kiss her. The camera makes a clicking sound as Celine sighs against my lips. I kiss her deeper, letting my hand cup the back of her neck, pulling her closer to me with a demanding grip. Another click.

Her lips are so soft and searching, and even though we barely know each other, the kiss is both tender and smoking hot.

Jeez.

I can see why Elias was so keen for an opportunity to date Celine. He'd already had a taste and wanted more.

And now, so do I.

Click.

Another photo.

I draw back, staring down into her glazed eyes.

"Are those good enough?"

She nods but doesn't check.

I run the tip of my nose over hers, lowering my eyelids while I catch my breath. "Did Elias and Dornan kiss you?"

"Yes," she whispers.

"Did they fuck you?" The question slips out without enough thought. They know Celine so much better than I do, and if that's where their dates ended up, it has no bearing on what might happen between us tonight.

Do I even want to go there? Stupid fucking question, Trav. Of course, you want to. Whether it's a good idea or not is another question.

"Yes."

"Do you want me to fuck you?" Am I really going there? I guess I am.

"Yes."

"But he won't know, Celine, will he? It'll just be you and me. What's the point in it if he can't see?"

She frowns and looks away, my comment touching the nerve I hoped it would. I want her to see that her actions don't make any sense. She's getting tangled and confused in revenge and lust, and it's a dangerous place to be.

When she turns back, the familiar fire is back in her eyes.

"Eddie doesn't control me, Travis. This isn't about him. It's about me scrubbing the stain of him from every part of me. But if that isn't something you want to do…"

Her eyes challenge me to back away, even as she leans closer to run her top lip between mine.

She's so damned sexy. Too damned sexy for her own good.

"If that's all this is about, then what the fuck are we doing here?"

She blinks, shocked, but I don't know why she is. This is what she's asking for. Was she imagining I'd be more difficult to convince?

Maybe that's it. Celine thought Gabriella's big brother would be less impetuous than her college friends. She thought I'd be mature and cautious and maybe harder to convince to play her games.

I should be.

But because I understand all the shame and feelings of inadequacy that come with being on the receiving end of a cheater, my desire to give her whatever she needs outweighs my need to be a mature and responsible man.

This won't really help her. Not in the long run. If anything, getting mixed up with three different men who are most probably only looking for physical release has the potential to crush all her shattered pieces into dust. My internal voice is correct.

It's a pain now or pain later situation.

I can take her to Molly's. I can do everything she wants me to do to her and more. I can help her hurt herself, but I don't want to. Not with everything I've learned going through the same situation. Not when she deserves so much more.

She's smiling as I walk her to the door. I pause to kiss her, hoping that it will be enough for those watching to make the assumptions Celine wants them to make.

And when we're inside my car, and the music is playing softly, only then do I tell her that I'm taking her home.

"I can't do what you're asking me to do," I say. "Not because I don't want to, because I do. I really do. But because I know using sex to mask feelings is a really self-destructive thing to do."

Celine gapes at me, and then her body stiffens. "You know what, Travis. You're not my big brother, okay? You don't need to take care of me. I'm not some fragile doll. I'm a grown woman, and I know what I'm doing."

I reach out to place my hand on her arm, but she pulls it away. "I care about you. You're a good person. I don't want to be on the same level as your ex."

"We're not dating, so you can't cheat. I don't get what you're trying to say."

"Sex shouldn't be a weapon or a bandage."

She huffs, turns to face front and folds her arms across her chest. "All I'm asking for is a good time, Travis. Not world peace."

This conversation isn't going anywhere, but I don't want Celine to hate me. I don't want her to feel humiliated because I've turned her down. "I like you, Celine. I'm happy to do whatever you want me to do to help you feel better, but this isn't going to work."

"Can you take me home?" she asks through a tight throat.

"Of course." I put the car into drive and focus on the road. My throat feels tight, and my hands tense on the wheel. I can feel Celine's energy, and it's unstable. I can't leave her like this. On the left, we're about to pass a fast-food restaurant that makes incredible desserts. If I pull in and offer her something sweet, it'll give us a chance to end the night better.

She turns to look at me when I signal and pull off the main road. As we approach the counter, I ask her what dessert she'd like to order. I can feel her warring with herself, wanting to turn down my offer but also wanting to go along with my attempt to lift the mood.

"A chocolate fudge sundae," she says, and when I've placed our orders, she thanks me.

When we've driven past the window to pay and collect our order, I pull into a space in the lot that's out of sight of the restaurant.

Celine spoons out a huge chunk of brownie that's heaped with soft-whip ice cream and chocolate sauce and puts it all into her mouth. The way she moans is so sexy, I almost drop my caramel sundae into my lap. That would be one way to chill out my semi-hard cock.

"Good?"

She nods, still chewing. There's a smudge of chocolate sauce on her cheek, which I rub away with my thumb. Her eyes widen in surprise, and she licks her lips.

Celine really is beautiful, like a medieval fairy transported into the twenty-first century, and given a sprinkle of sass in the process. It's a stupid description, but it fits.

"See, ice cream is better at fixing feelings than sex."

"Gabriella recommended cocktails and chocolate."

"Also great end of relationship fixers."

"Ellie suggested rebound sex."

"Did she?" That surprises me. Ellie always seemed quite conservative when it came to relationships. Before her stepbrother harem, she barely dated. Gabriella thought we might have been a good pair, but I told my sister that her friend was too young for me. It's funny that I'm now fake dating her other bestie, who's the same age.

"I know what you're going through," I tell her. It's time to come clean so she understands better where I'm coming from. "My ex cheated on me. It's why I left Germany."

"Oh." She tucks her spoon into the sundae and lowers it into her lap.

"It was a shock, and after, I felt like an idiot for not seeing the signs. The truth is, people who cheat are deceptive, and it's a good thing when you find out before things get serious and the stakes are higher."

"I was never going to go that far with Eddie."

"Thank the Lord. That guy is a douche of epic proportions."

She laughs and retrieves her spoon, reaching out to dig it in my sundae. I move it closer to her so it's easier to take a big enough sample. Her eyes roll, and she moans again at the caramel flavor, and I internally kick myself for turning down the sex. I'd like to make her moan just by pressing the flat of my tongue to her clit, but that's off the table for tonight. Plus, I don't get the feeling she'd be into my brand of fucking. Too bossy and confident to want what I like.

We spend another twenty minutes sharing our desserts and finding more music in common. Celine's cool. Definitely, a woman I'd like to date if things were different. I've had more fun tonight than I ever had with Lina.

We make our way back to Celine's dorms, and Celine sings all the way. She has shrugged off her sadness, and I'm relieved. It doesn't stop me thinking about what we could be doing if I'd agreed to what she wanted. We could have been at Molly's by now, sweat-slicked, and frantic.

I could have taken her mind off her stresses or, at the very least, relieved some tension.

Outside her dorm, Celine reaches for the handle immediately. I touch her other arm, holding her in place as gently as I can.

"I want you to know I'm here if you need me, okay?"

She turns then, and behind the bright smile, her sadness is just visible. I touch her face and kiss her sweet, pouty lips. Our mouths move like we've been doing this forever, like our lips were meant to touch and touch and touch until every nerve ending in my body is awake and ready. Being with Celine is like reaching out to catch a falling star.

If we were both less fucked up by the past, maybe we could enjoy the present together, but it's just not meant to be. Playing games doesn't feel right.

"Bye, Travis. And thanks."

She leaves me feeling more conflicted than I ever have.

7

CELINE

"Two cheese and ham paninis."

The man behind the counter taps Gabriella's order into the register.

"And these." She holds up two sodas, which he adds to the bill. "I'll get this." Gabriella turns to me with a smile. "You can get the next ones."

Alternating paying just makes things easier, and it's Gab's turn, so I'm fine with it. "Okay. Thanks."

A table by the window is vacated by a couple who were in the middle of a whispered argument when we arrived. I dash across the coffee shop to reserve it, leaving Gabriella to wait for our order.

Through the window, I watch streams of people moving between classes. I think I spot Elias's dark hair, but he disappears into a building across from my current vantage point.

I pull out my phone, open my Instagram account, and search through my notifications. There are a few likes on my most recent posts; the kissing shots with Travis. I can't look at those photos because there is too much passion there that I now know wasn't real. He didn't want me.

Gabriella carefully carries a tray of our food and drinks across the coffee shop, narrowly missing one of Eddie's friends, who stands and shoves his chair directly in her path. "Watch it," she yells, much to his amusement.

"I swear, the guys around here just become bigger jerks by the day."

"You're just spoiled by all your mature boyfriends."

She nods and unwraps her sandwich, focusing on the filling spilling from the end as she takes her first bite. "Mmmm..." Chewing with wide eyes, she watches as I do the same. "It's so good."

I nod in agreement as the hunger that built through my last lecture finally subsides into satisfaction.

"So, we can sit here and talk sandwiches all day, or you can tell me why my brother was sucking your face last night." She raises her eyebrows and stares pertinently at my phone.

"He's helping me with something...I mean, he helped me with something."

"By sticking his tongue down your throat? Travis is a regular good Samaritan."

"You and Ellie told me the best way to get over a bad relationship was with some rebound sex."

Gab's mouth drops open. "That was Ellie, and you had sex with my brother?"

A girl at the table next to us turns and gawps, and I stare at her for long enough to shame her into minding her own business.

"No. No sex. We made out in public so Eddie would know I'm moving on."

"Oh...so Travis is your rebound date."

"Revenge date." I correct her, and she blinks in surprise.

"And Elias and Dornan?"

"Revenge dates." I crack open my soda and take a long drink of the sweet, fizzy liquid.

"Revenge sex?"

My cheeks heat before I can reply, and the grin that splits Gabriella's face is enough to tell me it's pointless to deny it. "Revenge sex is hot."

"Jeez, Celine. I mean, Elias, I understand. You've been there already. A repeat of a one-night stand is easy. But Dornan. He's a friend. Wasn't it weird?"

"Strangely no," I admit. "It was…"

She holds her hands out before I can finish. "I'm not sure I want to know. If you tell me something that makes it hard for me to look at him, he'll know we've been discussing his sexual prowess."

I shrug, twisting off a piece of bread and popping it into my mouth. "I can keep it all to myself." I probably should have from the start.

Gab glances at the ceiling like she's searching for celestial intervention. When she's inhaled and exhaled a deep breath, she fixes me with her angelic blue eyes. "It's weird as fuck, but you have to tell me everything."

"We went on a date to Blue Bar, then he showed me a good time."

Gabriella shakes her head. "Do you seriously think you'll get away with giving me that limited summary?"

I tip my head to the side and purse my lips to stop the smile that's threatening. "It was so good. And not weird at all until it was over. Then, there was this moment when I thought he was going to tell me he wants more."

"He didn't?"

I shake my head. "He knows the score. He knows we're just messing around playing games to show Eddie how easily I'm getting over his ass."

Gab's mouth tightens, and she looks around at the other occupied tables surrounding us. Leaning in closer, she lowers her voice. "I heard Eddie's dating already."

My heart makes a weird squeezing pulse in my chest. "The one he cheated on me with?"

"Abbey Swanson."

"Abbey?" What the fuck? He didn't cheat on me with her, or maybe he did. Maybe he was dicking three of us around at the same time.

"Yeah. I overheard one of his jock buddies commiserating over the fact that Abbey's now off the market. Apparently, Eddie's taking her to that fancy new restaurant, Eclet, the day after tomorrow."

"Nice." My face feels hot, and the back of my neck is cold.

So much for showing Eddie. He's already replaced me with someone most guys at this university would regard as a ten.

I lower what's left of my sandwich to the plate, my hunger replaced by a wave of nausea.

"Hey." Gab places her hand on my arm. "Eddie's the king of the douches, Celine. A fleck of dick cheese. Just forget about him. Focus on the good things in your life."

That's easy for her to say. She's got three men who love her. What have I got? Two men who can fuck like gods, and one who told me I was trying to bandage my wounds with sex. I've got some sexy photos on Instagram and some hot memories. None of it keeps me warm at night or makes this terrible sinking feeling disappear.

But I know what will. Turning up at Eclet with three of the sexiest men in this town and showing Eddie that I've beat him three times over.

Elias will come, and Dornan. Travis's parting words were that he's there for me if I need him. Well, I need him now.

"You're plotting something." Gab narrows her kohl-rimmed eyes at me, tucking her hair behind her ear and leaning closer. "Tell me."

"What do you think about me turning up at Eclet with Elias, Dornan, and Travis?"

"I think it's unnecessary."

Leaning back in my chair, I focus on my plate. "It feels necessary to me."

"Well, then you should do it...if they agree." When I meet her gaze, it's filled with concern. "I'm just worried about you, sweetie. You're not acting like yourself. Half the time you were with Eddie, you were moaning about him and trying to find ways to escape the relationship."

"Exactly. But that's what I wanted when it was on my terms. None of what's happened has been on my terms."

"So, you don't want him back?"

I screw up my nose in disgust. "No. Ewww."

"You just want to prove that you're unaffected by what he's done?"

"Moving on to bigger and better things."

"And do you have feelings for Elias or Dornan...or Travis?" It's her turn to wrinkle her nose at her brother's name.

I think about how it felt to be in Elias's and Dornan's arms and the soft way Travis spoke to me about not wanting to hurt me. None of it could be labeled as feelings, but I'm not dead inside. They're gorgeous men who are caring enough to bother wanting to help me out. I enjoyed my time with them, even when Travis was trying to do what he thought was the right thing. He challenged me, and I like that.

"It's all just a big game."

Gabriella seems reassured, and she doesn't press me any further. Instead, she tells me about Dalton's catering successes and Blake's new tattoo. Kain doesn't go unmentioned, either. He's almost entirely recovered from the incident that nearly took his life and back to giving her non-stop orgasms. Seeing her so happy leaves me with mixed feelings. She's my friend, and I couldn't be more ecstatic that she's found 'the ones'. But my envy is sharp and only adds to my hurt.

I don't finish my sandwich before we both have to leave for our next lecture.

When I'm done for the day, I grab a box of donuts and a carton of milk from the store and head back to my dorm. It's not exactly a nutritious dinner, but I'm in the mood for a sugary overload. When life is sour, only sweet will do.

As I eat a chocolate-glazed donut, I start to type out a request to Dornan. He's the most likely to agree to my crazy plan on the basis that we're friends above everything else. Then, I pause and stop chewing while I consider a different approach. If I send each of them an individual message, they won't see that I've asked the others. If I set up a group, maybe that'll make each of them more likely to want to say yes. A little peer pressure driven by a smidge of jealousy. The friction between Elias and Dornan has built up over years. Regardless of whether they're possessive over me, the competitive spirit lingers. I don't get the feeling that Travis is competitive about women. He seems relaxed about life in general. But at least this way, I'm being transparent.

I call the group Fake Dates and invite them all. Then, I type out my message.

Emergency! Eddie is taking a new girlfriend out to a restaurant tomorrow. Please, can you guys take me there….all three of you for maximum impact? I'll owe you for life!

When I send it, the piece of donut I've been chewing gets caught in my throat, and I have to glug down half a glass of milk to stop myself from choking. The message is delivered, and Dornan is the first to start typing a response. But then he stops. Elias looks like he's typing something out too, but then he stops. Travis doesn't type at all.

I wait and wait, wondering if anyone will answer either way. They agreed to help me with this fake dating game, but now it seems like they're backing out. I rest my phone face down on my desk and press my hands to my face.

An image of Eddie and Abbey sharing food and making a toast with glasses of bubbling champagne floods my mind, making me want to scream. His smug face grins at me from my own imagination, and a bubble of fury swells up inside me, so visceral that I slam my hand down on my desk. My pen pot overturns, and the remaining donuts jump on the plate. The bones in my hand vibrate and then ache from the impact, and I'm immediately regretful. Using my good hand to rub my hurting palm, I grumble. *Stupid. Stupid. Stupid.*

Why can't I just do what Travis and Gab suggested and forget this whole thing? Why does Eddie's infidelity grate at my skin and crush my soul? I want to be able to put this all behind me, but even considering it makes Eddie the winner in my mind. *Stupid. Stupid. Stupid.*

I think about my dad and how easily he left and let the contact between us reduce to almost nothing. Eddie didn't even think about cheating because he didn't think I was worth worrying about losing.

I twist my hands together in my lap, hating the slick, dark pulse of rejection that fills me.

Maybe this final date will be enough? I can put all these ideas of revenge games behind me and move on.

The trouble is that I can't imagine what my future looks like.

My family is shattered.

My mom is resentful, and my dad is absent.

My friends are all partnered up and living their best lives.

My sister is blissfully married with a gorgeous baby.

And I'm just stuck. An outsider. Rejected.

My phone vibrates, and I grab it and check my messages. It's Dornan. He says he'll do it. One down, two to go. Now, I just have to wait to see whether Elias and Travis will step up to the plate.

8

CELINE

"When I return your test papers, I want you to look at where you've gone wrong. For some of you, this might be your first failure. Take note of your errors, apply yourself, and you'll be back on track. For others, this test may be another in a line of below pass marks. If that's you, I'm afraid you'll find it difficult to pick up your grade at this point in the semester."

I stare at the red mark of failure and swallow against the lump in my throat. This isn't my first bad grade in this class. I've been struggling to find time to do the required work and focus enough to take in what little I have been doing.

I glance around the room at the other students. Some are happy. Others, like me, have furrowed foreheads and grim mouths. Elias is at the back, packing away his things and smiling. Did he seriously pass this? It was tough. Our eyes meet—it's the first time I've seen him since our night together—and he raises his eyebrows expectantly. He wants to know if I passed. I shake my head, and his smile fades into a concerned grimace.

I turn back to force my notepad and pen into my

stuffed bag. When I follow the crowd from the room, Elias is waiting for me in the hall.

"Hey."

I move with the stream of exiting students, inadvertently forced to stand close to him. His scent is different today. Something woody with an orange undertone that floods my senses. When he touches my arm, I'm overwhelmed with memories of him naked and fierce, looming over me and thrusting powerfully. "You didn't pass?" God, his voice is just so rough and deep.

Shaking my head, I stare down the hallway, embarrassed to meet his gaze. He's going to make fun of me. I know he is, but I can't avoid answering. "I'm flunking," I say. "It isn't just this test."

"Why didn't you say something? We could study together."

I blink, surprised. Where are his usual snarky comments? This isn't like Elias at all. "I didn't think to....you know...because we're not..."

I want to finish the sentence by saying 'close' or 'friends,' but that sounds ridiculous in light of what we did a few nights ago.

And in the past.

Not close enough to share class notes, but close enough to share bodily fluids.

My life is ridiculous right now.

"You're happy to ask me out on a fake date and do stuff with me, but not to tell me you need help with a class?" His confused expression makes me flush hot with embarrassment.

"No one wants to own up to flunking."

Elias tips his head to the ceiling and blows out a long breath. "You know, this makes no sense. I can help you. All you have to do is ask."

"Yeah, well, asking for help isn't exactly easy. Especially when people don't reply." I pretend to look down at my watch rather than face him.

"I wanted to talk to you about that."

"You know what, Elias? Don't worry about it. Forget I asked. It's fine. And I don't need help studying. I'll manage on my own."

I turn away before he can reply and speed-walk through the building until the doors to the exit are in view. He doesn't follow, but I don't expect him to.

When Gabriella and Ellie turn up at my dorm with a bottle of wine and a massive bar of chocolate, my instinct is to tell them I'm fine and they can go home to their men. All I want is to be left in peace so I can curl up on my bed and stare at the wall. But their faces are so overly bright, and they seem so pleased with themselves that I can't find it in me to reject their efforts to help me through a dark time.

"So, Colby said this is a good wine. I know nothing about wine, but since he's been working, he's picked up some adulting skills that are coming in useful."

"Soooo mature and grown up." Gabriella wrestles with the expensive bottle of wine, trying to pull out the cork.

I find three plastic tumblers for us to drink out of. "Would Colby cringe if he saw these glasses?"

"Probably." Ellie unwraps the chocolate, breaking it into long rows and places it on my desk. "He does like things to be done properly, which is mostly a good thing."

"If he puts as much effort into sex as he does into choosing wine, you're onto a winner." Finally pulling the cork from the bottle, Gabriella holds it up and whoops. "I thought that fucker was never coming out."

We all giggle as Gab pours us almost overflowing cups of wine. I gulp mine with more enthusiasm than I should, bearing in mind I'm supposed to be cramming to improve my grades.

"So, Gab told me about Eddie and Abbey. How are you feeling about it?" Ellie bites off a chunk of chocolate, chewing it with her eyes focused on me.

"You know how I feel."

"Well, Dornan mentioned you asked him out for another fake date?" She eyes me carefully as though she's conscious that she might be pushing too hard but feels justified in doing so. Her friendship with Dornan dates to kindergarten, so I get why she might feel protective.

"I asked them all: Dornan, Elias, and Travis. Dornan is the only one who agreed."

"He's worried about you. We all are."

I bristle because this surprise wine and chocolate night is starting to feel like an intervention. "I'm fine," I lie. "This whole thing is just a bit of fun. You're the one who told me that rebound dick beats this." I wave my arms around to indicate what we're doing.

"Yeah, well, I kind of meant a one-night stand with a hot stranger, not hooking up with all the single men in our circle."

I frown. "It's not all the single men in our circle. Elias and Travis aren't even part of our circle. Do you not want me to hook up with Dornan? Is that what this is?" Ellie blinks and presses her lips together. Turning to Gab, I shrug. "Do you feel the same about Travis?"

She offers me a sympathetic expression. "It could get messy. Is it worth it?"

I put my now empty cup on my desk, feeling the alcohol warming my body already. "Men do this shit all the time, and no one has a thing to say about it. I just want to show Eddie that he means nothing to me and that I've moved on spectacularly and am fine without him."

"Well, you've done that." Ellie raises her glass in a toast. "Your Instagram is burning up with heat."

"All I wanted was one more night. To go out with all of them to the same restaurant as Eddie is taking Abbey. But Travis and Elias haven't replied, and it's just…" Feeling suddenly overwhelmed with emotion, I press my face into my hands. "I just…I can't talk about this with you. Can we change the subject?"

"No, honey." Ellie rests her hand on my shoulder. "We're friends through everything, okay? Good stuff and tough stuff. Don't shut us out when you need us the most."

"I'm flunking my classes. Everything's going wrong."

I can't look at either of my friends, but I sense them sharing unspoken communication. Ellie squeezes my shoulder, and Gab pats my leg.

"You've got a lot going on. I'm sorry that all this is happening to you."

"It's okay to feel overwhelmed, sweetie," Ellie adds. "When things pile up, it can feel like you can't catch a breath."

"I need another shitty cup of amazing wine," I say, forcing a bright smile on my face. Their pity is grating at my emotions. Gab pours me some more, and I gulp it down. It seeps through my brain with a tingling warmth that makes everything feel better. Even though I'm on my way to getting drunk, I can still register that drinking away pain isn't a good thing.

Mom did this after the divorce. I think she might be an alcoholic, but I haven't confronted her about it. On my rare visits, there are way too many empty liquor bottles in the trash than there should be.

"Just give us a second and eat some of that chocolate. It is soooo good."

Ellie and Gab stand and search for their phones in their purses. Both disappear into the hallway, and their muted conversations are only a light murmur through the door. The chocolate is delicious, melting on my tongue and coating my throat. I close my eyes and moan, contemplating whether Ellie was wrong, and alcohol and chocolate actually beat rebound dick hands down.

Oh, who am I kidding? Between Dornan and Elias, I might be ruined for other men. Just thinking about those evenings of mindless passion makes me simmer inside and flush brightly on the outside. And Travis's kisses. My lips tingle when I recall how he worked to help me with my stupid fake dating games.

I finish two delicious rows of chocolate by the time my friends reappear in my doorway. "It's all sorted," Gabriella says. "Tomorrow. They'll pick you up and take you to Eclet."

"Who?"

"Dornan, Travis, and Elias."

I pace to my closet before pivoting to face Ellie and Gab. "A pity fake date? This situation is bordering on a joke!"

"But they're stepping up for you, Celine, because they want to help you. We all do. Just enjoy the date. Have fun. Wear your sexiest dress and blow out your gorgeous new hair into tantalizing waves. Forget about all the shitty stuff for one night. And when you've done what you wanted, we're here to help with the rest."

Their expressions are so earnest and hopeful that I stop myself from speaking the sadness-inspired bitter words on the tip of my tongue. I glance at my closet and the new clothes I've bought to suit my 'life after Eddie' style. Most of them still have tags attached.

"Help me pick something," I tell them.

So, instead of wallowing in my own sadness, I let my

friends help me put together an outfit that will knock the socks off of three men who have been reluctant to take me out and an ex-boyfriend I wish would take a running jump off a short pier.

These are crazy times.

9

DORNAN

Travis collects Elias first and then me before heading to Celine's building. The atmosphere in the car is strangely charged, and I'm grateful to be in the back seat where I feel less pressured to make conversation. This whole situation is weird. Not so much the three men to one woman ratio. That part has become almost ordinary in our small circle of friends. No, it's the fact that we're nearly strangers to each other, and there is this buzz of competitiveness rolling off the car's other occupants, which I don't appreciate.

Celine is my friend first and foremost, although, after our last date, I'm less sure about the simplicity of that statement. I know what happened between her and Elias, which makes my skin prickle. Her date with Travis was after mine, so I have no knowledge of what went on between them. I guess it must have gone okay because Travis is here for round two. I mean, date two.

I sigh because who the fuck knows what any of us are doing right now?

Playing stupid games, and to what end?

Elias is here for the sex. That's for sure. Travis is an

unknown quantity. And me. Well, I don't know what the fuck I want. To help my friend. A repeat of the other night. More.

Admitting that I have feelings for Celine that don't fit into the friendship mold is tough, especially under the circumstances. Jealousy isn't an emotion that sits well with me. Celine isn't serious about any of this, so jealousy is the least of my worries. Having feelings for a friend who's on the rebound is a recipe for disaster.

Elias clears his throat as though the silence in the car has become overwhelmingly uncomfortable for him. "So, what's the plan for tonight?" He twists to assess my expression and then stares at Travis's shadowy profile.

"Wine and dine Celine," Travis says. "Show Eddie she's a desirable girl so that he'll hopefully kick himself for being such a douche. And then watch Celine walk off into the sunset as a changed woman."

"That sounds like a lot to achieve on one fake date," I say.

"Did you fuck her?" Elias asks, and I almost choke on my own tongue.

"No." Travis's answer is quick and firm. "That's not my style."

"Did she want to fuck you?" Elias isn't dissuaded from asking what's on his mind by Travis's tight jaw.

"She did…"

He doesn't elaborate on why he didn't go through with it, but I make my own assumptions. He's a better man than both me and Elias.

"And what about tonight? What do you think she'll want to do after this four-way date?"

Travis's jaw ticks, and when he doesn't reply, Elias turns to me. "Did you fuck her?"

I nod solemnly because I'm not a kiss-and-tell kind of

guy, and answering this question is awkward.

Elias's eyes flash, but he doesn't ask about the specifics, which is a relief.

"What do you think, Dornan, about tonight?"

"I think we need to play everything by ear. Celine's on a revenge mission. Who knows where her head is."

"We should be on the same page." Elias stares at Travis's profile as though his comment is aimed solely at him.

"And what page is that?" Travis glances at Elias before refocusing on the road again. "The page where we don't make Celine feel worse than she does already. She's failing classes, and this thing with Eddie is affecting her way more than it should."

I don't have a chance to give my opinion because Celine is waiting outside her dorm, looking like a million dollars. I mean, she always looks good, but tonight she could rival any celebrity on a red carpet. When I glance at Elias, his tongue is practically hanging out of his mouth. Travis's eyes widened at the sight of her. He might not have been on Elias's page before, but he's halfway there now.

Celine tugs open the door and slides into the seat next to me.

"Hey, boys." Her voice is bright and upbeat, but there's something a little artificial behind it that I'm not used to hearing. A tremble of nerves, maybe.

"There's our girl." Elias puts his hand behind Travis's headrest to turn himself. He shakes his head and then folds his lips as though she looks good enough to taste. I can't disagree with him there.

"Has anyone been to this restaurant before?" she asks.

"Nope," we all say in unison.

"It's supposed to be good. And tonight is on me, by the

way. Please don't make any kind of deal about that. I asked you all out. I'm flexing my dad's credit card tonight."

I can't be the only one who doesn't feel great about going on a date and letting the woman pay. I was raised to be a gentleman, and I don't even want to think about how my dad would view this whole setup.

Travis fiddles with the radio, putting on an old tune that my dad used to play in his car when I was growing up. "Are you seriously listening to this? This is old man music."

"Errr..." Celine puts her hand up. "Don't even think about criticizing, Dornan Walsh. Music from this era is the best. Nothing new comes close."

Travis chuckles. "She's got good taste. I'll give her that."

Their back-and-forth breaks the ice and we spend the rest of the car journey joking about how Travis listens to dad-music and how Celine is deluded not to appreciate newer bands. Even Elias joins in the jokes, shrugging off his usual surly attitude. I start to dread tonight a little less.

We find a parking spot near Eclet and gather around Celine like she's a celebrity client, and we're her security detail.

"Ready?" Travis holds out the crook of his arm, and Celine eyes it for a couple of seconds before sliding her hand through. We're greeted inside by an impeccably dressed server who escorts us to a table in the middle of the restaurant. I take a furtive look around for Eddie but don't see him. Travis drags Celine's chair out from under the table and helps her to take a seat. He's really pulling out all the stops tonight.

Elias and I take seats on either side of her, and Travis

opposite. We each take the menu offered and begin to work our way down the long list of food with difficult-to-pronounce names. "What is this stuff?" Elias fixes me with a panicked look over the top of the menu he's clutching tightly with both hands. I'm glad I'm not the only one out of my depth.

"Mostly French food." Travis runs his finger down the menu and nods. "If you don't know what something is, I can try to work it out."

"Not just a pretty face," Elias says sarcastically.

Celine doesn't seem overwhelmed by the menu. She's already folded it neatly and is arranging a crisp white serviette in her lap.

"What are you getting?"

She smiles at me sweetly. "The duck."

"Duck?" Elias gasps.

"It's delicious. The lamb also looks good."

"There's lamb?" He looks down to search, then puts the menu down in frustration. "Travis, can you order me the lamb?"

"Sure."

"I'll take that too."

"All right. And drinks?"

"Beer." Elias blurts the word as though he's parched.

"We should have red wine."

"We should?"

"We should," Travis agrees. He opens the drinks menu and looks down at the list. "Here's a good one."

I swear the guy is only a few years older than us, but he's making me feel like a preteen. When my eyes meet Elias's, I can sense he has the same feelings.

Before we have a chance to order, Celine stiffens in her chair. I turn to find Eddie sauntering into the restaurant, holding the hand of a girl I assume is his date, Abbey. Beneath the table, I rest my hand on Celine's thigh. "Take it easy."

Her leg is rigid, and her jaw is tight, precisely the kind of expression Eddie would love to gloat over. I lean over, sliding my hand into her nape, and pull her face to mine so I can kiss her. She seems surprised at first but then softens into the kiss. I don't let her go until I hear the server asking Eddie and Abbey if they would like to order drinks immediately or take a look at the menu first.

Celine's eyes are dazed when she lifts her lids, and they brush over each of us. When they reach Elias, he wastes no time in doing the same as me. Watching him kiss Celine when my mouth still tastes of her is strange. A pang of jealousy is immediately swamped by heat that swells my cock. Jesus. The way Elias grips Celine's hair and controls her kiss is hot.

Across the restaurant, my eyes meet Eddie's, and the fury in his expression is like iced water down the back of my neck.

I don't fear the guy. Not at all. He's all talk and minimal action. We play on the same team but manage to avoid ever having to speak to each other except when Coach demands it.

Celine and Elias separate, and I mutter, "Eddie's not looking happy."

For the first time since we saw them arrive, Celine smiles.

"Well, this is just going perfectly."

The server returns to take our order, which Travis relays perfectly in a French accent that sounds native. I thought he worked in Germany, but maybe I'm mistaken, and it was actually France.

Eddie's concentration is focused on Abbey, but his shoulders are tense, and he's angled himself, so I can only glimpse his side profile.

"I feel sorry for the girl," Travis says, sipping the wine poured into our tall bell-shaped glasses.

"I do, too." Celine licks the blood-red stain from her lips, stirring my cock again. "She doesn't know what she's letting herself in for."

"Maybe you should talk to her?"

Celine shrugs. "I wouldn't have listened. When he smiled at me, every reservation I ever had about him melted away. If I can be a fool, she probably will be, too."

"You're not a fool," Travis interjects abruptly. "He is."

"And he's looking over here again," I whisper.

Travis reaches across the table and takes Celine's hand. I don't know if it's for effect or because he genuinely feels she needs reassurance. Either way, it makes Eddie's cheeks heat and his eyes narrow.

"Keep doing that," I say. "It's working."

Elias takes Celine's other hand, pressing her knuckles to his lips, and I try to stifle a smile. This shouldn't be fun, but it is. If Eddie was less of a douche, then maybe I'd feel bad, but he deserves everything he gets.

The servers bring our meals, and everything looks delicious. At the same time, Eddie and Abbey are also served their food. I cut into my lamb and take a bite, savoring the deliciously soft, salty meat covered in a slightly sweet, wine-flavored gravy. I cut another piece and extend my fork to Celine. "You have to try this."

She opens her mouth, and I gently ease the meat between her lips. The moan she makes as she chews reminds me of the way she sounded during sex. "Mmmm...that is sooooo goooooood." She rolls her eyes the same way she did when I made her come.

"This is fucking delicious," Elias says, shoving a huge mouthful of lamb and potatoes into his mouth. The portions might be smaller than I'd like, but the flavors are all there.

"In Europe, these kinds of restaurants are everywhere. Apart from fast-food joints, the standard of food is way higher." Travis is scooping mussels from their shells as he speaks, grossing me out.

"I can believe that. What's Germany like?" Celine asks.

"Interesting. The culture is very different. The people are more reserved in some ways and freer in others, and the humor is drier."

Celine takes another sip of her wine. "Did you get to see a lot while you were there?"

"I did. The German people are proud of their culture and history. I enjoyed sightseeing. The beer and bratwurst were the best, though."

"That's a sausage, right?" Elias glugs down half his red wine without savoring the expensive flavor at all.

"Yep. A big sausage."

"I've got one of those." He laughs. "You don't need to go to Germany for that."

Celine snickers at his ridiculous attempt at a joke. She holds out both hands with her palms up. "Elias's dick, or German food, culture and history." The hand she metaphorically placed Elias's dick in moves up and up.

With an accompanying grin, Elias says, "Nothing beats my dick."

Celine reaches out to touch his thigh. "You're right, baby. Your dick is the best."

"Can we not talk about dick right now?" Travis wrinkles his nose, holding a quivery mussel on the end of his fork and eyeing it with an air of disgust.

Celine laughs loudly, attracting the attention of a couple of the other diners.

And Eddie.

He's staring over with blazing eyes.

"Yeah. Maybe the dick talk is better reserved for a less expensive restaurant," I say. A prickle of weird energy runs over my forearms, like the moments before a storm when the air starts to feel charged.

"Well, I recommend you guys all travel when you're done with your studies. The world is a big and fascinating place."

"I don't even have a passport," Elias admits.

"My dad is in Canada right now," Celine says.

"Have you been to visit?"

She shakes her head and presses her lips together into a grim line. I don't know much about her family other than her parents are divorced, and she's already an aunt.

"You should go." Travis spoons up some of the broth around the mussels. "Beautiful country."

"I haven't been invited."

Elias glances in my direction, silently asking if I know about this. I shrug back that I don't.

"Where would you like to go if money was no object?" Travis tips his glass to Elias.

"Romania."

We all stare at Elias in shock. "Romania. As in Dracula country?"

He shakes his head and rolls his eyes at me. "My country. Well, my mom's at least. I still have family there...distant family."

"So that's where Mazur comes from?"

Elias shakes his head. "It's Polish."

"Same as Gabriella's boyfriends," Travis says.

"Lauder is Scottish," Celine offers.

"Walsh is Irish," I add.

"Cross is English. We don't know much about our

family history, though." Travis looks over at Eddie. "What about Eddie? Where's his family from?"

"The depths of hell." Celine scowls. "The flaming center of the Earth. I met his mom once. I swear that woman has an unhealthy obsession with her son. That's probably why he's so toxic. She hated me."

"She must be an idiot," Travis says.

"Definitely an idiot," I agree.

"Awwww...thanks guys!" She reaches out to touch our arms again and I decide that it's time for another kiss. Celine acquiesces, and it's sweet and tantalizing. I'm so lost in the feel of her lips against mine that I miss Eddie rising from his seat and approaching our table. I only know he's getting close when Elias and Travis stand abruptly, their chairs skittering backward with a terrible grating sound.

"What the fuck?" Eddie yells. "You're getting passed around this lot like a fucking whore?"

"Back the fuck up." Elias looms over Eddie like a dark knight, ready to slay whatever's in his way. "What she does is none of your fucking business anymore, so get your cheating ass out of my face."

I'm up and making my way around the table to join Elias and Travis, keeping Celine behind me so she's out of sight. With the three of us standing shoulder to shoulder, Eddie seems to wilt. His eyes flick between us, narrowed and filled with hatred, but his face is twisted with a smirk. "Are you enjoying the pussy I rejected? It's already ruined enough for you guys to fit right in."

Celine begins to get to her feet behind me, but I grasp her arm and hold her tightly away from Eddie. There's no way she's going to face him when the three of us are here to protect her from his vicious words and who knows what else.

"Talk like that again about Celine, and you'll be swallowing your own teeth," Travis growls.

"Back up, Eddie. You're not going to win here." I jerk forward, and Eddie responds by stumbling back. Elias laughs, and Eddie's face flushes bright red with embarrassment.

"Three small men," he says. "For one stretched-out woman. You're perfect for each other." Big words, but he's returning to a shocked and horrified-looking Abbey. The manager of the restaurant stands close by. A small man, he seems to realize that intervening in an argument between four huge men isn't a sensible idea. I hold up my hand and apologize before retaking my seat. We eat in silence as people around us return to their meals and whisper hushed criticisms of our behavior. Celine is quiet, but as she eats a slice of duck, she smiles at me with a genuine spark I haven't seen for a while.

"That was frickin' awesome," she says after a while, and I have to admit that it felt damned good.

10

CELINE

Eddie leaves the restaurant before us, and when he's gone, I breathe a sigh of relief. It felt amazing to watch Elias, Travis, and Dornan stand up to him and defend me against his ridiculous slurs. I mean, seriously. He sounded so bitter; if Abbey doesn't take that as a serious red flag, she deserves him.

I pay for the meal on my way to the bathroom and before the men can object. When I say I'm ready to leave, they all pull out their wallets and seem genuinely aggrieved that I got there before them.

In the car, I settle back against the plush leather seat and exhale. "Thank you so much for tonight. It went perfectly."

"You thought that was perfect?" Travis turns in the driver's seat to study me. His dark blue eyes scan over my dress, lingering on my breasts before he checks himself.

"My revenge games don't meet with your approval, huh?"

He shrugs. "That man isn't worth the steam off your piss, Celine. Please, can you promise me that this is the last revenge game you plan to play?"

"I guess it is."

"Good."

He turns and puts the car into drive. "Time to go home?"

"I've got another idea," I say.

"Oh, yeah?" Elias sounds hopeful, which makes me smile. The way he kissed me in the restaurant left my panties wet and my pussy aching, and Dornan...well, Dornan almost finished me right there and then.

"Molly's?" I meet Travis's eyes in the mirror and almost melt in the intensity of his gaze.

"I can drop you guys there..."

"I want you to come, too."

Dornan makes a low rumbling sound in his throat.

Travis, who's trying to focus on the road in front of him, swallows loudly.

This is my one chance to convince him that I'm not just seeking comfort to recover from Eddie's rejection. One last opportunity to know what it could be like to be worshiped by three men, the way my friends are every night.

"I know what you said, okay? But this isn't about being on the rebound. This is about me choosing to have some fun. Are you guys up for showing me a good time?"

"Together?" Elias turns in his seat, glancing between me and Dornan. His dark eyes light periodically with flashes from the streetlamps. Behind us, someone beeps their horn, and inside my chest, my heart starts to pound.

"Together," I agree. "If Ellie and Gabriella can do it, why not me?"

"I'm in," Elias says quickly. "Dornan?"

I turn to face my friend, whose cheeks have reddened.

He reaches out to take my hand in his, studying it. "I'll do whatever you need."

It's a gentle declaration from someone who obviously cares about me. He's always been a giving person, but this is beyond everything that we've been to each other.

"Travis?" Elias asks. His tone is firm, urging Travis to agree before it all falls apart.

I stare into the rearview mirror, waiting for Travis to tear his eyes from the road. For a long time, he stays focused on the route ahead. Elias sighs and cracks his knuckles. Dornan squeezes my hand. I don't ask again. I won't beg.

Then Travis's inky-blue eyes meet mine, and he nods once. "Okay."

I don't realize I'm holding my breath until he says it.

At Molly's, Travis parks close to the reception, and Dornan books the room. When he returns with the key, I throw open the car door and pull myself onto legs that feel weak already. The walk to our destination is short, but the air is laced with so much anticipation, it's like wading through treacle.

I can't help myself from studying each of the men I've seduced tonight, remembering the heated moments we've already experienced, priming myself for what's about to happen.

Dornan opens the door and allows me to pass first. I slide off my heels, placing them against the wall, and then shrug off my light jacket, laying it over a chair in the corner. The door clicks shut, and the lock is turned.

When I face Elias, Dornan, and Travis, they're all gathered together, waiting.

There's a moment of awkwardness, but it's destroyed when I slide my dress from my shoulders and ease it over my hips until it pools at my feet. I want this so much that my fingers tremble and my heart races in a wild drumbeat.

I can do this. I can undress in front of three men. I can let them use my body and give me the kind of pleasure I'll be able to store away like warm summers in my memory.

This is exactly what I want to do now I'm living in my time. The freeness to decide without judgement or consequence is intoxicating.

Elias mutters an expletive as I reach behind my back to unhook my bra.

Three sets of eyes focus on my breast as my nipples harden in the cool air. I run my fingers over my soft flesh, gently pinching the tips as Elias breaks rank and steps forward.

He lifts me with one hand scooped beneath my ass, kissing me so deeply that my soul aches. But rather than pressing me up against the wall, he climbs onto the bed and deposits me in the center. "I have to share you tonight," he murmurs against my ear. "I'm not good at sharing."

"There's plenty of me to go around." He tugs my panties over my hips and spreads my legs wide.

"Yes, there is."

As Elias's tongue seeks out my clit, I seek out Dornan and Travis in the darkness. Dornan is close, moving to sit on the edge of the bed, his big, rough hand stroking up my arm and over my breasts. I moan as the sensation from my nipple, and clit collide, fizzing through my nervous system like sherbet on the tip of my tongue. Travis seems frozen, watching from the door.

"Travis." I hold my hand out to him, beckoning for him to come closer. He rounds the end of the bed, moving like he's sleepwalking or in a trance. When he's near enough, I take his hand and pull him close to kiss his lips. There has to be a way to make him more comfortable. I want him to let go and experience the same way I am. I know a secret about him that makes this desire even greater.

His lips are tentative but become teasing. But when Elias pushes two thick fingers inside me, I break away to moan loudly.

"That's it," Dornan murmurs. "That's it. She's getting close."

Elias's onyx eyes meet mine over my belly, flaming like he wants to devour me whole. I gasp as Travis touches my other breast, sliding his palm over every inch of skin he can find. All my worries that he'd leave, that he'd reject me, melt away.

"Oh god," I cry out. "Oh…oh." My hand grips Elias's thick dark hair to keep him exactly where I need him, but he's not going anywhere. He wants to make me come with a level of determination that borders on obsessiveness.

"Don't stop," I hiss as he pumps harder into me. "Don't… don't… don't….ohhhhhh."

I arch my back as the orgasm rips through me, my heart beating so fast I hear it thundering in my ears. White flashes blast behind my eyes, and my body quivers and spasms, totally out of control.

"That's it," Travis croons, lowering his mouth to my nipple and sucking. He keeps the orgasm going for seconds longer with the sharp tug of his lips on my flesh.

I close my eyes, dwelling in my own pleasure as the sounds of clothes being shed fill the room. Only when the rippling between my thighs has stopped do I raise my eyes to appreciate the men surrounding me.

There is so much to appreciate; I don't know where to look. Elias's broad chest fills my vision, the rounded bulk of his shoulders and biceps so potent a shiver passes through me. He fists his thick cock, gripping it so hard I wince on his behalf. I want to replace his fingers with mine and feel all of that girth and hardness.

Next to him, Dornan is just as muscular but has a bulkier quality that makes my mouth water. He shifts on his feet as though he's waiting for the ball to go into play. His huge quads shift, and his cock taps his stomach impatiently.

And Travis? Oh, Travis. I knew he'd be sexy beneath his classy clothes, but nothing prepared me for his lean, muscular body. He's built like a swimmer with a tight ladder of abs leading down to that V of muscle that makes me want to whimper.

It's like I hit a triple jackpot.

They eye me with three very different expressions. Elias with determined fervor, Dornan with tentative arousal, and Travis, like he's worried I might shatter at any second.

"I'm ready," I say, spreading my legs. "Look."

Stroking between my legs, my finger becomes slick with my arousal. I lick it and relish the groans of three men who appear so ravenous it's comical. I've always been sexually confident and being surrounded by three such gorgeous men has that amped up one hundred percent.

Elias is the one to break first, flipping me onto my front and yanking my body against his so my back is pressed against his front. His hand clasps my throat, slightly restricting my breathing. "You want us all at the same time?" he breathes in my ear. "Or one after the other."

"I'm not sure," I admit. I mean, I've thought about so many different scenarios when I'm alone in bed at night, but now, faced with the reality, my mind is blown at the options.

"Well, I guess we'll take the lead. Dornan, get in front

of her."

Dornan rounds the bed as Elias arranges me so I'm resting on my palms and knees. His cock is so big and blunt at my entrance that when he pushes inside me, it burns. I gaze up at Dornan, who's kneeling in front of me. "Suck his cock, Celine." The forcefulness of Elias's order is like a finger over my clit. I open my mouth wide and take Dornan as deep as I can, feeling him at the back of my throat before he pulls back. "Jesus, Celine. Take it easy."

I have to smile at that, even though my mouth is full.

Elias forces his way into me as deep as he can go. My belly aches with the size of him, but his hand on my lower back forces my hips to tip, and suddenly the depth is more manageable. "You feel so fucking good." He starts moving in gentle rolling waves at first, then harsher thrusts that make me gag on Dornan. I search for Travis in my periphery, and he's close, his eyes moving between what Elias and Dornan are doing to me, his fist wrapped around his cock.

That's an image I'll store in my masturbation library forever.

Pulling away from Dornan, I urge Travis to come closer.

His eyes are wide when I take his cock into my mouth. His hand goes to my cheek, not controlling but guiding. "Harder," he urges, and I hollow my cheeks, biting down through my lips to give him the tightest stimulation.

"Does she feel good?" Elias asks.

"So fucking good," Travis groans. He closes his eyes as I work him, barely maintaining a rhythm with Elias so deep.

"Her pussy's getting tighter," Elias says through clenched teeth. The pad of his thumb brushes over my asshole, once, twice, then presses harder, making me moan. "We can fuck you here too if you want," he says. He spits, and warm slickness slides between my cheeks. His thumb breaches and pushes inside too, and even though it's tiny compared to his cock, I feel totally full. "You're tight, Celine. So fucking tight."

"Oh shit," Travis grunts, as though the thought of my tight little asshole is too arousing for him to contemplate.

"Switch," Elias says, pulling out and leaving me empty.

Dornan slides off the bed and taps my hip. "On your back, Celine."

I quickly flip over, gazing up at the mountain of a man currently suiting up. It's a sight that will be burned into my mind forever. His hands work fast, rolling a condom down his thick length. His eyes flick up to mine, and he smiles. "Back up a little."

"But my head will hang over the edge of the bed."

"Trust me." Dornan climbs over me, bracing himself on muscular arms that bulge as they tense. As I tip my head back, Elias moves closer.

Oh...I see what they have planned. I've never sucked dick this way, but I'm game for trying. Is this what Ellie and Gab do with their men? I make a mental note to ask for at least some juicy details at some point in the future.

They time it so that they enter me at the same time. Elias fills my mouth, groaning as I take him deep into my throat. I close my eyes as Dornan thrusts into my pussy, his thickness stretching me wide. Not to be left out, Travis focuses all of his attention on my breasts, and I feel like an instrument being played for the beautiful music it can make. My mind swims, disconnecting as heat pools between my thighs and nerve endings fire wherever I'm being touched.

"I'm close," Elias grunts, but I already know he is because his thighs are trembling, and he uses my shoulders to brace himself.

"Me, too." Dornan speeds, using his hips to slam into

my clit. He's so big that my ligaments strain to accommodate him, and I hook a leg over his shoulder to deepen the penetration.

Higher and higher, they push me. Closer and closer to coming. My head spins, half from arousal and half from oxygen deprivation, as Elias thrusts into my mouth.

I lose myself as they use me for their pleasure, and the weightlessness expands inside me, setting me free.

"Oh, FUUUCKKK." Dornan seizes over me, his body becoming a wall of strained muscle, his face twisted and flushed as pleasure overcomes him. Elias pulls out of my mouth, using his hand to finish himself, groaning like he's expelling his last breath, and it's the sight of his cum leaking in ribbons over his fingers that triggers me to finish again.

"Fuck, Celine." Dornan pants, breath rasping, chest heaving. He's still inside me, thrusting to prolong my orgasm. The soft stroke of Travis's hands over my body sends me into a transcendent space I've never experienced before.

No wonder my friends risked everything for their unconventional relationships. If this is how good it can be, I don't think I'll ever want to go back.

11

TRAVIS

This is nothing like I thought it would be. When Celine suggested the four of us hook up, all I could think about was the weirdness of being in a room with two other naked dudes. Like, how would that work?

My sister has this kind of relationship, but I've tried not to overthink the practicalities of her sex life. In fact, I'm in total denial that she even has one!

Dornan and Elias are comfortable with each other because they play sports together. They've probably seen each other naked in the locker room more times than they can count. I'm not shy about my body. I know I look good, and even though they're built bigger than me, my physique is still trim and athletic.

But in the end, the only nakedness I've paid any attention to is Celine's.

Damn, she's beautiful, and it's not just what's on the outside. Yeah, she's got a pretty face, long hair, and a body that makes me feel hard just thinking about it. Yeah, she's petite but curvy, with nice natural tits and a narrow waist that my hands could probably span. But it's the fire in her eyes that lights me up. It's the way she asks for what she wants and how much she believes she deserves it that gets me hard. It's her vulnerability and the tough outer shell she's crafted for herself that makes me want to know her better.

She's asked for a one-night stand with three men who like her and care about her enough to play ridiculous revenge games to make her feel better. But I don't believe any of the men in this room are here for sex alone.

I've seen the way Elias stares at Celine like he doesn't want to like her but does. Dornan treats her like she's something precious he's scared of breaking. And me? Well, I don't really know what I'm doing. I returned from Germany with one goal. To forget what happened over there and get on with my life. I envisaged finding a new job and place to live, but not a new woman in my life.

It's just sex.

But it isn't. I know it isn't. Celine might be pretending, but the rest of us are getting tangled up, even though we might have reservations.

And now I'm the only one who hasn't come yet, and all eyes are on me.

Shit. When Celine touches my face and gazes up at me with dazed green eyes, the color of the forests on the outskirts of Berlin, my heart starts to pound. "Travis," she murmurs, pulling me closer. "It's time for you to take what you want." I kiss her deeply, grateful that Dornan has moved aside while my mind skitters over how I should play this. There are many things I'd love to do to Celine but don't have the courage to attempt in this scenario. My last girlfriend brushed off my desires like she thought they were weird and extreme. She made me feel shameful for even suggesting something outside the norm.

Celine pushes against my shoulder, forcing me to look at her. "I know what you like," she whispers.

"What?" I stare at her blankly, wondering what the hell

she's talking about.

"Kain has your porn collection in his closet. Gabriella found it."

She bites her bottom lip as I take in the fact that my sister has been discussing my sexual predilections with her friend. I will need to have a word with Gab about her loose tongue and lack of family loyalty.

Celine touches my arm. "Don't be mad at her. She didn't know we were going to get involved."

"What was in the porn?" Elias asks, disturbing the mortification I'm currently feeling.

I look over at him and his smug grin. Then he puts out his hands, palms facing me. "No judgments here, dude. All's good in the bedroom as long as it's consensual."

"Bondage," Celine says before I can decide whether I want to confess the room or not. "You like to be in control."

Shit. Shit. Shit.

What you want is sick. That's what my last girlfriend said to me. She thought I was a misogynist for wanting total control in the bedroom. That couldn't be further from the truth. I don't know why it turns me on to have a woman bound and helpless, but it has nothing to do with anything terrible. Bondage only works when there is consent. I'm not into anything non-consensual. In fact, the idea makes me feel physically sick.

Celine touches my cheek again, bringing my attention back to her. "I'm up for whatever you want to do. I brought some things in my purse, just in case."

My eyebrows shoot up to my hairline. "What did you bring?"

"Some silk ties...you know...so my wrists don't get bruised."

"Celine's like a boy scout for bondage," Elias laughs.

Dornan, still standing at the end of the bed, makes a strangled noise. "You guys are seriously going to get kinky?"

"Yeah." Celine's smile is wide and bright. "Why the fuck not? We're all here to enjoy ourselves. Might as well go all out."

I guess the idea must appeal to Dornan because his cock is rock-hard again.

I look away, the male nakedness thing still not sitting comfortably with me.

Celine asks Dornan to fetch her purse, which he does. She pulls out the silk ties and hands them to me. Elias gets off the bed so that Celine can move to the center.

The bed frame is old-fashioned and made of an orangy wood. There are struts for me to tie her hands to, but no footboard. I guess I'll need to improvise there. Without saying another word, I take Celine's arm and fasten the silk around her wrist, leaving enough space for her to be comfortable. She gasps softly when I lash the other end around the headboard and secure it tightly. The second hand is easier, and when she's fixed in place, I have to inhale a long breath and push it out in a rush to steady myself. Fuck, she looks good restrained for my pleasure. She brings her legs together like she's daring me to tie them, too.

"I'm going to need your help," I say to Dornan and Elias. Fastening ties around each of Celine's ankles, I feel the tremble in her legs. When I yank them open, handing the end of the left tie to Elias and the right to Dornan, Celine moans loudly.

"Hold her tightly, okay?"

"You all right, Celine?" Dornan asks.

"Yeah," she breathes. "Fuck yeah."

"I think she likes it." The smile in Elias's voice isn't mocking. He's happy that Celine is enjoying herself.

"Let's see how much she likes it."

I climb over her, taking in the stretched sinews beneath her arms and the way her breasts are pulled taut. I touch her top lip with my thumb, staring deep into her wide eyes. "How does it feel to be tied to this bed and held open by two men?"

Her tongue darts out to lick my skin. "Good."

My mind feels as blank as a clean white page, the realization of my fantasy almost too much. I run my fingers down the underside of her arm from her delicate wrist until the tips brush her tight little nipple. Her skin breaks out in goosebumps, and her whole body is racked by a shudder. When I circle the tight little peak with my finger, she moans, and when I tweak it with just enough strength to hurt a little, she cries out, arching her back. I repeat my actions on the other side, but instead of pinching, I pull her other nipple into my mouth and suck hard, finishing with a nip from my teeth.

"Yes," she gasps. "Oh fuck, yes."

I don't leave an inch of her skin untouched by my fingers or mouth. I explore each ridge and valley, the soft places that make her squirm and the unexplored places like each of her sweet ribs and the dip where her waist flares. I press them all with kisses.

When I'm close to her pussy, she tugs against her leg restraints, and Elias and Dornan hold firm, keeping her legs in a wide V, her pussy spread and open for me. When I run my fingers through the curls at the apex of her thighs, my mind goes back to the first night at Dalton's party, where her hair was red and vibrant. She's beautiful now, but I like her hair in its natural color.

Her pussy is pink and pretty, slick with her arousal. I lick the tip of my finger, stroking it over her clit, which is swollen and ready.

Celine curses, pulling again against the leg restraints.

"Lick her," Elias says in an excited whisper. "Let's see how much you can make her struggle."

His words make the ache in my dick so much stronger. I can't take on board how having my secret fantasy validated is amplifying my arousal. This kink that I saw as a burden or something to be ashamed of is now out in the open and being enjoyed by three other people.

When I lower my face to the apex of Celine's thighs, I'm hit by her scent, and a crank turns in my head. My desire for her is fierce, but suddenly, it's wrapped up in a layer of craving and need for possession. The thought of Eddie ever having had his hands on her makes me want to punch things. The idea that someone else will get to be like this with her when we're done is a rush of cold water down my spine.

Celine's binds are pulled tighter, and her movement is restricted even further. She groans as I touch the tip of my tongue to the spot directly above her clit, trying to shift but finding it impossible. Dornan and Elias are doing well at holding her immobile. "Please," she begs. "Make me come."

I smile against her thigh, then use my tongue to explore her folds, pushing at her sweet entrance and grinning when she cries out.

"Tease her," Dornan says. "Don't give her what she wants."

That's exactly what I intend to do. Make her squirm and pull against her binds. Make her internalize the knowledge that she's mine to do anything I like with.

I lick her again, resting my finger just inside her entrance. She tries to shift to make the penetration deeper, but Elias and Travis don't let her. Her groans grow in frustration, and I take hold of my cock, squeezing it and giving it three hard pulls just to relieve some of the burning tension which is driving me to bury myself inside her.

Her pussy flutters against my finger, a hungry little hole, but I don't give her more. The hungrier she is, the more I want to make her wait.

More slow licking sends my mind to a place where I feel like I'm hovering above our bodies, watching from outside myself. "Please," she gasps again.

"Maybe you should let her." Dornan kisses Celine's ankle, and her eyes focus on him, glazed with torment and desperation.

"Shall I let you come?" I ask her, already knowing the answer.

"Yes."

I hold my thumb above her clit and angle my cock into her pussy so I can push in with one thrust. She comes around my cock so violently that I see stars, fucking into her through wave after wave of beautiful contractions, watching her body twist and arch, stretching her breasts and making her hips writhe. "That's it, baby." She's done so well, put up with so much, and waited so long.

And now it's my turn.

"I want her on her front," I tell Elias.

Celine blinks up at me, surprised. Without any more instruction, Elias and Dornan drop her leg binds and begin to unfasten her wrists. They encourage her to turn over while I wait at the end of the bed, observing her being refastened on her front. Dornan and Elias are preparing her for me like a sacrifice at my altar.

Her ass is so tempting, curvy and round, with little divots at the top of her hips. Even with her legs pressed tightly shut, I can still see the swell of her sweet pussy pressed tightly together like a clamshell. She lays with her head turned to the left; her eyes focused on the middle distance. She doesn't help Elias and Dornan by spreading her legs. Instead, she waits for them to yank them apart using the binds, making a soft moaning plea as they do. I climb between her legs, spreading her ass cheeks so I get a clear view of everything that's mine. Hooking my thumbs inside her entrance, I spread her wider, groaning at the sight of all her pink, wet flesh.

"Shall I fill you up, Celine?" I ask, "Or leave you like this, gaping for us all to appreciate?"

"Fill me," she whispers. "Please."

"Such a good girl."

My cock slides into her so well at this angle. I cover her whole body with my weight, pressing so deep inside her that I bottom out, and she whimpers. Brushing my lips over the shell of her ear, I relish the shiver it induces. "Is this what you wanted, Celine? You wanted three men to own you. Have we given you what you need?"

"Yes." The word is strangled, as though her throat closed involuntarily halfway through uttering it. "Yes."

"I think you can come again," I say, even though I'm close and holding back will be a challenge.

"No." It's said on a gasp as I thrust into her hard. My hand pushes beneath her hip, searching for her clit. When I find it, all I do is press slightly above it as I thrust, knowing that indirect pressure is the most likely thing to get her off after so many orgasms. Damn, she looks and feels so good stretched out and captive on the bed. "Do it," I tell her. "Let go."

And as though my words are the trigger, she clamps around me, her body straining and spasming, and I see stars flashing before my eyes. My balls draw up, and I release like a tidal wave crashing on the shore, groaning long and deep.

Celine takes my weight as I collapse over her, burying my face in her sweet hair. Our bodies are slick, and I have a cramp in my left thigh. She's panting, and her heart is racing so hard, I can feel it against my skin.

All my reservations about getting involved with

someone new so fast after leaving Germany slip away. Finding someone who enjoys my kink has helped me shrug off all the tension I brought home with me.

But as I reach out to loosen Celine's wrists, and Elias and Dornan crowd around to kiss and touch her and tell her she's a goddess, the connection I crave retreats inside me.

12

ELIAS

"I don't want to go home yet," Celine moans, echoing my feelings. This room at Molly's isn't exactly Caribbean-Island five-star luxury, but the bed is soft and warm, and I'm dog-tired. Dog tired with a permanent raging hard-on thanks to Travis's kinky fuckery.

I swear, I never thought that bondage would get me so hot, but watching him control Celine, teasing her until she almost broke from pleasure, has opened my eyes to a whole new world of sex play.

"I don't want to leave either. It's fucking cold out there, and it's warm in here." I pull Celine closer to my body, and she hitches a lazy leg over mine, pressing her sweet pussy against my skin.

Jeez.

There is no way I'm leaving this room right now.

"I should go. I have an interview tomorrow."

"You're our ride," Dornan points out as Travis tries to rise from the chair he's slumped into. Travis flops back.

"I guess we could crash. I'll shower here, then I can throw my clothes on at home after I've dropped you guys back."

"I can do the walk of shame," Celine says with a hint of happy pride in her voice.

"There's nothing shameful about you, Red."

She swats my pec but smiles against the skin of my shoulder. "Did you just give me a cheesy pet name?"

"Well, you are our pet. Travis had you leashed."

"Fuck, Elias." Shaking his head, Travis's cheeks flush above his beard. "It's not like that."

"Like what?"

"She's not an animal. It's not about demeaning her."

"I know. I'm only joking. It was hot as fuck."

"You want a turn next time?"

I shrug, wanting to appear nonchalant, especially as Travis just assumed there would be a next time without Celine suggesting she'd want another night with us.

I want this to happen again. Even after the first time we fucked, I wanted more, but it wasn't an option. That idiot Eddie had his claws in her so deep.

Now, this has become a four-way arrangement, which can't go any further either. Too fucking complicated, and I'm an only child. Sharing is not something that comes naturally to me.

I'm a greedy asshole when it comes to Celine.

Dornan eyes me from where he's lying on the other side of her like I'm hogging her all to myself. Even though we've shared her, there's an unease between us that should prevent this from happening again. I see the possessiveness in his gaze as his eyes fix on where my arm is wrapped around Celine's waist, pinning her to me.

He wants her for himself in the same possessive way I do.

Travis is more complex to work out.

His kink must make it challenging for him to find partners. With Celine, he didn't have to go through any kind of confession stage because she already knew what he liked and accepted it.

And we accepted it, too.

No wonder he looks like the cat who got the cream.

"Are you seriously talking about more sex?" Celine yawns and shifts, easing out of my arms and turning to give Dornan some attention. Half my body chills at her absence, and I internally grumble as Dornan adjusts to gather her close.

"Did we wear you out?" Dornan asks, pressing a kiss to her forehead. So, now he's doling out easy affection. Now he's treating her like a girlfriend, not just a hookup.

"My body feels like it's been run over by one of those ice road trucks."

"Mine feels fine." I stretch out, resting my hands over my head. My cock taps my belly, ready to go at least another round, if not more.

See, that's why four won't work. The other men in this room have used up my time and my opportunity.

Travis groans and heads over to the empty bed, which has been pushed up to join the one the three of us are currently sharing. "You students know how to burn the candle at both ends."

"Are we wearing you out, old man?" I laugh.

"You wait until you've added a few years."

"You're only five years older than us." Celine raises her head to look at Travis. "You're making out like you're on the verge of collecting your pension."

Dornan laughs as her hand brushes over his abs. "Seriously, Celine. Don't do that. I'm ticklish."

Like a red rag to a bull, she pounces on him with wriggling fingers, and the biggest dude in the room is reduced to a quivery pile of Jello.

"I thought we were supposed to be sleeping." I tug the sheet over myself and turn to face away. Jealousy is an ugly knot in my belly and a lump in my throat that feels tight. It's fucking pathetic to feel rejected just because Celine has chosen to laugh with another man. None of us has a more significant stake in her time and affection. If anything, I've been intimate with her more times. That should put me on the front foot. But I can't help how I feel. I can't help that it makes me want to get out of this bed, drag my clothes onto my body, and storm out the door.

The laughter dies down, and the bed shifts behind me. Feet pad across the floor, and I turn just in time to see Celine's sweet ass disappear into the bathroom.

Fuck, she's got a sexy walk like girls in eighties music videos, hips swaying in a way that makes me feral.

Dornan whistles in a quiet, descending tone as Celine closes the door. "That girl is fire."

My throat swallows involuntarily, making a strangled sound.

"She is," Travis agrees.

I don't say anything.

"Elias, you want to do this again?"

It's obvious I'm not asleep yet, so I don't have a way of getting out of answering Dornan's question. If I say no, I'm out of the running with Celine for good. She's got two other men just waiting to fill my boots. But if I say yes, I'm signing up for more sharing, which feels good in the moment, but empty as a fucking cave afterward.

"Maybe you should ask Celine first before canvassing us."

"Travis?"

"If she wants to." He obviously doesn't have the same reservations or concerns. Great. Just great.

Sounds of splashing water emanate from the bathroom. Celine hums lightly to herself, but I can't make out the tune. My phone rumbles on the console table, but I'm too tired to check who it is. Probably one of the group chats, blowing up with gossip. There was a big hockey game tonight; if our team won, the players would be out, causing havoc.

When Celine opens the door, I crane my head to look at her just in case it's the last time I'm ever going to see her naked. She's twisted her hair into a messy bun, with strands hanging around her pretty elfin face. Her breasts are bare, and her nipples are still red from our mean fingers and mouths.

She hesitates, eyes the two beds like she's unsure what to do. She left a space between me and Dornan, but that doesn't mean she'll return to it. I want her next to me, even if she's cuddling up in the other direction, but three in one bed and one in the other doesn't make much sense.

She must think the same thing because she pads to the other side of Travis's bed and climbs in. "Room for another one?"

He grins and shifts, holding the comforter and settling it over her. He kisses her lips and cuddles up in her embrace like they've been sleeping together for a hundred years. I turn away, gritting my teeth.

"Guess it's just you and me." Dornan shifts lower on the pillow, and I become very conscious of the fact that I'm naked and in bed with another naked dude.

"We need to put on some underwear." I grab mine from my clothes pile on the floor and pull them on. "There's no way I want to wake up with your cock anywhere near me."

Dornan climbs out of bed, hunting for his lost boxer briefs. "Believe me, I'm more than happy to keep my junk to myself."

"Your junk is all mine," Celine murmurs contentedly. She makes a humming noise in her throat like a cat's purr.

"Greedy." Travis turns to find Dornan sliding into bed. *This is not how I imagined the end of this night.*

"You tell anyone about this, and your junk will be in a waste disposal," I growl.

The room erupts with laughter, but I don't join in.

Falling asleep doesn't come easy.

Travis's alarm wakes us all at the ass crack of dawn. Thankfully, I held my position last night facing away from Dornan, and he hasn't drifted across the bed to spoon me. I slide my legs off the edge of the mattress and rub both hands over my face and through my hair. Lumbering to the bathroom, I piss for so long that I start to worry. I take a two-minute shower, reluctantly washing off all evidence of Celine and what we did last night.

Back in the bedroom, Celine has already pulled on her dress and heels. She smiles at me with sleepy eyes and rosy cheeks, and my stupid chest fills with softness at her cute morning face.

"We have ten minutes." Travis barrels into the bathroom, flicking the shower on before relieving himself. Dornan's still tucked under the sheet like a giant tree trunk.

I throw a pillow at his head. "Dornan. Time to get up."

He groans and then flings his arm across the bed. As he turns, it becomes very obvious that he has morning wood. Celine snickers, and I look away, annoyed.

Even witnessing her staring at another man's accidental erection has me seething.

I dress in record time and adjust my drying hair in the mirror. My expression is more strained than it should be. Usually, the morning after I've gotten laid, I'm all sweetness and light, with a smile that can't be dislodged and dimples out in full force.

Usually, I can fuck away the tension that builds up inside me until I'm bordering on a grizzly bear.

This time, it's the after-sex part that's turned me grumpy.

"Hey." Celine comes up behind me, resting a gentle hand on my shoulder. "You okay?"

"I'm fine." I turn to stare down at her, finding her head tipped to one side. The churning of her mind is practically audible.

"Yeah?"

"Yeah. We had a good time." I shrug like it meant nothing other than that. Two bodies coming together for mutual pleasure.

"Yeah, we did." Her lips press together, and her eyes find a spot in the corner she focuses on. "I wanted to ask if you have time to help me with my class? I need to get my grade up before they start taking action."

She can't even look at me when asking for my help. Shit, this girl reminds me of me.

"I can help you. Travis can drop me off at your dorm, and we'll study."

Celine nods and then steps back, putting some space between us. I don't like the space. I want to pull her close and press a kiss on her forehead. I want to reassure her that no matter how far behind she is, she can improve her grade with some hard work and focus.

I want to behave in a way that I never have with a girl before, and it freaks me the fuck out.

Travis emerges from the shower, humming something. The dude has a seriously happy post-sex vibe going on.

Dornan disappears into the bathroom, picking up the tune, so now both men are humming. It's a chorus of satisfaction that darkens my mood even further.

Flicking through my phone, I try to pass the time until Travis is fully clothed and Dornan has emerged from the shower. Celine does the same, perching on the bed's edge, curling around her screen.

I catch sight of it from the side and find her adding a few of the selfies we took together last night to Instagram, and even though I know that our date was part of her vendetta against Eddie, it still sticks in my throat that she's focused more on that and less on me.

My hand swipes through my hair, frustration knotting my insides.

"What the fuck is he doing in there?" I huff.

"Easy." Travis glances at his watch. "We're good. Still two minutes to go."

Like clockwork, Dornan emerges from the bathroom, pulls on his clothes, and ruffles the towel over his wet hair. Four of us are ready in ten minutes. That's got to be some kind of record!

Travis blasts his dad-music all the way to campus and Dornan and Celine hum along with it. I'm left staring out of the window with tightly pressed lips. Dornan is the first to leave, reaching over to kiss Celine's cheek. "I'll call you," he says and then slides from the back seat, stopping to give us all a parting wave as Travis pulls away.

He can call Celine. They have that kind of relationship.

Their easy friendship twists my gut.

We drive for another minute before we reach Celine's dorm. The building looms next to us, and Travis turns to Celine, who's in the back seat. "Last night was…" He stops as though he's lost for a word to describe it. I know the feeling, and so, it seems, does Celine.

"It really was."

I'm out of the car before he can say he'll call her, too; I

lose the grip on my tongue.

"Good luck with your interview. I'm sure you'll blow them away."

"I hope so."

I open Celine's door, wanting to get her as far away from my competition as possible.

"Let me know if you need anything else."

Celine is halfway out of the door when he says it, and she pauses. "Okay. Thanks."

On the sidewalk, she glances around to see if anyone's going to spot her getting dropped off in last night's clothing. It's still early, and students are not known for their morning rising abilities. The coast is clear. I follow her inside and take the stairs to her room. Her walk mesmerizes me, and the memories of last night paint sexual flashes in my mind that thicken my cock.

I focus on the floor, not wanting to have a full-blown boner by the time we reach her door.

She's asked me here to help her, not fuck her, although the two don't have to be mutually exclusive.

What happens next is down to her, and I hate not being in control.

13

CELINE

Elias lumbers into my small dorm room, filling so much space, I don't know what to do with myself. I smell funky, and my pussy is so amped up by last night and his proximity that it has its own heartbeat.

Jeez.

I need to work on my grade but doing it with Elias under these circumstances is torture.

"Can I get you a coffee and some breakfast? I have cereal."

"Sure." He glances around my room.

"You can sit here. I'll fix it, and then I'll take a quick shower."

He moves toward the chair at my desk, passing me closely. "Don't shower on my behalf. You smell good."

"I stink of sex."

"Exactly."

I screw up my nose, and Elias chuckles darkly. "You smell like the best kind of fucking, Celine. No dude worth anything is going to find that smell off-putting. Shit, it's practically making me woozy."

"Men are gross." I stomp to the shared kitchenette to fix my guest an instant coffee and a bowl of muesli. He'd probably prefer something sugary, but I don't have any kiddy cereal.

Back in my room, he takes my offerings gratefully, looking at me with low-lidded eyes that tell me he'd rather eat me than the food. Before he has a chance to touch me, I disappear into the bathroom, locking the door behind me. Mr. Horndog out there would probably follow me in if he got half the chance, and although the idea of a naked and wet Elias pinning me to the tiled wall is delicious enough to bring saliva to my mouth, I have to restrain myself.

I smother myself in strawberry body wash and scrub my face. When I've dried my skin, I apply thick strawberry body butter and spritz my face with rose water. Then I realize I've forgotten to bring fresh clothes into the bathroom.

Jeez.

My towel is small and barely covers my ass. When I open the door, Elias has finished his breakfast and is resting against my chair with his arms folded and his legs spread wide. When he sees me, his tongue darts out to moisten his lips.

"Are you trying to kill me, Celine?"

"You're too big. I could never hide your body." Laugh sputters out of him as I rummage in my dresser for some clean panties and a matching bra. I haven't done my laundry for two weeks, so all that's left is plain white cotton underwear and a black lacy bra. It's not exactly an alluring combination, which is good because I don't need Elias to get ideas.

In reality, he wouldn't care if I was wearing a plastic bag. In fact, he'd probably like it. Easier to remove.

I find a shirt and a pair of jeans and set off in the direction of the bathroom.

"Where are you going?" His voice rumbles with a smile present.

"To get dressed."

"Celine, I've seen up inside your pussy, and you're acting shy?"

I swivel to face him and roll my eyes. "It's not classy to beg for a free porn show."

Elias reaches his arms up and rests his head in his palms, pressing back so his back cracks. I saw a documentary about body language once, and he's put himself in a classic dominant pose, displaying everything he's got going on.

"This already feels like the start of a stepbrother-stepsister porno. The next thing you're going to say is that you're short of money, and you'll give me a blowjob for fifty dollars."

My mouth gapes with surprise and disgust. "You seriously watch that?"

Shrugging, he switches his position, resting his forearms on his knees and leaning forward. There is wickedness in the gleam of his eyes and the quick flash of a smile on his lips.

"What do you think?"

"I think you're annoying, Elias."

"But you like it, don't you, Celine? So what does that say about you?"

Sparks fly between us because he's right. I like that he pushes boundaries. I like that his confidence rumbles off him like the after-effects of an earthquake. Everything from his bigness to his dark hair and slow, purposeful movements makes me hot.

"Fine." Tossing my clothes onto my bed, I drop my

towel to the floor. I don't bother looking in Elias's direction and focus instead on the corner of my room as I tug up my panties and hook my bra together. Once my shirt and jeans are on, I stomp over to my desk. "I'll get my books, and you can tell me where we should start."

I don't reach my bookshelf before Elias's big arm scoops me around the waist and tugs me onto his knee. I swat at him, annoyed, and when he tries to kiss me, I press both my hands to his chest and shove him back.

"I don't think so."

His cock is an iron bar beneath my butt, and wriggling against it only seems to make it bigger.

He presses his face into my neck and inhales. "Jesus, you smell good. Like strawberry pop tarts."

"Are you seriously comparing me to sugary, plastic breakfast food?"

He laughs, and it feels like it comes from somewhere deep inside him that he doesn't show very often. His hand slides up my side and cups my breast. "Nothing plastic about you."

I stifle a smile as my whole body flushes hot with arousal.

This shouldn't feel good. Elias is an arrogant douche who finds joy in pushing my buttons. Still, I can't help enjoying his metaphorical and literal button-pushing.

I take his hand from my boob and rest it on my thigh. "I need to study."

He takes an exaggerated breath and blows it out like an enraged bull, but he's smiling at the same time.

"You could have this..." He thrusts upwards to let me feel his boner. "But you want this." He taps the side of his head.

"Both would be nice, but this first." I touch his temple, and he snatches a kiss, then taps my ass, urging me to get up.

"Get your books, Celine. My cock won't wait forever."

14

ELIAS

We spend two hours going over Celine's understanding of the topic and the parts of the course that she struggles with the most. By the end, her eyes are wide, and her pen is practically tearing lines in the paper she's writing so fast. "Oh my god, I can't believe I didn't get this."

"I can't believe it either."

"Professor Callihan is a terrible teacher."

I shrug because I only half agree. He points us in the right direction for all the information we need to be successful. There's a lot of external reading that Celine obviously hasn't done. "I think he gives us what we need, but we can't just rely on the lectures. You've gotta spend time with the study texts."

Her frown deepens, and she clicks the end of her pen over and over.

"How much do you study, Elias?"

"A lot."

"But you have practice."

"That takes up time, but…"

But I need to make every second count while I'm here because I don't have Mommy's and Daddy's money to fall back on. I need to prove that I'm not the idiot my father told me over and over that I am. I need to show the world the man I want to be because the man I am isn't that great.

Fuck. I don't tell her any of that.

"But?"

"But you have to make time for what's important."

Celine places her pen on her notepad and slides off the edge of the bed. When she's in front of me, she stops between my legs and runs her fingers through my hair. My eyelids lower, the sensation over my scalp sending a pulse of awareness down my spine and between my legs. I think about her mismatched underwear and how badly I want to strip it from her body and sink inside her. How badly I want the bite of her fingernails into my skin.

Pulling her to me, I press my face into her belly and rest there while she pets me. Her fingers run down the back of my tense neck and graze my bunched shoulders. Even though our team physio deals with our aches and pains, I'm still tense from all the benching and drills and the rest of life's stresses.

"You're so big," she whispers. "So big and hard and..."

"...and?" I wait for the thought that dried on her tongue.

"...a quandary."

"Good word. How so?"

"You don't seem to take anything seriously, but you do. You brush off any kind of emotional contact, but you love sweet affection. I can't work you out."

I snort wryly, but beneath my flippancy, I feel exposed. "Sounds like you want to work me out."

Instead of admitting that she does, she tips my chin so I'm forced to look her in the eyes. The uncertainty I see there floors me.

"Take me to bed, Elias."

So I do.

I make it raw and sexy, and I know she likes it because it trips her switch until she's clawing at me and whimpering. But after, when I pull her close, I let my fingers wander over her skin with the same gentleness that she showed me, and allow myself to drift beneath her gentle caresses, pushing back the thoughts of Dornan and Travis, and even Eddie. Pushing back my own mumbling mind that tells me I'm a pussy for wanting Celine for anything else other than a fun and convenient fuck.

I let myself rest because the chance feels like one I won't get again for a long time.

15

DORNAN

Travis got the job. I find out from Ellie, who finds out from Gabriella and tells me over coffee in the afternoon. Later, when I'm chilling in my room, I use the 'Fake Date' group chat to share my message of congratulations. It seems like the right thing to do, but when it's sent, I feel a rush of uncertainty.

We're not a friendship group. We shared two nights at Molly's motel, one perfectly innocent and the other totally corrupt, but that's it.

I haven't seen Celine since, and it's been driving me crazy, wondering if she's just busy or avoiding me. Or even worse, is seeing the other two but has decided to leave me out.

Shit.

I run my hand through my hair and mumble that I'm an idiot for letting my feelings for Celine grow under circumstances that are far from ideal. Slumping down on my bed, I stretch out my long legs, wincing at the bruise I earned at the last game and my muscles that ache from training. My socked feet look huge, almost hanging off the end.

When my phone buzzes, I jump up, forgetting my aches and pains and snatching up my phone. It's Travis with a reply.

TRAVIS - Thanks, man. I'm pumped. It's a great role. Better than the one I left behind in Germany. They need me to start immediately, but I asked for a week off so I can find an apartment.

I can see that Celine and Elias are typing.

CELINE - Yay. That's awesome news. Go Travis!

ELIAS - Well done, man. Can I be you when I grow up?

TRAVIS - Are you trying to make me feel old again?

ELIAS - You are old, dude!

CELINE - Can I come apartment shopping with you?

ELIAS - You're supposed to be studying Celine.

TRAVIS - I'd actually appreciate some company. My mom and Gabriella have hair appointments, and my friends are all busy. I don't know what I'm looking for. I have five appointments tomorrow between nine and eleven.

CELINE - I'm in.

Elias is quick to reply.

ELIAS - I'm down.

If they're going, I'm not going to be the odd one out. I type quickly, **'I'm down.'**

TRAVIS - I'll pick you all up around eight-forty-five.

Celine responds with a smiley face. Elias drops a thumbs up. I send one of those green tick symbols just to be different, and I feel like a high schooler in the process.

Dropping back onto my bed, I smile at my phone and

then toss it next to me. It'll be good to see Celine, and part of me is looking forward to the stupid back-and-forth that flies around the group whenever we're together. I've seen Ellie have the same dynamic with her stepbrothers-turned-baby-daddies and Gabriella with her three neighbors-turned-boyfriends. There's something about three men and one woman that seems to bring out the humor in everyone.

Travis is chill, Celine is fiery and funny, and even though Elias seems to have a giant chip on his shoulder most of the time, he's got a dark sense of humor that amuses me. Before Celine brought us together to play her revenge games, I had a different view of Elias. I still don't like how he can be cutting and egotistical, but he seems to want to care for Celine. His willingness to step in for her when they weren't even very close beforehand says something new about his character that I can't ignore.

Elias and Celine are already in Travis's car when they arrive to collect me. I jump into the backseat with Elias, checking out Celine, who twists to greet me between the seats.

"I can't believe you guys were on time." Celine's hair is still wet, and she has it twisted in a knot at the back of her head. "I thought I'd have time to dry my damned hair."

"Punctuality is important." Elias cracks his knuckles in his lap as I fasten my seatbelt.

"Punctuality is necessary when you're an old man like me."

"Stop saying that." Celine rests her hand on Travis's knee and squeezes. "You're not that much older than us."

"It feels like a lot."

"Why?" I ask.

"I don't know. You guys seem way more chilled than I feel. It's like I'm already in the rest of my life, and you guys are still preparing for it."

Elias opens the window and rests his big arm slightly out of it. The wind whips through the car as he stares out. "I'm not chilled."

"Me, either," I say. "Trying to work out what the rest of my life will look like is way more stressful."

"Tell me about it." Celine turns, and her face is grim. "If I ever actually get through this course."

"You'll get through it," Elias says, sounding so confident, it makes me frown.

"Just because you're a friggin' genius doesn't mean I am."

"Wait, who's a friggin' genius?"

Celine nods in Elias's direction. "Him. He's getting top marks, and I'm flunking. It's depressing."

Elias's jaw ticks, but he doesn't say anything.

"He's trying to help me, but everything that comes easy to him feels like I'm dragging myself backward up Everest on my belly."

"You'll get there."

Travis signals to pull over outside an apartment building. It's in a decent-looking area, and the building seems tidy from the outside. A man, who I assume is a realtor, is standing by the front door.

We all assemble on the sidewalk and follow Travis, who shakes hands with the balding man in a suit and shirt stretched a little too tight around his frame.

"Mr. Cross?" His eyes sweep the group.

"Yes. That's me."

"Right, well. Let me take you inside."

It's on the first floor, so we don't need to take the stairs or the elevator. The entrance area is well-kept and smart. The realtor opens the front door and holds it open for us all to enter. He eyes us with interest. I guess that three men and a woman are an odd combination for house hunting.

"So, as you can see, it has a very large open-plan living area."

Celine immediately heads to the window to look at the view. Elias folds his arms over this chest, assessing the layout. I head to the kitchen to check out the appliances and cupboard space. My mom recently renovated our kitchen at home, and she spent ages going over all the things that are important for when I get my own home. "It looks like it's got everything you need. The built-in appliances are all good brands, and the cupboards are relatively new."

"Exactly." The realtor seems pleased with my summary. "The owner has just had all the sockets replaced with new ones, including USB ports."

"That's useful," Celine says. "What about the bedroom?"

Travis rubs his hand over his beard, and when his hand drops, I catch the end of his smile. Celine is the first to follow the realtor through a door into a large bedroom with a huge window, walk-in closet, and bathroom with a double shower and double vanity. Dark hardwood floors stretch through, giving the place a seamless and contemporary look.

"This is nice." Celine opens the closet and steps inside, staring around at all the space. Something about the way she peruses everything feels more considered than I'd expect, bearing in mind that she's not going to be living here herself.

"The current owner is single, so he only has a small bed, but this room could take something much bigger." The realtor looks between us as though he's waiting for us to confess our sins.

Travis's eyes meet mine, and his smile is back. "The place is just for me, but I like to have a lot of space to move around."

"To be honest, this place is the nicest of all the apartments you're currently booked to see."

"Yeah. Well, I like it. What do you think, Dornan?"

Surprised, I step forward and shove my hands into my pockets. "I mean, I've never had to think about getting a place that wasn't at the university, but I think this place is nice. I could live here. It has everything you need."

"I like it." Celine drifts to Travis's side and rests her hand on his shoulder. "And you could grow into it. It would definitely work for a couple...or more."

"There's a couple down the hall with a baby. They've converted the closet into an open-doored nursery and fitted other shelves for their clothes." The realtor shoots Celine a grateful look; she's helping out with her enthusiasm.

"A baby in a closet. That sounds messed up."

"You don't like it, Elias?"

"I think you should look at the others, too."

Travis's shoulders curve a little and I shoot Elias a narrow-eyed look. I swear, sometimes he seems intent on squeezing the joy out of other people. "Yeah. It would be good to get some perspective," I agree, to make it sound less disheartening.

"The appointments are there if you want them."

Travis nods at the realtor, who puffs out his chest with a long inhale and then breezes to the door. We all follow Travis out of the building. When we're outside, he glances up, taking everything in before we leave. "You can follow me to the next place," the realtor says. "Are your friends coming to all the viewings?"

"Yes." Travis presses his key fob, and the car opens, and we all jump into our same seats.

The rest of the viewings don't live up to the first. I guess the realtor ordered them that way to showcase the best upfront. By the end, Celine can list a million reasons Travis should only consider apartment number one.

"I can see you there," she says.

"I can see myself there," he agrees.

"So, what's the plan now? I'm as hungry as a bear," I say.

"Me, too." Elias stretches his arms over his head, and as his shirt lifts, exposing his abs, Celine's eyes drift and focus hungrily. The way she looks at him is purely sexual, and it sends a shooting stab of jealousy through me. She looked at me like that the other night, but I haven't seen the same craving in her eyes since. I thread my hand through my hair and stare up the road, hoping the distraction will diminish the stab to my gut.

"You can come back to my place. My mom cooked yesterday, and we have enough food to feed five thousand."

"Sounds good." Celine looks at her watch. "I did have a study group, but I can miss it."

"We have practice later," Elias reminds me.

"We have time." I shrug like I'm not bothered either way, but I am. Getting to spend more of the day with Celine might help my confusion, and there is no way I'd leave her in the company of these two horny men and miss out on what might happen between them all.

If anyone is going to get with Celine, I will be there to share.

I haven't been to Gabriella and Travis's family home before. It's a nice house on a nice street, and their mom keeps it spotless and homey, with traditional touches like flowers in vases and enough throw pillows to sink a small ship.

In the kitchen, there is a large wooden table that looks like it has been the site of generations of amazing meals.

Elias looks around like he's never seen the inside of a house before. Celine helps Travis empty the fridge of trays and trays of food.

"How come your mom cooked so much?"

Travis shrugs, passing me a plate. "She loves cooking. So does my sister. I've been spoiled by amazing food my whole life."

"Some people have all the luck." Elias reaches out for a plate, his comment landing flat. Seems I'm not the only one to experience jealousy, although the target of his is something unexpected.

"I know. I reckon I'm destined to marry someone who can't even make toast. That'll even it out."

"I burn toast." Celine pops a delicious-looking piece of chicken into her mouth.

Elias scoops out a considerable portion of lasagna, dropping it onto his plate with less consideration than he should. "Sounds like Celine might be your destiny."

Celine sneaks a peek in Travis's direction, but he stays focused on the food. Is that a snub? I'm not sure. Travis isn't the easiest man to read. "What about you, Elias? Can you cook?"

"I get by." He chews on a big mouthful of the lasagna, and his eyes light up. "My mom burns toast, too. If I wanted to get in decent shape to play ball, I had to get accustomed to making my own chicken, broccoli, and rice."

"You seriously eat that?" Celine wrinkles her nose. "Broccoli smells like…"

Elias puts his hand up to stop her. "I don't want to hear what you're going to say. I love all green vegetables, and I don't want you to make them ick."

She shakes her head, smiling. "Maybe I should get you to cook for me."

"In addition to tutoring you and fucking you? You're starting to sound like a lot of work."

"Jesus, Elias."

He turns his attention to me, focusing like he didn't realize I'd been standing there the whole time. "What? It's true."

"Tutoring and cooking seem like a small price to pay for the fucking!"

"This isn't a labor exchange, and if it was, I'd have to be compensated for the fucking, too, as Celine has twice as many orgasms as I do every time we fuck."

"Every time?" How many times have there been?

Celine's cheeks turn a deep shade of tomato, and the floor is suddenly the most exciting feature in the room. Have they been solo fucking? Leaving me and Travis out feels like a betrayal, even though it isn't. We haven't made any rules for this. I keep having to remind myself that I shouldn't have any expectations.

"Celine's horny." The way Elias chews as he carries his plate to the end of the table and takes a seat like a king at a banquet riles me.

She looks around, reading the room. "I'm horny. What can I say? And I'm used to fucking a lot. Eddie was the male version of a nymphomaniac."

"You mean a man?"

I snort at Elias's quip. He's not wrong. Most men would fuck every day if they got the chance. If not twice or more. There's a need for release that builds up like an ache between my legs that pulses in some unidentified lobe in my head. Like, right now, I'm talking and trying to act normal, but on a level running underneath, all I can think about is burying myself between Celine's legs.

"Not all men are like that," she says, sitting beside Elias. I take the seat opposite while Travis tosses us beers and a soda for Celine.

"Men are all like that. Some of us just do a good job of being less of an asshole about it." I twist the lid off my beer and take a welcome drink.

Celine opens a can of soda and takes a sip. Her hair has dried now, and her curls are crazy. "Yeah. Eddie did a good job of being king of the assholes."

Travis spoons some potato salad out of a large brown bowl. He looks around to see if everyone has helped themselves to enough food, then focuses on Celine. "Are you done with your games?"

"Yeah." She places the soda on the table but keeps her fingers wrapped around the condensation-covered tin. "He's not worth my time or effort. I've got enough going on without dragging him along with me."

"End of relationship baggage has to be shaken off, or it wears you down," Travis agrees.

"To being single." Elias tips his beer, waiting for us to join him in a toast.

Celine shoots him a look laced with disapproval, or is it disappointment? I can't be sure. "What's so good about being single, Elias? Casual sex? Sleeping alone?"

He shrugs. "No drama. No games."

The last comment feels like a dig against Celine for what brought us all together in the first place. "No joy."

"You guys are like a game of Olympic table tennis." Travis gulps his beer and licks the residue from his lips. "Life without love is empty. And the right person won't play games with your heart. They'll protect it like it's something precious."

Celine looks at Elias. "Thank you, Travis, for your mature perspective."

"He sounds like a chick." It's said with snark and a challenging raise of Elias's eyebrows.

"He sounds like someone with a soul." I don't mean

the words to sound rough, but Elias turns his head slowly to look at me as soon as they're out of my mouth.

"I have a soul, dude."

There's a ripple of disquiet amongst us until Travis smiles and shakes his head. "So, have y'all been thinking about the night at Molly's?"

"Yes." Celine says it so quickly that she makes us all jump.

"Definitely," I admit.

Elias shrugs in a non-committal way that I'm certain is only masking his true feelings.

"Wanna do it again?"

Celine draws in her bottom lip, her pretty eyes trailing between us all. "I'm game if you are."

"Three on one? Is it necessary?"

She pats Elias's arm. "Ahhh…you want me all to yourself?"

Shrugging again, he stuffs his mouth full of the last forkful of food on his plate, avoiding answering the question altogether.

"What time's your mom going to be back?" I ask Travis. It's a way to find out if today could be an option without directly asking each person for their availability. "Late. I'm not so sure about Gab."

"Well, it's not like it'll be a shock to her if she does come back. Three on one is her daily life experience."

"Yeah, thinking about my sister getting boned by three guys isn't my favorite way to pass the time." Travis rises to pack away all the food we haven't eaten, and Celine grabs the empty plates, taking them to the sink and rinsing them before placing them into the dishwasher.

The atmosphere is thick with anticipation, but no one seems to want to direct us all upstairs, at least until the kitchen is as spotless as we found it.

HUGE GAMES

"I guess we could head up?" Travis asks.

And like the horny sons-of-bitches we all are, we follow Celine up the stairs to heaven.

16

CELINE

"Everything you need is in this bag." Marie hands over a large cloth tote that's filled to the brim with all the things a toddler might require.

Lonie is in her highchair, using her fork to carefully stab pieces of the omelet my sister made her. After missing three pieces, she drops her fork in frustration and picks up her piece of bread and butter, stuffing it into her mouth. Her eyes widen as she chews, focusing on me.

I grin at my beautiful niece, desperate to wipe her face. Marie is a great mom, don't get me wrong, but she's way more laid back than I would be. Then again, Lonie seems capable of a lot of things other toddlers seem to struggle with. Maybe Marie's relaxed approach has contributed to that.

"I'm aiming to be back at around six."

"Six?"

When I agreed to babysit, it was on the basis that I'd be able to make it to watch Elias and Dornan's game.

"Is that the earliest you can get back?"

"Yeah. Why? Is there a problem?"

"I've got a game to go to. Am I okay to take Lonie?"

"Sure. Make sure she has a good lunchtime nap. I'm sure she'll love all the cheering and excitement and those big men in their tight pants." She winks and grins, then finally bends to wipe the food from Lonie's sticky face.

"Marie!"

"What? She's just like her aunt. A terrible flirt."

"You got me!"

"So, is Eddie playing?"

I grit my teeth at the mention of the scumbag who I'm trying to banish from my memory. "Yes, but I'm not going to watch him. He can fall over and die in a ditch."

"Who are you going to watch?" She lifts Lonie from the chair and sets her on her feet. Lonie toddles off to her play corner and finds a board book to leaf through or destroy, depending on her mood.

"I may or may not be having a fling with a couple of the team."

"A couple?"

"I'm sowing my wild oats."

"Men sow the oats, Celine. Women get plowed."

I grin, shaking my head at all the delicious memories still fresh from an afternoon tied to Travis's bed. They did things to me that I swear are illegal in at least a few states.

"You have no idea."

"Do they know what you're up to, or have you taken a leaf from Eddie's book?"

"Oh, they know about each other...they were all present. And I'm not a cheater."

"All?" The way Marie's mouth hangs open inspires me to push up her chin with my finger.

"Three of them. I've gathered my own casual harem for three times the pleasure."

She shakes her head, folding her lips over a smile. "How long have I been married? I swear things like this weren't a thing when I was single."

"When were you ever single?" I snort. "You were a child. Then you met Aiden. Then you got married."

"Yeah. That's it, pretty much. And he is more than enough man for me. I just...what do you even do with three men?" She immediately holds her hand up with her palm facing me. "Scrap that. I don't want to know. You'll only create images in my head that I don't want to carry around with me for the rest of my life."

Lonie shouts for her momma, and Marie heads over to kneel next to her daughter. As she points to a duck in the book, she swivels to face me. "Two football players?"

"And my friend's brother."

"Is he the size of a football player?"

"Almost." A flash of a memory of Travis, Dornan, and Elias all staring down at me from the end of Travis's bed flashes into my mind. Naked, erect, and potent, they were enough to make me swoon.

"My god." She shakes her head. "I'm not sure that I should be letting my daughter out with her sexually corrupt auntie, but I really need a day for myself."

"It's fine. It'll all be very wholesome. She can wave a flag and eat healthy snacks from your mega-bag-of-doom."

"Okay." She bends to kiss Lonie's sweet head. "I'm going to get ready. You should read this book to her...distract her from the fact that I'm leaving."

"She loves me," I reassure. "We'll be fine."

As I squat down and read "Duck Swims in the Pond" to Lonie, I say a silent prayer that we're both going to make it through the day in one piece.

"Are you serious?" Gabriella exclaims when I take my seat next to hers. The stadium is packed, and the rumble of so many people talking excitedly before the game has Lonie looking around with wide eyes.

"I'm totally serious," I say, dropping Marie's huge bag onto the floor and dropping into my seat, adjusting Lonie so her legs are facing Gabriella. "Marie asked me to watch her, and I didn't want to miss the game."

"She's totally gorgeous." Gab touches Lonie's cheek and then her red curls, which sit like a halo around her sweet, elfin face. "She looks just like you."

"She did before I dyed my hair."

"I still think you're crazy for doing that. Your natural hair is gorgeous."

"I feel good like this." I touch my brunette curls, bringing one in front of my face to study the color. "I feel like a different me."

"I liked the original you." Gab reaches into the bag and pulls out a stuffie. "Who's this?" she asks Lonie.

"Mimi." Lonie snatches the fury creature and squashes it possessively to her chest.

"I love Mimi." Gabriella presses her hand to her heart and sighs. "I swear my ovaries just popped out an egg in readiness."

"And what would your men think about that?"

"Dalton's ready. Blake and Kain, not so much."

"And what about you…Jesus…how come I didn't know this?"

"I'm not ready, either. Not really. I mean, I can imagine our cute little babies in my head, and I can see how awesome their daddies are going to be, but I can't see myself as a mom yet. I'm still recovering from seeing Ellie's splintered nipples a week after she had Noah."

I wince at the reminder. They didn't look good.

"And forget about the damage to her lady garden. I swear, she was out of action for weeks."

I squirm, clenching my legs together in the imagination of a shared pain. "Yeah. I'm definitely nowhere near ready for that."

"But we're spending a lot of time practicing, you know." Gab's exaggerated wink and grin make Lonie laugh.

"Yeah, the practicing is the part I enjoy, too."

"You still messing around with Dornan, Elias, and my brother?"

"I am."

My words are lost beneath the cheering as the team runs out onto the field behind their mascot. Lonie, spotting the costume-clad person skipping along with a flag, reaches out like she wants them to come to her. Gabriella claps and whoops, pumping her right fist in the air. I'm limited by Lonie's warmth on my lap, but I still yell out my support.

I spot Dornan first by his number, then Elias. A thrill travels up my spine and settles between my thighs at the sight of their sheer size and power. The tight pants leave nothing to the imagination, not that I need to look to remember what they're packing underneath all that spandex.

Eddie is towards the back, waving like he's the sole reason everyone is cheering like crazy. My teeth grit of their own volition as the marching band plays and the cheerleaders whip up the crowd into a frenzy.

Elias and Dornan stand at the forefront, their faces etched with determination as they exchange nods with their teammates. What must they be feeling? Excitement? Anticipation? Fear? The opposing team is huge, but Elias and Dornan don't have to worry about that.

Lonie, sensing the anticipation, squirms on my lap, her wide eyes filled with wonder at all the excitement in front of her.

A hush falls over the stadium as the national anthem plays. The crowd stands, and I struggle to my feet with Lonie, who is a heavy weight in my arms. She stares down at the field, but her gaze is still drawn by the mascot, who looks uncannily similar to her stuffie.

Our team is set to play offense first, and my heart skitters as the referee's whistle pierces the air.

"They've got a good chance," Gab says as we retake our seats.

I say a silent prayer, knowing that if they lose, Dornan and Elias will be in a terrible mood for days after.

The game is exciting. Each team pulls ahead but is quickly caught. With the score tied and the tension palpable in the air, the spotlight falls on Josh, the quarterback, as he takes command of the game. The stadium echoes with the roar of the crowd, their collective breath held in anticipation. He surveys the field with a steely gaze, the weight of the moment evident in the determined set of his jaw.

As the ball snaps, Josh drops back, skillfully evading the defensive linemen with a graceful dance of footwork. I hold my breath, the suspense building with every passing second. In the periphery, Elias, always attuned to Josh's movements, sprints down the field with lightning speed, creating an opening in the opposing defense. With a swift glance, Josh locks eyes with Elias, signaling a play. Josh unleashes a powerful spiral, the ball hurtling through the air with precision. Elias leaps into the air, fingertips grazing the ball. The crowd erupts into cheers as Elias secures the catch, landing gracefully in the end zone.

"Touchdown," Gab yells, on her feet, jumping up and down, the moment of triumph setting the stadium into a frenzy of celebration. I want to yell too, but Lonie's ears are likely already overwhelmed with the shouting around us.

In the midst of the celebrations and high-fives, pride surges in my chest. Lonie claps as Dornan throws his arm around Elias's shoulder and presses their helmets together.

"Ah, look. There's a new bromance building." Gab grins. "Must be your pussy of unity."

"Yeah. It's the thing that can bring about world peace."

Lonie grabs a fistful of my hair and pulls it, making me squeal. I think all the excitement is becoming too much for her, and she must be tired, too. I'm wrecked from my time spent taking care of her. I make a mental note to offer to help Ellie out more often. I forgot my friend has this level of responsibility around the clock, and she's still studying, too.

"Shall we head out?" Gab asks me as the teams leave the field.

"Yeah. Elias and Dornan want me to wait around."

"Okay. Let me help you with the bag."

We make our way down, and Lonie insists on walking with her sweet little hand clutched in mine and her stuffie trailing in the other. Everywhere we go, people stop to tell me how adorable she is. We grab sodas and ice cream for Lonie to keep her quiet, and I message Dornan to find out where they are. It takes them over an hour to shower, change, and handle all the post-game expectations. He asks me to meet them outside and sends me a location, and with Gabriella's help, I somehow make it with Lonie and the giant bag through a quieter stadium.

"Hey." Dornan's smile is warm enough to melt chocolate as he eats up my outfit with his baby blues, cut off jean shorts, and a team shirt tied into a bow at the front. My Converse are new and super cute. "Who is this gorgeous girl?"

"You know who I am," I snort, then lift Lonie to greet

him as he laughs. "This is Princess Lonie, my niece."

"Does everyone in your family have red hair?" Elias asks, appearing behind Dornan.

"Not everyone, but a lot of us."

"Not you anymore," he points out.

For the first time since I had my hair dyed brown, I feel a wisp of regret. Having family similarities has always made me feel securely rooted. Now, I could be mistaken for Lonie's nanny instead of her auntie.

"I got her this." Elias bends down and hands Lonie a fluffy bear wearing the team's jersey. Lonie quickly looks up at me, seeking permission to take the gift. When I nod, she hands me Mimi, then uses two dimpled hands to grab the bear. "I think she likes it."

Elias watches as Lonie presses three vigorous kisses onto the bear, which includes some ice cream residue.

"Have you seriously been watching her all day?"

"Yes." I swat his shoulder with Mimi, insulted that he has so little faith in me.

"Hey, Dornan." A man in his forties, with blonde hair like Dornan's, lumbers over.

"Dad."

I do a double take as Dornan and his father embrace, slapping each other enthusiastically on the back. He passes his son a bag filled with bags of chips, candy, and other snacks. "For you and the team." His smile is the same as Dornan's, except his front teeth cross over a little.

"Thanks, Dad." Dornan opens the bag wide, whistling at its contents. "That's awesome."

"You played well."

"You think?"

"You won, didn't you?"

"Elias got the winning touchdown."

Dornan's father's attention drifts to Elias. "That was a great play, son. Your family must be very proud."

Elias, who should be puffing his chest out with pride, instead looks like he could crush steel with his teeth. His masculine jaw pulses at the side, and his dark eyes flash. "You wanna get out of here?" He tips his head in the direction of the exit.

Dornan frowns at the snub of his father's kind comment, but I step in to answer Elias quickly before anything can be said. "I have to get Lonie home. Her mom should be back by now."

"I'm going to get pizza if you want to come?"

"I could eat pizza. Luizos?" Dornan rests his hand on his dad's shoulder and steers him away from us, leaving Elias staring after him, annoyed.

"Jeez, Elias. He was only trying to be nice. What's with you?" I hiss.

He focuses somewhere over my shoulder. "Do you want pizza or not?"

I should say no. I don't like how he's talking, but then Eddie walks past, fixing me with scary wild eyes that prompt me to twist so Lonie's out of his way. "Pizza would be great." My voice is artificially loud, and Elias seems confused until he spots Eddie's retreating form.

"More games, Celine?"

Lonie drops the bear, and Gab, who has remained silent until now, bends to scoop it up and hand it to Lonie again. "I'm going to head off, okay?"

"Yeah. Sure. Say hi to your men from me."

Straightening, she leans in to kiss me on my cheek and whispers. "Don't settle for another red flag, Celine," in my ear as a parting thought.

Is Elias a red flag? Sometimes, he acts that way, but then I remember all the effort and care he put into coaching me and the sweet aftercare he provides after we've had sex. When he thought I needed help to get revenge on Eddie, he didn't even think before volunteering. That doesn't fit with the traditional toxic archetype in any way.

I watch her leave, but Elias's attention never drifts from me.

"I'll see you at Luizos, then. In thirty minutes."

"See you there."

Elias drifts away while I hoist the tote onto my shoulder and pray that Lonie will walk.

"See you at Luizos?"

Dornan tears his attention away from his dad and waves. "See you there."

Marie is home, and Lonie is asleep in the car seat. I help my sister lift Lonie out and take the bag into the house. "How was your day?"

She nods with an expression of serenity that hadn't been present this morning. The miracles of a spa day. "The game?"

"They won."

"That's great."

"I'm going out for celebration pizza," I say.

"Followed by celebration group sex?"

"What?" Aiden sticks his head around the living room door into the hallway.

"Nothing." Marie waves him off, then presses her fingers over her lips. "Shit. Sorry."

"It's okay." I kiss Lonie's sweet forehead, but she nuzzles into her momma's neck, no longer interested in me now that her best buddy has returned.

I say my goodbyes and drive to the pizza place Dornan suggested, finding Dornan, Elias, and Travis waiting at a table. They must have gotten hungry because the table is already dominated by three tire-sized pizzas, already missing a few slices.

"Hey, Celine. Dig in."

Sliding next to Travis, I don't waste any time. The first bite is a slice of heaven and pepperoni. "Oh my god," I moan around my mouthful. "This is like the best kind of sex."

"I like pizza, but I could never compare it to sex." Travis shakes his head. "Especially not the kind of sex we've had."

"Ahh…" I rest my hand on his arm, flattered, even though it's a strange compliment.

"Eddie wasn't happy." Elias wipes his mouth on a serviette and tosses it onto the table.

"I don't give a fuck about Eddie."

His eyebrows rise with disbelief. "Really. Then what are we all still doing here?"

"It's called hanging out for a beer. You know, socializing with friends."

"Friends?"

Elias doesn't say, 'you're not my friends', but his comment comes out that way. I don't rise to it, though, because the truth is that he wouldn't be here if he didn't want to be. He likes this as much as the rest of us.

"You did good today, Elias. That play was insane."

He studies me, and I see the flicker of uncertainty in his expression. He was expecting me to bite back, but instead, I gave him a compliment. He's trying to work out if it's genuine. I get the feeling he isn't used to positive affirmations.

"I did what any other player would do."

"She's right." Dornan drops his half-chewed crust and picks up another loaded slice. "The drills you've been working on with Coach paid off."

"I wish I'd been able to watch," Travis says. "Sounds like a great game."

"It really was," I tell him. "It really was."

For the rest of the evening, we eat and talk, and Elias goes from being a grumpy bear to sharing our laughter. Travis tells us funny stories about his time at college and even funnier ones about his antics with his neighbor's best friends—Gabriella's boyfriends—and their mission to tease Gabriella mercilessly.

Dornan shares many embarrassing tales from high school when he was a geeky, skinny dude who had to struggle to grow into his Adam's apple. I can't imagine it, but there you go.

I show them one of my high school pictures, and they laugh their heads off at my crazy, frizzy orange halo hair and weird heart-embroidered jeans.

Elias laughs and jokes, but it's not until I'm home and in bed that I realize he never told us a thing about himself.

17

ELIAS

It's seven pm, and I'm stretched out on my bed in my boxers, catching up with game highlights when my phone rings. Celine's name flashes on my screen.

"Whatup?"

She snorts. "Is that your way of saying hello?"

"Are you calling to bust my balls, or do you want something?"

"Nice." The accompanying huffing sound makes me smile. "I need your help."

"This is becoming a habit, Celine. Have you forgotten I'm not your boyfriend?"

"Ugh. Elias. Seriously. You are not boyfriend material. But you are my fuck buddy, and as far as I can tell, you enjoy our little games, so maybe you should listen instead of being snarky."

"Fuck buddy?"

"Friend with benefits? Booty call? What would you call it?"

"Pussy," I say, knowing it's going to piss her off. I like

Celine when she's riled up. Plus, her snideness about my boyfriend abilities pisses me off.

"Fuck you."

"I'm nearly naked, Celine. If that's what you want, you know where I am."

Her frustrated growl amuses me so much I bring my fist to my mouth and bite down. After a few seconds of pause and a few audible deep breaths, she changes tack.

"Please, Elias, can you help me with my class? My test is tomorrow."

"Come over, but I'm warning you now. I'm not putting on any clothes." I cup my dick which has stirred and stiffened at the words pussy and naked. It's so easily aroused.

"I can't. I'm at my sister's babysitting again. Aiden's mom is in the hospital, so they've both visited."

"I'm sorry to hear that," I say, frowning. "But are you seriously calling to ask me to drive over and help you?"

"I'm seriously asking that. Forget asking, I'm begging. I don't know what the hell I'm doing. They're going to kick me out, and then I won't be around for any more booty calls."

The desperation in her voice is real, and although I like to pretend to be an asshole, when a friend is in need, I can never say no.

Groaning, I slide my legs off the edge of the bed and reach for my discarded sweatpants. "Message me the address."

"You're an angel," she squeals. "Did anyone ever tell you that?"

"No."

I hang up, trying to find a clean shirt. I really need to do some laundry. Maybe I could do some at Celine's sister's house? Kill two birds with one stone. I reply to her message, asking if using the washer and dryer would be out of the question. She replies, **Bring your stinky clothes, and I'll do your laundry as payback**. I counter-reply with **Pussy is payback. Laundry I can manage on my own.**

Pulling all my dark clothes out of the hamper, I stuff them into my gym bag and lumber to my car. The air is cool, which wakes me up from my evening drowsiness. I toss the bag into my trunk and climb into my car, tapping the address into Google Maps.

Celine's sister's house is fifteen minutes away in a nice neighborhood of small family homes. Celine's car is in the driveway, but I pull up on the road outside. A wide porch area flanks the front door, with a few nice pots of flowers and shrubbery. Her niece, Lonie, has a plastic playhouse and a trike in the corner.

When I make it off the sidewalk with my bag held high on my shoulder, Celine's standing in the open doorway. She has her hair drawn into a high ponytail with wispy bits framing her face. There's a pen stuck in it and a deep v grooved between her brows. I wait for her to thank me for making the trip, but she doesn't. Instead, as I get close, she presses a soft kiss to the corner of my mouth and puts out her hands for the bag.

I follow her inside, enjoying the way her ass looks in camel-colored sweatpants. Her feet are bare, and her toes are painted in a light orange, reminding me of her original hair color.

The home is filled with warmth. Family photos are on practically every wall and surface, kiddie paintings spread over the refrigerator, and toys littering the area in front of the TV. Celine has her books spread out over the kitchen island, but she walks past them and into a small side room. "I'll put these into the washer first. Hopefully, there's a fast wash setting so we can get them dried before you leave."

"Your sister won't mind?"

"Marie is grateful that I drop everything whenever she needs me."

I wince as Celine pulls my training clothes out of the bag and stuffs them into the drum. Coach has us working hard, and my stuff is usually wet by the time I'm done. Wet and stinky. "Doesn't your mom do this stuff for you?" she asks.

I don't reply because telling Celine anything about my family is off tonight's agenda. "This is a nice house. Has your sister lived here long?"

Celine twists to look at me, then stands to shut the washer door. "A couple of years. They moved here when she was pregnant with Lonie. They wanted a yard for her to play in."

Her boobs look good in her white V-neck shirt. It shows off her creamy cleavage, dusted with pretty freckles.

"Makes sense."

I saunter back into the kitchen and take a seat on a stool next to the one Celine vacated to open the door.

"So, tell me what you need."

She takes a seat and begins to explain the areas of confusion. It's nothing I find difficult, so I do my best to go through each point step by step. She takes notes in scribbled handwriting that I struggle to read. Maybe that's her problem. She can't read her own writing.

After thirty minutes, I see her eyes light up. "Oh my god, I get it."

I shrug one shoulder and then stretch my arms over my head, leaning so my spine bends and my back cracks. My body aches from training, but the ache in my balls is something else entirely. That's good. You ready to fuck now?"

Her narrowed gaze only narrows further when I snort. I make my pecs jump, first one, then the other, knowing it's a douche move that is going to piss her off.

It does.

"Can you chill out? My niece is asleep upstairs."

"Is she in a crib?"

"Yes." Confusion clouds her expression.

"So, she can't come down."

"Elias. I'm not fucking you on my sister's couch."

"You're obviously not an experienced babysitter, Celine. That's the standard protocol for every babysitter I've ever had."

"You fucked your babysitters?" The horror she feels makes her mouth drop open.

"Not the old ones. Fuck, that's gross. The hot ones, sure."

"How old were you?"

"I don't know...twelve...thirteen. Not old enough to stay at home by myself."

Her hand flies to her mouth. "You fucked your babysitter when you were twelve? Had you even gone through puberty?"

I shrug. I don't remember when I became capable of fucking. The first time was an accident. Our neighbor, Justine, came over when Mom had to go to the hospital in the middle of the night. She was fifteen, and we hung out together on the sofa. We put the TV on, and there is a film that must have been rated way above our age. Somehow, we ended up fumbling around, and I ended up sticking my dick between her legs.

I remember feeling like I was in a dream. Afterward, she arranged her clothes, and we sat next to each other like nothing happened.

Her family moved that fall, and looking back, I wonder how she was so cool about what we did. Most likely, something bad was going on in her house. Looking back, the signs seem clear, but at the time, I was stuck in my head and swamped by my own problems. I don't tell Celine any of it.

"She was horny. I was horny. The rest is history."

In the other room, the washer beeps its finale, and Celine slides off her stool. "I didn't offer you a drink," she says. "Help yourself while I move the stuff into the dryer." She points to the refrigerator, so that's where I head. It's filled with fruits and vegetables, healthy smoothies, and glass containers of home-cooked food. I search for a soda, but there are only expensive brands of fizzy water or juice. I opt for juice. I'm pouring it into a glass when the front door opens, and a woman who's a double of Celine, when she had red hair, strolls into the kitchen.

"Oh, hi!"

"Hey." I lower the juice carton. "I'm Elias. Celine's friend. She's in the laundry room."

"She is?" Her brows quirk in surprise. I guess Celine isn't usually a domestic goddess when she babysits for her sister. "I'm Marie. And this is Aiden."

A big dude, with brown hair and a reddish beard, lumbers behind Marie, surveying his home and the invader in it with suspicious eyes.

"Hi." I step forward to do the manly handshake thing, making sure to offer a firm grip so he doesn't think I'm a pussy. "Celine needed help with her work."

I indicate our study material with a sweep of my hand. Marie snorts. "Of course she did."

My eyebrow jumps, and I shove my hands in my pockets, wondering what she knows and what she's assuming. Maybe Celine told her everything about what's been going on between us. Maybe she's spilled the whole sordid foursome thing. Or perhaps Marie's just assuming I'm here to hit the babysitter's ass like in all the teen movies.

"Marie. You're back earlier than I expected." Celine

emerges from the laundry room to the sound of the dryer beginning to turn.

"What are you drying?" Marie asks, her expression quizzical.

"Elias's laundry. It's payment for the lending of his genius."

Aiden's expression is amused. "Is that what they're calling it these days?"

Marie's eyes drift to where my junk is outlined against my gray sweatpants. She's so like Celine that I can't stop staring.

"Leave him alone." Celine drags me by the arm and pushes me gently back onto the seat. "He's really helping me. In fact, he might be the only thing standing between me and the life of a college dropout."

"Get this man a drink." Aiden pats me on the back, reaching into a cupboard for a bottle of whiskey that looks like the good stuff. "Marie's on a health kick, so beer's out, but this is the stuff for special occasions." He raises it high like we should all worship its greatness. I'm not really feeling whiskey, but the dude's just been to visit his sick mom in hospital, so if he needs a drink, I'm gonna drink with him.

He pours what looks like a double and hands it to me. "Cheers, man," I say, lifting the glass and taking a swig. I can tell this is good stuff. It's warm and oaky in my mouth and slides like lava down my throat.

"Don't get him drunk," Celine says. "How will he help me with my work if he's drunk?"

"I can do a lot when I'm drunk."

Aiden and Marie snicker and Celine shakes her head. "You know what. I think I'm good. I had a eureka moment before I pulled your boxers out of the washer."

She shuts her books and stacks them in a pile. I lower the drink, wondering if she's hinting that I should leave.

"How's your mom, Aiden?"

Marie answers for her husband. "She's definitely turned a corner. She had some color in her cheeks."

"That's good." Celine nods, then fixes me with her pretty eyes. "Want to hang out while your underwear dries?"

"It's not just underwear." I feel my cheeks heat. It's stupid to feel embarrassed that my personal items are going round and round in this dude's dryer. It's not like he caught me fucking his wife.

"Sure."

"I'll put out some snacks." Marie opens a huge cupboard door and begins pulling out bags of healthy chips and popcorn. She empties them into bowls and then chops apples, strawberries, and plums, placing them alongside.

Celine takes the tray into the seating area and places it on a low coffee table. I drift behind her, unsure of where to put myself. She flops onto the sofa and grabs the remote. "You can take the weight off." Pointing at the space next to her, she smiles at my uncertainty. I take a seat, sinking against the plush throw pillows. Damn, this couch is comfortable.

Aiden and Marie carry some glasses and a jug of what looks like fresh iced tea into the den and flop onto the couch next to ours. Celine finds a standup comedy special and grasps a handful of popcorn, tossing it into her mouth.

I don't know how it happened, but I've slipped into a scene of domesticity with a girl I'm not even dating.

"This one's fucking hilarious," Aiden says. "Have you seen it, Elias?"

"Nah, man."

"Watch this. His jokes are off the charts."

The comedian is funny as fuck, and I find myself

munching on sweet apple, and spicy lentil chips, laughing along with Celine and her family. It's kind of cozy and easy, and I forget why I'm here. I don't notice the beeps of the dryer coming to the end of its cycle, and neither does Celine. We laugh so much that my belly aches, and Celine's freckled cheeks are pink.

In the end, Lonie's cries on the baby monitor prompt me to look at the time on my phone. It's eleven pm and way past the time I should be hanging out at two strangers' house on a weeknight.

"I should get going," I say as Marie jogs up the stairs.

"Yeah. Me, too." Celine rises as I do, so much smaller than me when we're standing close. The red in her hair is just growing through at the root and my fingers itch to touch it. She's the same girl, but different since she covered it with brown.

"I need to grab my stuff."

She leads me into the laundry room, and we quickly share the folding responsibility. Everything smells fresh, and I'm relieved to have something clean to throw on for tomorrow's classes.

"I had fun." She places my last pair of boxers into my bag.

"Me, too." I lift the bag onto my shoulder and watch her hesitate with what to say next. It's on the tip of my tongue to say something crass, like 'it would have been more fun if we were naked,' but surprisingly, I keep my mouth shut.

Celine does, too. Her eyes drift from me to the door and I take the hint. In the kitchen, Aiden is clearing up the dirty glasses and loading them into the dishwasher. Celine gathers her books, shoving them into a black tote. She kisses Aiden's cheek and tells him to say bye to Marie for her.

"Thanks, man," I say.

Aiden wipes his hands on a cloth and shakes mine again. "It was good to meet you, Elias."

He's not much older than me, but the gulf between us is wide.

Travis would probably feel totally at home hanging out with Celine's family. And most likely, Dornan would as well.

"Yeah. You, too."

At the front door, I hold it open for Celine and follow her to her car. "Thanks for helping me," she says. On tiptoes, she presses a kiss to the corner of my mouth like she's not sure where we stand. I cup the side of her face and pull her into a deep and searing kiss that I've been craving for hours. She makes a sweet squeak of shock but rests her hands on my chest and goes with it.

I don't know what the fuck I'm doing.

This thing is messy. Celine is rebounding hard. Dornan and Travis lurk around every corner. She's using me for my dick and my brain. That's it.

I don't fit into this world of happy families.

Nothing about this thing between us works, but I still have this craving that I squash, leaving her wet-mouthed and wanting in her sister's driveway as I toss my bag into the trunk and drive off into the night.

18

DORNAN

"Fuck. My ankle hurts like…" Nathaniel's words are replaced by a wince as he tugs his sock down over his ankle and inspects his blooming bruise in all its glory.

"Shit, who got you?" Elias asks.

"Fuck knows. There was way too much flailing out there today."

"Put some ice on it," I tell him. "That kind of bruise can start out minor and end up causing the whole joint to immobilize."

"Yeah. I'll go show Freya."

She's our sports therapist. She'll know exactly what to do.

"That was a great play." Elias addresses me as he towels his cock. This is one thing I'm not going to miss when my football career is over. I've seen enough junk over the years to render me blind."

"Thanks. It felt good."

He nods, dropping his towel to the bench and searching for his underwear in his bag. It's been over a week since the afternoon at Travis's house. Over a week since Elias last got his cock out in front of me, although then, I didn't really notice. I was too busy focusing on Celine's naked body to care about anything else. But the sex had been hot. Hotter because watching Celine come over and over again at the hands, mouths, and cocks of other men just about blew my mind.

Elias might be arrogant, but he knows how to fuck.

"Celine was watching," I tell Elias.

He pretends not to be interested, but the corner of his mouth twitches, and I know differently. "There were a lot of people watching."

"Right."

I shove my foot into my sneaker, pulling the laces tightly and twisting them into a bow, then repeat with the other foot. This locker room smells like a marinated jockstrap dunked in blue cheese. The poor air freshener has given up trying.

"I'm gonna go and find her. You coming?"

Elias shrugs but grabs his white shirt and yanks it over his head, rummaging for his sneakers.

I wait for him, even though he hasn't said yes. Around us, the team chats shit about the girls they're intending to celebrate their victory with. Eddie's in the middle, yapping on about some other girl he's fucking. The guy is such a piece of shit that I can't even stand hearing his voice. Everything that comes out of his mouth involves inflating his own ego or putting someone else down.

Elias glances in his direction with a side-eye that's so vicious Eddie should drop down dead as a result.

"Fucking asshole," he mutters under his breath.

"He really is."

I stand and lift my bag. Elias grabs his hold all, and we make our way out of the locker room door.

"There they are. Celine's bitches." Eddie laughs loudly

at his own joke, and there is a small ripple of laughter from the men surrounding him that dies when Elias and I turn our heads slowly to look at him in disgust.

"You say something?" Elias asks.

"Yeah, I said you're Celine's bitch."

I half expect Elias to drop his bag and punch Eddie in the face, but instead, he just laughs. It's a big booming, full-bellied laugh that stops Eddie in his tracks. His expression turns from smug to pissed. "You seriously running with this shit, Eddie? Like, seriously. Are you so jealous that your ex is getting to experience the kind of dick you could never provide, you need to toss out stupid comments in the locker room? Like, dude, get a fucking life."

He turns to me, shaking his head, then leaves Eddie behind with his cronies.

Outside the locker room, I breathe in a long lungful of fresh air. "You handled that well."

Elias shakes his head and rolls his eyes. "That guy is just so fucking pathetic. Who can take anything he says seriously?"

"I still can't believe Celine was with him for so long."

"He wore her down, but she's learned her lesson."

As though we conjure her with our conversation, Celine appears with Gabriella, Kain, Ellie, and Colby. "That was so good," she squeals, running into my arms and squeezing me around my neck. I envelop her in a huge hug, breathing in her sweet scent. But before I have a chance to really relish the press of her body against mine, she lets go of me to focus her attention on Elias. The hug she gives him matches the one she gave me, but he doesn't hug her back. I fix him with a stare because I can't work out what's going on with him. Is he trying to make her feel like shit? If he is, he's no fucking better than Eddie.

"That play." Kain claps me on the shoulder with his big hand, jolting me from my thoughts and nodding appreciatively.

"Makes me want to play again," Colby admits.

"It felt good," I admit, rubbing my hand over the back of my neck. "I mean, who doesn't want to set up the win?"

"ELIAS."

The name is yelled out by a gruff voice, which slurs slightly at the end, lingering on the s. We all turn to find a man wearing Elias's face but with at least twenty years of wear and tear. In jeans, a plaid shirt, and worn boots, he has a scruffiness about him that makes me do a double take. It's the combination of his rough clothes and his reddened face that makes me pause.

My uncle is an alcoholic, and this man has the same ruddy, disheveled look about him.

Elias mutters something under his breath and turns away, looking like he's considering striding off in the opposite direction. He doesn't, though. Instead, he fixes his face with a blank expression. "What are you doing here?"

"Came to see you play," the man says. Is this Elias's dad? It couldn't be anyone else, could it? They look so alike.

"You shouldn't have bothered."

The man's face drops, then flashes anger in less than three seconds. "Who the fuck do you think you're talking to?" It comes out with three flecks of spittle, which fall to the floor.

Elias flinches. It's almost imperceptible. He does a good job of holding his ground, but I catch that motion out of the corner of my eye, and my stomach drops. Fuck.

This is his dad.

"Just go home." It's a brush off, but there is a cool edge to Elias's tone that ripples around the group. Celine takes a step closer to him, and so do I. It's an instinct to provide him with support, especially against someone who appears to have hurt him in the past. Elias is bigger than his dad, but that wasn't always the case.

"Embarrassed of me? Am I causing a scene?" He holds his hands out and looks around like he's daring someone to say something to him. Colby moves Ellie back, and Kain does the same with Gabriella. Anticipation of an impending confrontation settles into the air around us all. I'm ready to step in to stop it from happening.

"Dornan!" My dad chooses this exact moment to appear with a big bag of treats and groceries, grinning from ear to ear. I've never been more conscious of what a good man my dad is than right now, faced with Elias's father.

"Dad."

I can't move because I'm the only one close enough to get between these two men who are staring at each other with palpable malice.

"That play...I got it on video. I'm going to watch it over and over."

"Thanks, Dad."

Elias's father turns slowly, his gaze fixing on my oblivious father. The atmosphere must finally register, and my dad's eyes flit from face to face, trying to work out what's wrong.

"You need to leave," Elias tells his dad again, his tone arctic.

"It's a fucking free country." His dad stumbles back and spreads his arms to regain his balance. We all stare, unable to take our eyes off the car crash happening in slow motion in front of us.

Before Elias's dad has a chance to say anything else, my dad puts out his arm. "Come on. I've got snacks for you guys. You must be ravenous."

Elias doesn't take his eyes off his father for a minute, but as the rest of the group crowd around my dad to accept the bags of chips and sweets, whether they want to or not, the atmosphere is diffused. Celine's arm and shoulder are just in front of Elias, her face tilted into his body. She's trying to shield him, and when Elias realizes, the look on his face is enough to tug even the blackest of heartstrings.

His dad is the first to break the standoff. He wanders away like nothing has happened, swaying and unsteady on his feet.

Elias seems to shrink as he does, all the tensions crumbling from his body. "It's okay," Celine says, turning to touch his arm.

He closes his eyes, shutting out the world for a few seconds. "It's never okay."

"At least he came to watch you play. My dad doesn't even bother to call me anymore."

"I wish he didn't bother."

I take a bag of chips and offer it to Elias. He takes it, eyeing my dad suspiciously or maybe jealously. I wouldn't blame him for feeling either way.

"Let's go grab a beer," I say, looking directly at him. "I think we deserve it."

Elias nods, and Celine whoops and Gabriella tells Kain to call his brothers.

By the time we hit the bar, there's a big group of us, and everyone is chatting. Travis has arrived with Dalton and

Blake. Seb and Micky have come, too, leaving Noah with Ellie's mom and their dad. It's a raucous celebration, but Elias is still quiet. I buy him a beer and pass it to him. He downs the whole bottle in one go, slamming it onto the bar hard enough to draw the attention of others around us.

"Don't let him get to you," I say.

He fixes me with stone-cold eyes. "Says the man with the world's greatest father."

What do I know about what Elias has been through? Nothing, that's what. But I clap him on the shoulder and avoid getting drawn into any back and forth. "We don't get to pick our family, Elias. You might have a let-down of a father, but you have friends. You're on track to ace your degree. You can leave the past behind if that's what you want."

He could have Celine, too. I'm sure if he asked, she'd date him.

I might want her, but I don't need her in the same way Elias does.

Could I give up my claim on her?

I'm not sure.

"The past follows us around like a mangy dog." He indicates to the barman to bring him another beer.

"Celine wants you, you know."

His eyes cut to mine, emptier than I've ever seen them.

"Celine doesn't know what she wants."

We might not be playing games anymore, but somehow, this thing between us all seems even more tangled than at the start.

19

ELIAS

My head is banging in time to the beat. I didn't want to come to this stupid bar, but I knew Dornan would have made a big deal about it if I refused. He's on a mission to save me. He thinks he knows what my life has been like, and now, because he has a great father who loves him, and I don't, he wants to fix me.

I knock back a shot of tequila, not even bothering to suck on the lime. The sour, bitter taste jolts me, and the burn down my throat sears like bile.

I still don't know why my dad picked tonight to watch my game. It's been years since he turned up to anything of mine. In fact, I can't actually remember the last time he showed me any interest. Maybe he needs money. Maybe that's what he planned to talk to me about? Not that I have any to give him. Even if I did, I wouldn't share it with him.

Instead, Dornan's dad and his generosity and kindness highlighted what an asshole my dad is.

The way they all looked at him made me sick to my stomach. Having a shit family is bad enough. But people finding out I have a shit family is peak humiliation.

Celine and Travis are dancing. Well, Celine is dancing, and Travis is watching. Dornan's talking to Ellie, as usual. The others are around here somewhere, but none of them care enough about me to notice if I leave. Now's my chance to get out of here and lick my wounds privately.

I'm unsteady on my feet, and the weight of my bag doesn't help. I nod to the bouncer as I exit and am hit in the face by cool air, which goes some way towards clearing my mind.

I don't have my car with me, and money for a cab will wipe me out. It'll take me thirty minutes to walk home from here, but that will be enough time to sober up. I might even grab myself a burger on the way.

By the time I reach my dorm, my legs are dead, and my head feels like it's about to explode. Even the greasy burger didn't have the power to soak up all the shots I drank without wanting to. I fumble to get my key into the lock and dump my bag onto the ground with a thud.

I should clean my teeth and wash my face. Maybe drink some water and find some pills. I'm already anticipating a mighty hangover.

Ultimately, I manage the water, the Advil, and a rough clean of my teeth before flopping on the bed. I'm about to slide into the black abyss of drunken dreamland when my phone rings. Cracking one eye open, I answer when I see that it's Celine. "Open up. I'm outside."

"What?"

"Open the door."

She hangs up, and I blink, unsure if the call really happened or if I had imagined it.

I groan as I roll out of bed and rub my stomach as I make my way to the door. With every footstep, my head pounds. I buzz the front door open and wait, listening for Celine's footsteps, holding onto the top of the doorjamb for stability. Multiple sets of footsteps thud against the stairs. Voices rumble, and Celine laughs. When she finally comes into view, she's flanked by Dornan and Travis. What the fuck?

"I was sleeping," I groan.

"You left the bar without saying goodbye."

"You're not my girlfriend," I grunt.

Celine's hands rest on her hips as she surveys me. Luckily, I have my black boxer briefs on, but the rest of me is naked. "It's polite to let people know if you're leaving, Elias. We were worried about you."

"Yeah? Well, you don't need to worry about me. I'm good."

"You don't look good," Travis says. He runs his hand down his shaggy jawline. Celine steps forward.

"We just wanted to make sure you got back okay."

"You wanted to make sure I didn't do something to hurt myself because my dad is a worthless cunt."

She winces at the c-word in a way that I don't understand.

"That didn't cross our minds," Dornan says. "We just worried you were drunk and that you might have gotten into trouble on the way back."

"Well, you can see that I'm fine…in one spectacular piece."

I sway as I try to stand without support, and Celine is there in a flash, resting her hand in the center of my chest. I gaze down at her fierce expression. My drunken haze makes this whole exchange blurry. Why are they here? What is Celine doing? Slow-motion thinking has me blinking in confusion.

"Come on, big boy. Let's get you inside." Taking my arm, Celine walks me backward. Her hands on my skin make my cock hard, even though by right, I should have alcohol droop. She notices my erection and chuckles softly. "Are you serious with that right now?"

She eases me down onto the bed and attempts to lift my legs to get me to lie down. They're too heavy, and in the end, I scoop my arms around her body and pull her with me until she's splayed out on top of me. Her shocked laughter settles my soul. Her hand on my stubbly face is gentle. The way she eases my hair back from my forehead is so soothing, I close my eyes and relish every sweet touch.

Footsteps in the room remind me that we're not alone. It's weird because I don't give a shit. Dornan and Travis being here doesn't feel like an invasion of my space or privacy. There's a comfortableness about us all being together.

I take Celine's hand and wrap it around my cock, laughing as she squeals. "What? You guys come to my room in the middle of the night, and we're not going to have sex?"

"You're drunk," Dornan says.

"So are you. But you want to fuck, don't you?"

My hand roams Celine's side, finding soft skin and a warm breast. She's braless. I'm so fucking horny.

"Elias." Her warning voice is breathy, but her objection dies when I wrap my lips around her sweet nipple and suck. Celine's body goes slack beneath me as she gives into my wandering hands.

"Celine." I say her name in the same feminine tone, and Dornan and Travis laugh.

It takes me one shove to push my boxers far enough down my legs that I can get my feet out. It takes a little longer for my fumbling hands to get Celine naked. While all that's happening, Travis loses his shirt and boots, leaving his dark jeans unbuttoned at the waist. Dornan drops most of his clothing, leaving only his gray boxers. Why he bothers, I have no idea. It's not like they're doing anything to cover his monster erection.

Jeez.

I know more about these guys' cocks than any straight man should know about another.

While Celine pretends to object to my frantic clothing removal, Travis asks me if I have anything to tie her up with. In my closet, I have precisely one black tie that I use for formals and team functions. If I had a funeral to go to, I'd use it for that, too. I have some longish socks somewhere. Oh, and a few belts.

"Belts," I grunt, waving in the direction.

Celine shakes her head. "Too hard. I don't want my wrists getting fucked up."

"I only have one tie, and I don't want that getting fucked up, either."

Travis shrugs. "There are enough of us to hold her down."

"You could use her panties to tie her wrist together," Dornan suggests.

I have them balled in my hand. "They're wet. Sopping, even."

"And I'm not embarrassed about that in any way!" She laughs. "I mean, look at you guys. You're every woman's pussy-wetting dream. It's a miracle I'm not dehydrated."

"Jesus," I mutter as she wriggles beneath me. I want to get up inside her so badly, but it's Travis's turn to go first. Not that the order matters, but I don't want to be accused of being a selfish lover in any way.

I take Celine's panties, which are pink lace and barely there. They make a good tie for her dainty wrists and forcing her to keep her hands over her head stretches her pretty tits out perfectly.

"Travis, you're up, man."

Surprised, he pushes his jeans off and climbs onto the

bed. I shift so I sit with my back against the wall, anchoring Celine's hands.

Travis's blue eyes narrow as he assesses her body, considering what he wants to do to her. I get the feeling if they were alone, he'd tease her for hours before he'd let her come. It's weird because, in the darkness of a bedroom, a very different man comes out to play.

Celine trembles, and her eyes meet mine.

She pretends to be brave, but inside, she's just like me. Afraid she's pushed herself too far and won't be able to live up to promises and expectations.

Afraid she's not worth the effort.

It's why she stayed with Eddie for so long.

I run my hand down her torso, skimming her nipple as Travis eases open her legs. Dornan sits on the other side of Celine, so we're like bookends. He mirrors my hand and its movements over her skin, watching as Travis bends her legs and pushes them apart, spreading her pussy wide.

Travis licks just the tip of his finger and runs it over her clit with hardly any pressure. Celine's body reacts like he whipped her hard.

Travis's smile is as wicked as it is pleased. He rests the same finger at her entrance, not quite inside but with just enough pressure to hint at penetration. She starts to wriggle, but he holds her firmly with a hand spread over her belly.

"Tell me what you want," he says.

"I want what you want."

I swear a shiver runs through him.

Over the next thirty minutes, Travis teases Celine to the point of delirium. Her body writhes, and her skin develops a sheen of sweat as she strains for pleasure but never quite reaches it. She begs to come, but he doesn't let her. First, I hold her hands high above her head, and then

Dornan takes over. We take turns to enjoy the heat of her mouth and the vibrations of her moans.

And when she's crying out loud enough to wake the neighbors, Travis finally wraps his cock and fucks her.

She comes on his first thrust, arching, then going slack, her face twisted and then serene. She looks like an angel with her hair spread out over my pillows. I trace the bridge of her nose and the freckles there as Travis grinds into her, over and over, his face almost pained. When he roars his release, he earns a pounding fist on the wall from my awkward, geeky neighbor who doesn't ever look me in the eye and now never will.

After, Travis touches Celine's face, kissing her tenderly on each corner of her mouth before gently sucking on her bottom lip. She moans, still out of it from his kinky style of torture.

My head is still pounding, but there is no way I'm missing out on getting inside Celine again. I'm quick to release her hands and pull her onto my lap.

"Are you okay?"

She rests her hands against my chest, flexing her fingers against my skin. Her eyelids flutter as though she's trying to regain focus, and her hips move, sliding her slit up and down the rigid underside of my cock, coating it in her arousal.

I close my eyes and drop my head back, focusing on the sensation. I'm dizzy. So dizzy.

The bed shifts, and Dornan has moved behind Celine, cupping her breasts so her nipples peek out between his huge fingers. He lost his boxers in the process.

He tosses me a condom and sheathes himself with a tear of foil and an efficient roll of latex. My hands feel like shovels, and Celine ends up getting me ready.

"Who's next?" She glances over her shoulder at Dornan.

"Want us both at the same time?"

Her eyes widen, staring down between her legs at where my cock is big and hard and waiting. "At the same time? Like last time?"

I reach between her legs, pushing a single thick finger inside. "Both of us, here."

Her little hole clenches. I'm not sure if it's fear or anticipation. "How?"

I touch her face, brushing her damp hair from her forehead. "I'll push in first, then Dornan will work his way in. I grab her hips, lifting her so she's suspended over the head of my cock. It's easy to get inside now Travis has opened her up, and she slides down onto me with an open-mouthed gasp. I pull her over my chest and nudge out her knees, spreading her legs wider. I keep her face close to mine, kissing her mouth while Dornan moves into position. Her lips are soft and warm, and she lets me slide my tongue in, stroke after stroke.

My head spins.

Dornan's cock presses against the underside of mine, pushing to get into Celine's tight wet heat, as my hands caress down her spine, knowing she needs to relax, and I can help her.

Travis watches with his cock in his hand, already hard again.

"That's it, baby," Dornan croons. "Let me in. Let me in this sweet pussy. I'm gonna make you feel so good."

She whimpers against my lips as Dornan grips her ass cheek with one of his hands, using his thumb to pull her pussy open just a little more.

"Oh…oh…" she pants, hot breath gusting over my jaw. I close my eyes at the intensity of such tight penetration and the strange sensation of Dornan's cock rubbing against mine.

I've had my fair share of women and fucked them in

positions that the Kama Sutra would be proud of, but this is so much more than I've ever done before.

"I'm in," Dornan practically growls. I want to hit him with a snarky reply, but the words die before they reach my tongue.

Celine moans as Travis rolls her nipple between his fingers, making her pussy clamp down.

"I'm gonna move," Dornan warns and tests the first thrust, pulling back and then pushing in. I grip Celine tightly against my chest, fearing she might move and this whole crazy sandwich position we're in will fall apart.

"I can't," she says. "Oh fuck. Oh... don't fucking stop." It's a garbled mess of different statements that makes me chuckle.

"Make up your mind, girl."

She pinches my nipple, which shocks me at first but actually feels good. "You try fitting two massive dicks inside you, and then we'll talk. Oh...Oh..." Her eyes roll as Dornan mashes her pelvis into mine. Her clit must be rubbing against me with every thrust.

"She's close," I gasp, as the tight clench of Celine's pussy steals my breath, then it's rippling and rippling as she digs her nails into my arm.

I don't get even a second to relax into her pleasure.

"I'm fucking close," Dornan gasps.

"Just... don't fucking stop." I sound like Celine does when Travis has his tongue hovering over her pussy, but I don't care because my dick feels like the top is about to blow off, and I know my impending orgasm is going to be record-breaking.

"Fuck..." Dornan roars.

Celine turns to watch what her body has achieved; Dornan, looming over her like Thor, his face twisted with pleasure-pain like he's about to destroy a legion.

I close my eyes as my own pleasure surges. I lose control, thrusting up into Celine as Dornan withdraws. I roll her until I'm on top, crashing my mouth into hers as everything that's been building spills out of me in wave after wave.

"Fuck…Celine…fuck…"

More pounding against the wall makes us all look in the same direction. I laugh because this situation is fucking crazy. I have two naked men in my dorm room and one woman who probably won't be able to walk for a week.

Celine reaches out for me. "Elias."

My head spins with alcohol and hope.

Up until tonight, we've been playing stupid games, but this feels different.

They came to find out if I was okay, my mind whispers. They didn't have to do that.

It shows a level of care beyond what games should involve, but believing is hard for me. Hoping for more feels impossible. My own parents don't give a fuck about me. Why would these three people?

"Elias?" Travis's voice cuts into my racing thoughts. "You okay, dude? You look gray?"

I touch my forehead as the spin seems to get worse. Celine touches my forehead, too. "He doesn't feel hot. It's probably just the alcohol. Are you okay?"

Three people's attention is all on me, and I don't like it. It's like having a microscope aimed in my direction. Fuck.

I pull Celine into a searing kiss, driven as much by my fear as by my desire.

Sex is the only safe place for me when these three people are around me.

Sex is a place where I can hide from my ghosts and from my hopes, but for how long.

20

TRAVIS

After we make sure Elias is okay, forcing him to drink two glasses of water and eat two slices of bread, Dornan decides to walk home for the fresh air, and I drive Celine back to her dorm.

I say goodbye and yawn halfway through, and she insists that I sleep at hers rather than drive home. It's sweet that she's worried for my safety and even sweeter that she wants me to snuggle up in her bed and fall asleep.

I lay awake with her in my arms, wondering what the hell I'm doing when I made so many mistakes the last time I got into a *situationship*. I touch her face, marveling at the red of her eyelashes that cast pretty arcs of shadow over her cheekbones. Her lips are pouty when she sleeps.

Tonight was good for many reasons.

Hearing Celine and Dornan's concern when I pointed out that Elias had left dispelled some of my concerns about this complicated situation. The sex is epic, not only when it's me and Celine but when the others are involved, too. We laugh a lot together like I used to with my best mates.

I'm still friends with Dalton, Kain, and Blake, but since they fell in love with my sister, they have less time for me. I'm happy for them, but it's an adjustment.

If I was a sensible man, I'd walk away from this four-way confusion.

What good can come from catching feelings for a woman who quite obviously has feelings for other men? They might be willing to share her while we play games, but how long until they want her for themselves? And what kind of friendship could I develop with two men who've shared a woman with me? This would make the world's weirdest friendship origin story.

The pipework in the dorms makes strange clunking and gurgling noises. Someone, somewhere in the building, is showering or flushing a toilet. My feet hang off the end of Celine's bed, and I feel like Daddy Bear in Baby Bear's bed, an imposter in a life not meant for me.

I'm supposed to be past this.

I'm supposed to have my shit together, but I obviously don't.

Allowing myself to get drawn into this situation is another sign that the boundaries I try to set aren't firm enough.

I'm in danger of digging another hole of misery for myself.

I resist waking Celine and sinking into her sweet body again. Somehow, I've gotten used to the fact that Elias and Dornan need to be around for that. Eventually, I drift off to sleep.

In the morning, Celine wakes me with a soft kiss on my lips and scrambles from beneath the comforter to use the bathroom. The shower starts up and Celine hums as I turn over in bed and breathe in her scent. When she emerges, she's freshly scrubbed, with pink cheeks and damp tendrils curling around her face.

She dresses in front of me, pulling on a sports bra and tight leggings. I have to wait a few minutes, channeling images of my ex-boss, who had a mustache and body odor, before I can get out of bed without morning wood.

I don't shower because I don't have any clean things with me, but I do rinse my mouth out with mouthwash and quickly scrub my face with one of Celine's face products.

My hair is messy, but wet hands and finger combing do the trick.

When I emerge from the bathroom, I only have to pull on my jeans and shirt. Celine watches me dress with what can only be described as a wicked smile on her face.

"Seriously," she says. "Your body is just..." she makes a gesture with her hand and a sound with her mouth, "...chefs kiss."

I cock a brow and run my hand over my beard. It needs a trim, but I'll have to deal with that later.

"It's all yours, baby."

"Seriously."

Celine slowly sways across the room and lets her fingers trail down the center of my chest, her eyes opening wider with each ab she passes over. "Insane," she mutters.

I grab her wrist and bring her hand to my lips, kissing her knuckles softly; then I pull out the center of her gym bra, getting a good look at her perfect cleavage. "Now, that's insane."

She laughs and swats me away. "Keep doing that, and we'll get absolutely nowhere today."

"That sounds like an awesome plan." I pull her top again, this time pushing my finger between her tits. She squeals and jumps back, but not before I snag her wrist and twist her arms behind her back, holding them in one of my hands at the base of her spine. I loom over her shoulder, pressing my mouth close to her ear. "If I want to touch you, Celine, I will."

"Yes," she whispers. Her nipples tighten, poking the fabric of her sports bra, and she presses her thighs together. I shouldn't work us both up this way, but I can't resist it. She brings out the wickedness in me so perfectly.

Dropping her hands, I adjust my hard-on.

Celine is red-faced and flustered, just the way I like her.

"I have to go," I tell her.

"Can I come with you? I told Gab we can go to the gym together this morning."

That explains the outfit. "Sure."

Mom has a day off. It should feel weird to rock up at home with a girl, but Celine's different. She's already part of the family, in a way.

We make the drive with the windows down. The wind whips at Celine's hair, and she smiles into the breeze like a happy dog leaning its head out of the window. She finds music she likes on my phone, and we blast it, singing loudly and not caring who can hear us when we stop at the lights.

I laugh and feel a wave of happiness surge inside me, unfamiliar and brilliant. Before Germany, this was my constant state of being. I'd hang out with Kain, Blake, and Dalton, and somehow, we'd always be able to find a way to turn even the most boring of situations into something hilarious.

I felt comfortable in my own skin and in my surroundings.

The build-up to going to Germany had been mixed. The job opportunity was too good to turn down, but I was filled with regret at leaving my family and friends behind. I told myself that it wouldn't be for long. Just a year, maybe two. Enough time to get some experience under my belt. Enough time to work out who I am when I'm not surrounded by everything that's familiar.

It had been much shorter than that and returning felt like failure.

I didn't have a chance to settle into my new life or go through any of the self-discovery I had hoped for. I fell into the trap of a new relationship and let all my goals fall by the wayside. And when it all went wrong, I returned with my tail between my legs.

But Celine, Elias, and Dornan have brought some joy back to my life. I feel rooted again, as weird as it sounds. And happy.

We pull up outside my house, and I look at the place that has been my family home since before I can remember. The familiarity of walking up the front path and putting my key in the lock is like a balm. Celine bounds behind me on her bubble trainers. In the hallway, she looks around, her eyes trailing the family pictures with a new interest. "You were such a cute kid." She points at a photo of Gab and me when I was around nine and Gab was around four. With our summer tans and white-blond hair, we look like a pair of cherubs.

"Cute adult, too." I grin and wink, and Celine smiles before her eyes drift to a point over my shoulder, and her face falls a little.

"Travis?"

I turn at my Mom's voice, detecting a strangeness to the way she said my name. "Mom, you know Celine."

"Of course. Gabriella's upstairs." She glances back into the den. "Travis, there is someone here to see you."

If it was someone Mom knew, she wouldn't say it that way. She'd say Blake is here. So it must be someone she doesn't know, and I have no idea who that might be.

Celine's still standing next to me, and it's as if she can sense something's off, too.

"Who, Mom?"

"Lina from Germany?"

She says it like a question, and my heart seems to thud in one big, weird pulse and drop to the floor. All the darkness I felt when I got on the plane from Berlin and managed to push into the recesses of my mind barrels forward.

Celine's hand rests on my arm, and I turn to her like she's my safety in a warzone. "Are you okay?" she asks.

My head moves from side to side of its own volition, and Celine, picking up on my sudden change in mood, still makes no move to climb the stairs. Instead, she lets her fingers slide into mine.

Mom's gaze drops to where we're now joined, and her lips part like she wants to say something, but we're all trapped in a vortex of the silence that swirls around when things remain unsaid.

"I'll make coffee," Mom says eventually. "And I have blueberry muffins. Would you like one, Celine?"

"Sure."

My feet won't propel me forward even though I know I need to follow Mom and face the woman I flew over an ocean to escape.

"I'll come with you," Celine whispers. Never letting go of my hand. It's her presence that propels me forward.

In the den, Lina is relaxing on my family couch like it's the most normal thing in the world. Her arms are draped across the back, her legs are crossed, and her pointed shoe bounces up and down as she swings her leg. She always was an impatient person, so finding that I was not home when she arrived must have pissed her off. Her eyes brighten when she sees me, but her expression shifts into something darker when she sees Celine and follows my arm down until she notices our hands are linked.

"What are you doing here?" She doesn't deserve any pleasantries. She doesn't deserve to feel comfortable on my home ground when she made my life so difficult on hers.

"I'm here to see you, Travis."

Celine shifts closer to me until her shoulder is pressed against my upper arm. She squeezes my hand just enough to let me feel her reassurance. "Why?"

"This isn't the greeting I thought I'd receive after flying so far to see you."

"You shouldn't have bothered." I turn to where Mom's stirring the coffee so vigorously it sounds as though she will wear a hole in the mug.

Lina rests her hand on her belly and smiles in a way that doesn't meet her eyes. Smile is too nice a word for it. Smirk more accurately reflects the situation. I stare at her as my brain glitches. Why the fuck is she in my house? How the fuck did she find me?

"I have good news," she gushes, her eyes lifting from Celine's hand in mine to my face. "I'm pregnant."

The words penetrate my skull but don't truly register for a few seconds. Celine flinches like she's been slapped but still doesn't let go of my hand. It's as though she wants to tell them that she's with me no matter what. Except she can't be with me through this.

"Pregnant?" The word comes out through a throat that sounds strangulated. I stare at Lina with an expression that can only be described as horrified.

"Yes." Her hand caresses her belly again. "I couldn't believe it either, but the pregnancy tests, it's true."

I want to scream at her that I always wore condoms, but that wouldn't matter, would it? Condoms can fail. It says on the box that they're only ninety-eight percent effective.

"It's not mine." I bark. It can't be mine. I won't believe it.

Mom chooses that moment to return with a tray of coffee and blueberry muffins. She fumbles with the tray, and it drops to the table, sloshing some of the liquid.

"Oh...look what I've done." She bustles back to the kitchen, and Lina and I exist in a weird stare-off.

"Of course, it's yours," she says.

"You cheated on me. It must be his."

"He had a vasectomy, and we used condoms, so no. It can't be his." She shrugs like the cheating was nothing and describes another man's sexual function as though it's something normal to do.

My heart skips in my chest. Da-dum, da-dum, da-dum, da-dum. My stomach lurches, and I have to swallow the bile that threatens to rise. This can't be happening. I got away. I saw what this woman was like, and I left, and now she's trying to pull me back in.

My legs feel like they might go out from under me. The only thing keeping me standing, keeping me functioning, is Celine's presence. I don't want her to see me weak. I don't want her to witness me lose my cool or, worse, see how fucking broken this situation is making me.

"I want a paternity test," I say.

Lina's spine stiffens, and she smooths her long chestnut hair. Her tongue slicks over her teeth, pushing out her reddened lips. Mom returns with a cloth and the grayest pallor to her face. Upstairs, Gabriella laughs loudly, in another world where people aren't being trapped by their psycho ex-girlfriends into a lifetime of misery.

Because that's what this will be. If the baby is mine, my life is ruined. She'll use it to embed her nails into me permanently. She'll control the child to control me. I'll have to live in Germany because there is no way I'll leave a child of mine to be raised solely by a woman like this. My dad chose another woman over his family and ended up dead before he ever confessed his secret. There is no way I'd put a child of mine through what I went through. They'll know I love them and am prepared to sacrifice my life for them.

"Of course." She says it like she's confident that nothing will come of it. She says it as though she knows for sure that I'm the father.

I want to sit down. I need her to leave so I can get my head together.

Mom hovers like she doesn't know what to do. This woman is a guest, and Mom is hospitable to a fault, but this woman is obviously not my friend. Mom knows I wouldn't be standing across the room as stiff as a plank of wood if this woman was someone I care about.

Celine's hand is warm in mine, and her closeness makes me want to rewind time to the moments when we were singing in the car, laughing, and joking, where happiness felt like a thing that was possible. I could dwell in that moment forever if I knew that what came next was this.

A noose around my neck.

Dreading that my first child might be on its way into the world because its mother would be the worst kind of person, capable of ruining its life like she ruined mine.

"But the test will have to wait until it's born because there are risks." Her tone is smooth and confident.

"When's that?"

"Five months." Lina stands and makes her way closer, and I'm reminded of the school tarantula I looked after in the summer holidays. It had a way of walking that gave me the creeps.

She touches my arm and peers down her nose at Celine as though she's hoping she'll just disappear by wishing. "I know this is a lot to understand, but it's a good thing, yes? We were happy once. We can be happy again. I made some mistakes, I know. But with a baby, I won't make the same mistakes again." Her smile, that's all teeth and thin lips, could turn me into dust.

The audacity of her to give me this speech while I'm holding another woman's hand isn't lost on Celine. Her fingers tighten around mine, and I feel she's ready to unleash. I squeeze her hand gently, urging her to keep calm.

"That isn't going to happen." I shift on my feet, my fight-or-flight instinct telling me to run as far away from this toxic woman as I can. She touches her stomach again, and the panic I feel that it could be my child contained inside her sends a trickle of sweat down my back.

Her eyes narrow into the same slits that I remember so well from when I confronted her about the rumors. There was no shame. No apology for sleeping with another man. There was just anger that I found out and rage that I dared to ask her about it.

"I can go back to Germany, and you won't hear from me again." She tips her head to one side, smiling again like she didn't just threaten to take a child that might be mine and disappear. "Or you can come back to Germany with me, and you'll have a chance of spending time with your child when it's born. Those are the options, Travis. There are no others."

"Now hang on a minute," Mom says, her hand reaching out towards Lina. "Don't you think that's a little radical? Travis has a life here, and if he's not certain the baby is his, shouldn't you be willing to take some time and work at things? I don't understand why you're treating this as a black-and-white situation."

Lina cuts my mom a withering stare. "Travis should understand that this situation is very difficult for me. I need to prepare for this baby. The preparation can be with him or without him. If it's without him, then me and the baby won't need him."

"A child always needs a father."

"A father doesn't have to be genetic."

Mom's face reddens at the idea that I could so easily be replaced in my child's life. Celine is still holding her tongue, but I don't know how. She's conscious of overstepping, maybe. Conscious that this is a family matter, and the stakes are high.

Feet pound down the stairs, and Gabriella appears in the doorway, dressed in purple gym gear with her hair braided into two long blonde strands. "I thought I heard voices." She looks between us all, waiting for a response, but no one says a word.

"I'll come to Germany if the paternity test proves the baby's mine."

Lina shakes her head. She puts up two fingers. "Two options, Travis. You don't have to decide now. I'm flying back tomorrow. Come with me or don't. It's your choice."

She turns to my mom. "I'm sorry we met under these difficult circumstances."

Mom grimaces, a flush settling high over her cheeks. "It seems to me that you are making the circumstances more difficult than they need to be."

With a blasé shrug of her shoulders that indicates zero remorse, Lina walks past Gab, down the hallway, and out of the front door, slamming it behind her for effect.

It's only when the lock clicks into place that I slump into the chair behind me. I clutch at my chest. I can't fucking breathe.

"Jesus." Celine drops to her knees in front of me and takes my face in her hands. "That woman is awful." I close my eyes, inhaling slowly to the count of four, and exhaling at the same speed until I have some control over myself again.

"What am I going to do?" I ask the question even though I don't expect Celine to have an answer. Even hearing advice at this moment won't help. I just need time to decompress and face up to what's just exploded in my face.

Gab steps into the room and takes a seat next to me.

Celine drops her hands, defeat etched into her expression. Gab's arm drapes over my shoulder and she gives me a fierce hug. "Trav. She's pregnant?"

"So she says."

Mom slumps onto the opposite sofa, resting her face in her hands. It looks like she might cry and I couldn't deal with that, knowing that the impact of my decisions are the cause.

"I don't know what to do," I admit. "I don't know what I believe."

"She wouldn't have flown all this way if she wasn't pregnant. If she gets you to go back with her, she'll need to be showing within four weeks, or it'll be pretty obvious she's lying." I meet Mom's eyes and she shakes her head. "Do you believe what she said about not letting you have any contact if you don't go immediately?"

"Yes."

She blanches, twisting her hands in her lap. "So, you either go now, or you have to fight a foreign legal system to get a paternity test and access to a baby in five months."

"Or the baby isn't his, and he doesn't have to do anything." Gab leans into me and rests her forehead against my temple.

"He can't plan for that." Mom straightens. "He can't take that risk. He has to plan as though the baby is his."

"Why?" Celine voices my question.

"Because if there's even a small chance that the baby she's carrying might be Travis's, he has to put himself into the best position with the courts. If he stays here, the courts won't look favorably on him. He'll be seen as a foreigner who wasn't prepared to make any sacrifices for a child who is a German citizen. She'll use Travis's denial of the child against him."

"Fuck," Gab mutters, dropping her arm from around me.

Celine rests back on her feet, as defeated as I feel, because Mom's right.

Mom lays her face in her hands for a few seconds, then straightens again. "That is not a woman who will be a nurturing mother for a child, especially if she resents or hates the father. Travis, you need to see the next few months as a possible investment in your child's safety. If it's not your baby, you can walk away."

"But he can't go back to Germany," Gab moans. "He just found a new job...he just signed for a new apartment."

"None of that compares to his responsibility for a child."

Nausea surges, filling my mouth with saliva, which I swallow. I push my hands over my head and blow out a long, ragged breath. Celine's eyes are filled with unshed tears. She rests her hand on my knee, and I reach for it, holding it so tightly, I expect her to complain, but she doesn't.

"I have to go," I say eventually. "She's not going to back down. You don't know what she's like. If I don't go now, and it is my child, she's going to make it suffer for being a part of me."

"She can't do that," Celine pleads, but I can tell she doesn't believe her own words. Even though she only met Lina for a few minutes, she knows. Mom knows, too. How I didn't see it before, I don't know. I'm an idiot who was blinded by her brilliant smile and stark beauty. I wanted to believe that a girl like that could love me. It sounds pathetic now.

"You and Gab should go to the gym. I need some time to think." Celine's hand drops from my knee, and the loss of connection with her aches.

"I want to stay."

I reach out to take her hand in mine. "You should go. I

need to talk to Mom."

"Take a muffin each," Mom suggests weakly.

Celine meets Gab's eyes, and she nods. "We'll come back after," she says.

I touch Celine's cheek, my heart aching now I'm having to push her away. "I'm sorry."

She covers my cheek with her hand. "You have nothing to be sorry for, Travis. You made a mistake. Now you have to deal with it. We're all here to support you, whatever you decide."

I want her to tell me she'll wait for me. I want her to tell me that the happiness I felt when I was with her isn't something I'm about to lose to return to a life that fills me with misery and dread. But none of that is fair. Celine has come out of a tough situation of her own. She doesn't need to be dragged into my drama.

Mom stands and presents Celine and Gab with their muffins, and they take that as a sign to leave. When they've gone, I stand, intending to hide out in my room to try to come to terms with all the ways my life is about to change, but Mom doesn't let me. Instead, she pulls me into a long hug and tells me that everything will be okay.

I wish I could believe her.

21

CELINE

After the gym, I go back to Gabriella's house, expecting to see Travis. There is so much I want to say to him that I couldn't with an audience. I want to hear what's in his heart and help him find a way through this terrible situation. But when we return, Gabriella's mom is crying on the phone, and she tells us through sobs that Travis has gone out. Gab calls Dalton, but he hasn't heard from Travis. It's the same with Kain and Blake. They're all so worried when they listen to what's happening, but worry isn't going to find Travis or solve his problems.

"Where do you think he's gone?" Gab shakes her head and shrugs, which is zero help. I want to scream and find that woman so I can scratch out her eyes. Who the fuck does she think she is, threatening Travis that way? She needs to be taken down a peg or fifteen.

Shit.

The prospect of Travis leaving tomorrow to return to Germany hurts my heart so severely that I have to press my hand to my chest to contain the ache.

Gab drives me back to my dorm, and I shower and try to catch up on an assignment that's due, but I can't concentrate. For the first time since Travis, Elias, and Dornan agreed to play my stupid revenge games, I feel alone.

I didn't realize how much having them all in my life meant to me.

I didn't realize that letting any of them go would hurt worse than finding out Eddie had made a fool of me.

I send Dornan and Elias a quick message, asking them if they're free. Both reply to say they have practice but can meet me after. I don't tell them about Travis. I'll wait to do that in person. Instead, I agree to meet them near the locker room. Time moves so slowly, I want to scream.

Dressed in a black sweater, black leggings, and black chunky boots, I stride out into the afternoon. The wind whips my hair, but I don't bother trying to smooth it. Nothing superficial matters. I already feel as though I'm in mourning for what Travis and I have started to mean to each other and all the days, weeks, and months that we could have shared. I'm in mourning for the man Travis was becoming and desolate to see him return to the closed-off person he was when he returned from Germany. It's like witnessing a butterfly fold its wings and curl back up inside its chrysalis.

Elias is the first to leave the locker room, with Dornan close behind. Their smiles are wide and welcoming, but they must see my dark expression.

"What is it?" Elias stops in front of me and drops his bag to the floor. I collapse into his embrace, sobbing as all the pent-up worry overspills the moment that I'm close to him.

"Travis is leaving."

"What?" Dornan's voice is a confused boom, and he tips my chin, forcing me to look at him. "Why?"

"His ex-girlfriend says she's pregnant with his child. She told him he has to go back to Germany now, or he'll never get to see his kid."

Elias stiffens against me. "What the fuck?"

"She's horrible. A terrible, toxic person. And he's considering it. He's really considering it."

"Does he believe it's his kid?" Dornan tucks loose strands of my mussed hair behind my ear. He stoops to hear my raspy reply.

"He doesn't know. He says he always used condoms, but they're not one hundred percent reliable. She cheated on him, but she says the other guy had a vasectomy and used condoms, so there's almost no chance it's his."

"That sounds shady as fuck."

I release Elias and do my best to wipe my eyes without smudging my makeup. I feel like a mess of frayed emotions. Everything I want is slipping through my fingers like sand. "It does, but Travis's mom told him he needs to go, just in case it is his baby. She thinks he'll struggle to get access to see the child if he doesn't."

Dornan cups the back of his neck with his big hand and stretches back. "She might be right, but this is fucked up. He's just got himself settled here."

"I know. And she's such a bad person. She gave me the creeps."

Elias shakes his head, and by his sides, his hands flex into fists. There's no fight here. Not a real one, anyway, but he's ready for one on Travis's behalf.

"He shouldn't go. This sounds like the desperate grasp of a toxic woman."

"He can't risk it." Dornan sounds genuinely pained. "His mom's right. When it comes to kids, everything else goes out the window. If she's as bad as you say, he can't risk his child being left in the sole custody of a malicious woman like that."

"I don't want to lose him," I admit in the smallest,

weakest, most pathetic voice.

This time, Dornan embraces me, and I sob against his warm, fresh-smelling shirt.

A rumble of laughter spills from the locker room behind us, and Eddie's voice rings out. "There she is. College girl enjoys getting fucked by the team."

I pull back from Dornan, but I don't want to look in Eddie's direction. He's the kind of pathetic loser who'd assume I was still upset over him, and I'm not about to reveal anything about Travis to make him understand it isn't true.

"Shut the fuck up, Eddie." The menace in Elias's voice should chill the heart of any man, but Eddie isn't a normal person. It's suddenly clear to me just how much he reminds me of Lina. They have the same air of superiority and the same expectation of control. They even have the same kind of self-satisfied smirk that makes the hair rise over my scalp like some kind of primitive danger warning signal.

"What? Am I not speaking the truth?" A couple of his friends laugh but hang back so that if Elias and Dornan lose their shit, then they're not the ones in the firing line.

Elias takes a threatening step forward so abruptly that Eddie jerks back in response. When he realizes that he's made himself look like a frightened coward, he puffs out his chest. "I told you she's not worth it. You'll see just how worthless she is."

It's a weird threat like he's anticipating something happening in the future. Dornan takes two steps forward with the same speed as Elias, and Eddie backs off again. This time, he walks away, trying to find some swagger.

"Ignore everything that fuckwad said." Elias stares after him with menace darkening his already shadowed eyes.

"Everything," Dornan reiterates.

In my pocket, my phone begins to ring and vibrate. I

pull it out, finding Ellie's name flashing across my screen. When I answer, she says my name in a panicked voice. "Celine. Have you seen it?"

"Seen what?"

"The video?"

My heart thuds within the cage of my chest as Eddie's threat echoes. *'You'll see how worthless she is.'*

"What video?" I pace away from Elias and Dornan, unable to meet their eyes.

"Someone sent me a link—I'm not going to say who because I don't want to compromise them—but there is a video of you on a free porn site."

"A what?"

"A video of you having sex."

"Me?" I don't understand how a video of me having sex could be anywhere. I've never let anyone video me or take photos of me. I'm not an idiot. As soon as a digital image or video is created, there is a risk that it will find its way into the public domain.

"Yes. You. It's definitely you."

"You watched it?" The idea that one of my besties has seen a video of me having sex feels like a huge violation.

"I had to, sweetie. I wasn't going to call and freak you out on another person's say-so."

"And it's me?"

"It's you. I'm sending you the link now. It's under the title 'College girl enjoys getting fucked by the team.'"

Eddie's words pound in my mind like a bass drum of doom. My phone pings with a message, and I click the link. The volume on my phone is set to loud, so when the video comes up, the sounds of moaning and slapping flesh are loud enough to draw the attention of a few passersby as well as Elias and Dornan.

I slap my hand over my mouth when I see what is

clearly me being fucked from behind. I'm naked, so my breasts are visible. My face is slack, and my mouth is open. The man pounding into me from behind isn't visible above his navel. It's like whoever set the camera to video purposefully excluded themselves from the shot. Dornan snatches the phone out of my hand and deals with the volume. He shares the phone with Elias, and I turn away, so fucking mortified at what they're seeing.

"Your hair was red," Elias says. "It has to be Eddie who posted the video."

"You fucked me when my hair was red," I remind him, although I'm not sure why. It has to be Eddie, doesn't it? Or could it have been someone else, and he saw it and wanted to gloat? Suddenly, all my previous sexual partners become potential perpetrators.

"I didn't fuck you like that. This dude has no fucking style, pounding away like a jackhammer." He shakes his head in disgust. "Look at the background, Celine. Look at everything you can see. Your face...anything that might tell you when it was."

"I feel sick." It hits me with such violence that I stagger and vomit next to a trash can. It splashes onto my boots, and I have to grasp onto the can to stabilize myself.

"Fuck." Dornan grabs me around the middle as I heave again. "We should get her home." He must address that part to Elias.

"I'm going to go and find that cocksucker and skin his dick."

"Not right now, you're not. If Eddie's pencil dick is getting skinned, I want to be there. We need to look after our girl."

Even bent over and in distress, the words 'our girl' slide over me like the softness of a feather. Wiping my mouth on the back of my hand, I straighten my spine and exhale. "We need to find Travis," I remind them. "It can't wait."

Dornan and Elias exchange another look, reminding me of Colby, Seb, and Micky, who always seem to have a triplet sense that enables them to communicate with only their facial expressions. Dornan and Elias aren't related, though. Up until recently, I didn't even think they liked each other. Now, they seem to be working as a team. "You take her home," Elias confirms. "I'll go looking for Travis."

"I want to come," I say, but Elias shakes his head. "Go home and deal with the video. I'll call you as soon as I know anything."

22

ELIAS

Celine wants me to find Travis, but every fiber of my being wants to hunt down Eddie and tear his intestine through his asshole. It's him in that video. I'd stake the last hundred bucks I have in my bank account on it. He didn't like the revenge games Celine played and lashed out. He couldn't stand to see her with three decent men who want to treat her like the queen she is.

He had to find a way to shame her, even though he was the guilty party that caused the end of their relationship.

Men like that make me sick. Weak, vicious men who can't take it when their woman moves on. Petty fucking jerkoffs.

But Celine's right. Travis has to come first. He's someone who deserves my attention. A man caught in the kind of tight spot I would never want to be in. A decent man who's contemplating leaving his life behind on the off chance his cheating-bitch-ex-girlfriend might be carrying his child.

I jump into my car and make my way to Travis's mom's house. The traffic is terrible, and with each passing minute, my head pounds with more tension. I'm famished from training hard and in desperate need of a protein-rich meal, or my muscles will scream at me for neglecting them.

As I pull up outside the house, the scent of home cooking wafts through my window, making my stomach growl in reply. Someone's cooking up something good. If the last meal I had at Travis's is anything to go by, it's probably his mom.

It feels weird to approach Travis's front door. We're not friends in the true sense, just men who have come together because of a shared appreciation of a woman. But over the past couple of weeks, he's proved himself to be a good man, and that's rare as fuck.

I knock on the door, glancing down at my beat-up sneakers and ratty faded black joggers. I'm not exactly dressed for visiting. A woman with short blonde hair, and stunning blue eyes opens the door and stares at me curiously. She looks so much like Gabriella; it's uncanny.

"Hi, I'm Elias. I'm here to see Travis. Is he here?"

"He is." She sounds wary, and I get it. He's gone through a lot today, and she doesn't know me from Adam. "Travis." She yells his name and ushers me inside.

Travis appears at the top of the stairs, looking bleak. "Hey, man."

I tip my head in greeting. "You got a minute?"

He nods and waves me up. I take off my shoes, remembering my manners even though I wasn't raised with many. My sock has a hole in the toe, which Travis's mom spots with her eagle eyes. She doesn't say anything, but I feel her pity or maybe her question. Why is his mom not taking care of him?

This is why I don't hang out with other people's families.

The hallway is lined with pictures of Gabriella, Travis, and their mom over the years. I avoid looking at them in too much detail, not wanting to see the happy smiles because it's a reminder of how few photos I have of my childhood, and even fewer when I'm cracking anything other than a grimace.

Travis is standing in the hallway at the top of the stairs, his shoulders curled forward, and his head held lower than usual. He shuffles into his room and slumps onto his big bed, resting back against the dark wood headboard. There's a chair in the corner that I sit on because standing would make this whole thing feel pressured.

"What's going on, Travis?" I eye the open suitcase next to him on the bed. His attention drifts there, too.

"I have to go," he says.

"Celine said that's what you thought."

"If I don't go and it's my kid..." He trails off and shudders.

"Is she that crazy?"

He nods, and I crack my knuckles, first on one hand and then the other. I grew up with crazy, except it was my dad. My mom's a little on the edge, too, mostly because of my father's behavior.

"What are the chances it's yours?"

His eyelids lower and stay closed for a few seconds before he opens them. Frustrated, he scores lines into his hair with his fingers. "We fucked for three months. I used condoms the whole time."

"Any breaks or tears?"

He shakes his head.

"Did you leave the condoms in the bathroom at her place?"

Travis blinks fast. "No. I always wrap and flush. My mom taught me that when I was a teen."

"Clever mom."

He nods.

"So, next to no chance."

"There's always a chance."

I blow out a tense breath, knowing that he speaks the truth. No sex comes without risk. It's why dudes need to choose their partners carefully, even if they're only intending to share one night. My own actions with Celine were risky, but I don't regret a thing.

I wish I had words that would help Travis. He's stuck in a situation where there's no winning. A situation I'd never want to find myself in.

"When can you get a paternity test?"

"She says only after it's born because of the risk to the pregnancy."

"So you'll know when?"

"Five months."

"Jesus. That's a long time to wait around in a foreign country. Do you even have money? And what about a visa?"

"Money is tight. I just put a big deposit on the apartment, and I have to find the rent for that while I'm away. Visa is still in force."

"So, where are you going to stay?"

"She says I can stay with her."

"Holy fuck. You're not going to move in with her?"

"What choice do I have?"

He's right. The dude is out of options. He's going to leave his life behind, his family and friends, and everything that he's been working to establish since his return, all for a one percent chance there might be a baby that's his in five months. It's fucked up. "Listen, whatever happens, we're on your side, okay?" I run my hand through my hair and focus on the point where the wall meets the ceiling. Fuck. I'm not good at this kind of thing. Not good at all.

Focusing back on Travis, I want to say something that

will help. He needs it. "I know this situation between us all hasn't exactly been normal, but we're buddies now, right?" The label sounds stupid but I don't know how else to describe it.

He nods, a twitch of a smile pulling just one side of his previously grim mouth. "Buddies."

"So, call us. Especially Celine. She's really sad about this. She's going to miss you."

He nods, but the way his eyes widen makes me realize he didn't know.

"I'll call when I can."

"Okay, buddy."

We both laugh uncomfortably as I stand.

I decide not to tell Travis about the video because he has enough on his plate. If he finds out, maybe he'll feel like he should stay. He'll feel torn, and the guy doesn't need that. Me and Dornan are more than capable of handling shit with Eddie and supporting Celine through it all. It's what we've been doing from the start.

I shift on my feet and drift to the door, but Travis says my name. "Elias. Take these." He holds out a set of keys. "Someone might as well get some use from the place."

I nod solemnly, as though he's trusted me with his castle rather than a half-empty apartment he never even got the chance to move into.

Maybe we can set the place up for his return. Make it feel lived in. I believe he's coming back. The alternative just wouldn't be fair, and Travis deserves a good life.

"I'll see you in five months." I reach out to shake his hand. We both grip firmly, and he clasps his free hand over mine.

"Maybe."

When I get to the bottom of the stairs, Travis's mom comes breezing out. "Dinner's ready. Will you stay, Elias?"

"I shouldn't," I say, even though I'm so hungry, it feels like I'm digesting my own stomach. Right on time, my belly growls like an angry bear in an echoey cave.

She looks down at my sock again. "You absolutely should."

Bustling away, she leaves no room for me to object. Travis laughs softly, as though this is the usual situation in his house. He claps me on the shoulder, and I follow him into the kitchen, my eyes bugging out at the table that is overflowing with food. It's like a medieval banquet. "You eat like this every day?"

"Sure."

The guy is so blasé. He has no idea how lucky he is to have the normal things every child should grow up with. Travis indicates where I should sit, and he takes the place opposite. His mom gestures for us to serve ourselves, so I start by spooning small portions onto my plate. She tuts and takes over, doubling the portion of everything. "You're big," she says. "You need to eat."

"Mom!" Travis shakes his head. "You can't go around telling people they're big."

"Why not?" She looks between us, bemused. "Big is good for a man."

I accept the plate, trying to keep my smile suppressed while inside my chest feels hollow. Travis has a great life here. He has so much good that he's going to leave behind.

"And you eat." She nods at her son. "I've made extra for you to take with you."

"I can't take food through the airport."

She sighs and slumps into a chair before serving herself. Her weariness at the situation scores lines into her forehead. "Elias, you'll take some with you?"

It's my instinct to say no, but her need to take care of Travis through me is evident. "Sure. That would be awesome."

We eat, and everything is delicious. Darleen offers me seconds and then tries with thirds, but I'm almost fit to burst. Conversation is light, and rather than feeling like a spare part, I can tell they're grateful to have me with them to distract them from what's coming. Halfway through our meal, Gabriella arrives with Kain, Dalton, and Blake. She's obviously updated them on the situation, and all the men's expressions are concerned. "Trav, man. You're seriously going?" Dalton rests his hand on his friend's shoulder.

"I have to."

"Sit and eat," Darleen says, shoving a plate towards Blake. He accepts it gratefully.

"Dad is coming over in a minute. He's just washing up."

It's a hastily organized goodbye meal for a man who doesn't want to say goodbye.

When I've finished what's left on my plate, I make my excuses to leave, not wanting to invade their privacy any further. I'm handed three large containers filled with food by Darleen, who has glassy eyes. Saying bye feels like a line drawn through an experience I wasn't looking for and would never have thought I wanted.

At the door, I'm at a loss for what to say, so instead, I slap Travis's shoulder with my big hand and tell him not to forget us.

As I drive away, I can't shake the feeling that this is the first step to everything good in my life falling apart.

23

CELINE

Elias calls to say he's outside my building, hours after he left to find Travis. When he knocks on the door, I ask Dornan to open it. I'm exhausted and rung out. The tears I've shed have left my face blotchy and my eyes so swollen I can barely see.

Dornan and Elias have a rapid, hushed conversation that I can't really hear. When Elias enters the room, he makes a beeline for me, squatting next to my bed so he's closer to my level, reaching out to touch my face. "Celine. Don't cry."

I curl up so I'm facing away from him, not wanting him to see my face in this state.

"Did you find Travis?" I ask.

"Yeah. He was at home."

"And."

"He's going."

"You couldn't convince him to stay?"

Elias's hand moves down my arm in a soothing stroke. "I couldn't. He's too fearful, even though the chance that it's his kid is almost nothing, in my opinion."

The lump in my throat burns like the surface of the sun.

Dornan sits at the end of my bed, resting his hand on my foot, and Elias pats my arm. "What happened with the video?"

"We watched it again," Dornan says. "It's definitely Eddie, and he must have posted it."

"That fucking asshole... I'm going to tear off his balls and make him eat them."

"I feel the same." Dornan's voice matches Elias's growl. "But it's not going to help Celine."

"But it'll make me feel better."

"We need to do this right. We need to get the police involved. We need to contact the website that's hosting this video to let them know she didn't give permission for it to be shared. Celine needs to tell her parents."

"I don't want to." The prospect of telling my mom and dad fills me with dread. Mom will be angry that I've gotten myself into this situation and that it's taking the focus from her misery over the divorce. Dad will probably not have time to deal with it and not really want to. He's barely interested in my life. He won't want to deal with something so embarrassing and mortifying.

"What about Marie?"

I turn to Elias, swiping my hand over my face. "She has enough on her plate with Lonie and Aiden's mom."

"She's your sister... She'd want to know what you're going through."

I could speak to Marie, even just to get her perspective on what I should do. Half of me is worried that reporting this to the police will only make the situation between me and Eddie spiral more out of control. Who knows what other videos he might have made of me without my knowledge.

I also can't deal with the prospect of Marie watching the video.

"I'm going to have to deal with this myself," I say it firmly, hoping they'll both understand that arguing for something different is pointless.

"You're not going to be alone in this." Dornan is firm, and he looks to Elias to make sure he's in agreement.

"We'll be with you all the way."

Tears burn in my throat and trickle down my face. I hide in my hands as my shoulders shudder with stifled sobs. Elias cups my chin in his palm and tips my face up. "This isn't like you, Celine. You're a fighter. Don't play Eddie's games. Don't let him win. You need to face this with your head held high and know that we'll be here to support you while you do it."

I blink, startled at his fierceness and the way my tears dry with his words. He's right. This isn't like me. So, I fucked someone, and they were enough of a jerk to put it on the internet. I'm not the first, and I definitely won't be the last. Eddie isn't going to win. He's done something illegal, and he's going to pay for it, but only if I'm strong enough to report it.

"I'll go to the police," I say, my determination hardening every word. "Fuck Eddie. He thinks he can humiliate me. Let's see how much he likes being taken away in handcuffs."

"That's my girl." Dornan smiles, proud of my resolve.

Elias rises from his squat position, straightening his legs with relief. "Do you want to go now?"

I shake my head. "Tomorrow," I say. "After our classes are done."

Sliding my feet over the edge of the mattress, I stand to find a tissue so that I can blow my nose. I strip off my sweater, feeling hot and gross. Dornan finds his phone. "I'm going to message Ellie and let her know what you've decided."

"Sure."

As he begins typing, Elias's phone rings. It's the first time I've ever heard his phone make a noise in all the time we've spent together. He pulls it out of his pocket and looks at it but doesn't answer it. When it stops, he pushes it back into his pocket. Then it starts to ring again. "Aren't you going to answer it?"

He shrugs and lets it ring out again.

I toss the tissue in the trash and take a long drink of water from the glass on my nightstand.

Elias's phone rings for a third time. "Maybe you should get that," I say.

He shrugs, retrieving it and staring at the screen. I can't work out if he recognizes the number or not. He swipes the screen. "Hello?"

A woman's voice speaks rapidly into his ear at a volume I can't decipher. I watch as Elias's color changes and his expression hardens. Dornan and I exchange a concerned glance. "Which hospital?" he asks.

The caller continues.

"Okay. I'm going now."

When he pulls the phone from his ear, he stares at it for a few seconds before shoving it into his pocket. His eyes fix to the floor, not meeting mine or Dornan's gaze.

"Is everything okay?" Dornan asks.

Elias turns to the door as though he's intending to run. His fists ball at his sides, a strange reaction to someone being taken ill and needing to go to the hospital.

"Who's at the hospital?" I ask.

Elias's cheeks begin to redden, and he seems on the brink of raging.

"Elias." I take a step closer, but he moves away.

"My mom." His voice sounds strangely dead.

"We're coming with you." Without waiting for his agreement, I gather my phone and a hoodie, twisting my messy hair into a quick bun. Dornan slips on his sneakers, and still, Elias doesn't look at us. He doesn't tell us what's happened to her. But most importantly, he doesn't tell us we can't go with him.

My problems slide away at the sight of Elias's suffering. He's such a big, strong man with so much resilience, but I see how his eyes flit around the room that he's panicking.

"I'll drive." Dornan jingles his keys in his hand, which seems to jolt Elias from his strange trance. "Come on."

I want to touch Elias, take his hand, or rest my palm on his shoulder. Anything to let him know I'm present and concerned, but he seems to have folded within himself, so I leave him be. He rides up front with Dornan as we drive to the nearest hospital. Marie gave birth there, so I'm familiar with the parking lots in relation to the location of the main entrance.

When we arrive, he tells the receptionist his mom's name, and she directs us to critical care. Elias strides ahead, and Dornan and I trail a little behind, giving him the space he seems to need. Dornan takes my hand in his, and we walk like a couple through sterile corridor after sterile corridor.

At the ICU, Elias gains entry, but we have to stay outside. He doesn't even acknowledge us before he disappears through the door to face whatever's brought his mom into such a dire health situation. When he's out of earshot, I face Dornan, finding his expression worried. "What do you think has happened?"

"I don't know." He shakes his head. "But his reaction isn't normal. Who gets enraged when their mom's sick."

"Either she's brought it on herself, and he's frustrated, or someone has done something, and he's mad."

"You think his dad did this to his mom?"

The question hangs between us uncomfortably. We both saw his father and how unhinged he was. Elias was clearly uncomfortable with him around. Elias never talks about his family. I don't even know if he has siblings. I didn't even know his mom was still in his life.

I think about how much I avoid discussing my own family. I haven't always been this way. When they were married, I'd often refer to them or talk about my home life. Since they divorced, I don't bring either of my parents into conversation at all. Dornan talks about his family a lot. I can tell they're good people and that he loves them. His dad is always around, making sure to treat Dornan whenever he can. I'm happy for him, but the absence of my own parents makes me more envious than I'd like to be. I guess Elias and I have more in common than I thought.

We lean against the wall in the hallway, letting silence rest around us. I'm glad Dornan is with me and that we're both here to support Elias. Imagining him here alone hurts my heart, although how much of a support he will allow us to be remains to be seen.

"I don't know. I don't want to make judgments after meeting someone once, but…"

Dornan nods. "I got a bad feeling, Celine. A really bad feeling about that man."

"I just want to go in there and help him," I whisper, staring at the door, keeping Elias from me.

"It sucks that we can't go inside as support."

I nod in agreement as a wave of anxiety clenches my stomach. "Do you think he'll come back out?"

A doctor bustles past, carrying a takeaway cup of coffee. His shoes squeak against the floor with every step.

"He'll come out. He knows we're waiting."

My phone buzzes in my pocket. It's a message from

Ellie, asking if I'm okay and if I can talk. I reply to say I'm okay and busy right now. I don't share Elias's situation because it's private. If he wants to tell people what's happened, that'll be up to him.

I call Marie, knowing I need to tell her about the video now before it finds its way to her by other means. Too many people watch porn these days. It's become mainstream. For all I know, Aiden might go to the site it's trending on. Would he tell Marie if he saw the video? Probably not.

Ugh. The idea of my brother-in-law watching me fuck only exacerbates the anxiety.

As the phone starts ringing and I wait for Marie to answer, I start to sweat.

"Celine." Her voice is bright, and happy to hear from me. It only makes the news I have to pass on feel worse.

"Hey, Marie. Sorry to disturb you this late."

"It's okay. Aiden's sleeping, and I'm watching that cheesy series I told you about."

"Cramming in your free time after hours?"

"Something like that. You'll understand when you have a Lonie of your own."

"Lonie is one hundred percent original."

Marie laughs. "I just love the relationship you guys have," she says. "You're an awesome aunt to her."

My throat tightens and burns, but I rush to speak through it. "I don't think you'll feel that way when you hear what I've got to tell you."

"What? What is it?" I hear her pause the TV in the background.

"Eddie circulated a video of us having sex. I didn't know he made the recording. It's up on a free porn site."

"He did what?"

"I know. It's the worst attempt at revenge."

"Revenge for what? He's the one who cheated on you."

"I know." I sigh, meeting Dornan's eyes. He gently touches my face and then steps away, looking at his phone. I dread to think what kind of messages he might be getting about me. The location of the video must be circulating around the university like wildfire.

"So, what the fuck is his problem?"

"He didn't like the games I played with Dornan, Elias, and Travis. I guess he felt humiliated."

"What a fragile ego, small dick man."

I'm not used to my sister speaking that way, so I snort a surprised laugh. "That's about it."

"You need to go to the police. There are laws against this kind of bullcrap."

"I will. I'm going to."

"I'll come with you," she says, then as an afterthought, she asks in a lower tone, "Are you going to tell Mom and Dad?"

"Thank you, and no."

"I know why you wouldn't want to, but maybe you should. I know they've been shit recently. I mean, they never bother to call me to find out about Lonie. When I see Mom, all she wants to do is trash Dad. And Dad has turned into the invisible man."

"I thought it was just me," I admit. Marie was always their favorite, or so I thought.

"Definitely not just you. But they're still our parents. They're self-obsessed, but something this big could yank them out of their funk."

"You're more hopeful than me."

"Should I ask where the video is?"

"I don't want you to watch it," I squeak.

She makes a disgusted noise. "You think I want to see

you fuck. Jesus, Celine. I just want to do some research."

"I'll message you the site. Don't tell Aiden."

"I won't, but he might be able to help. He has friends in law firms. We might need to draw on some free advice." She always was the practical thinker of the two of us.

"Okay. Maybe. I want to go to the police tomorrow."

"I can come with you. Lonie will be at preschool in the morning."

"Okay, great. Thank you."

"You sound okay about this. If it was me, I'd be freaking out."

"I have been freaking out, but some stuff has happened to put it into perspective. I'll call you first thing, okay?"

Marie agrees, and we say our goodbyes just as Elias appears at the door of the ICU. His face is like a frozen mask; he's white as a sheet, but his jaw is clenched as though he's furious. Before he can speak, I walk over and wrap my arms around him. It takes a few seconds, but he eventually buries his face into my neck. Dornan shoves his phone into his pocket and moves closer, too. "How is she? What did they say?" he asks.

"She's really bad." Elias's voice sounds weirdly strangled. "She fell from the top of the stairs to the bottom. Her face is messed up. She broke fingers and her arm and collar bone. She has a busted-up ankle. They say her brain is swollen from the impact of the fall, so they've put her into an induced coma."

"Jesus." Dornan shakes his head.

Elias straightens and pulls away, running both his hands through his hair and turning to face the wall. His broad back heaves, muscles bunching beneath his shirt. "He's gone too far this time."

Dornan steps between us as though he's worried Elias is going to lose his shit. I'm not worried, though. Elias would never hurt me. I know that. Dornan should know it, too.

"Who? Who did this?"

"My fucking asshole dad."

Dornan's wide eyes meet mine. We speculated, but hearing it's true is shocking. "Was there a witness?"

Elias spins to face us. "There doesn't need to be a witness. He's been violent since I was a toddler."

"Are you serious?" I regret the words as soon as they're out of my mouth because who the fuck would joke about something like this. "I'm so sorry, Elias," I add before he can respond.

"He's going to be the sorry one."

Elias starts to stride down the hallway towards the exit, and Dornan is quick to keep up. I have to run to match their long strides. I catch up to Elias and grab his arm. "You can't do anything to him, Elias. I'm not going to lose you, too."

He whirls, fury narrowing his eyes to slits, but when he sees the unshed tears in mine, he seems to soften. "Please." I'll beg and plead…whatever it'll take to make him see. "We can go to the police together. I'll tell them about Eddie. You tell them about your dad. You can hold my hand, and I'll hold yours. Dornan will come to back us up. You don't have to deal with this alone."

He blinks and turns away again as though my words are making him want to escape. I touch his arm, seeing how hard he finds it to accept kindness and affection.

Sex, he can handle.

Stupid jokes and holding people at arm's length are fine.

But accepting care from another person seems like a foreign thing to him.

It breaks my heart.

So much falls into place. His tough exterior and his preference for being on the edge of friendship groups. It has all come about because of what he experienced when he was too young.

A flash of the innocent boy he once was breaks my heart.

"Come on." I take his hand. "Let's go."

When he lets me lead him, I can hardly breathe from relief.

24

DORNAN

Everything is falling apart.

Elias's mom is in a coma. Celine is reeling from the circulation of a video she didn't even know existed, and Travis has been dragged out of the country by a toxic ex. I'm the only one currently not dealing with a crisis, but I feel frustratingly helpless as a result.

I battle through a boring class, knowing that Celine and Elias are at the police station, reporting their separate issues together. Celine decided that she should leave Marie out of it for now.

It's hard to concentrate because my brain wants to anticipate every possible outcome. I'm just thankful that I haven't seen Eddie yet. The rage I feel towards that fleck of dick cheese is unlike anything I've ever felt before. Watching Celine with him on the video destroyed me, not because I'm jealous but because he never deserved to touch a hair on her head, let alone take pleasure in her body.

I text Travis to let him know what's happening. Halfway through, Professor Letterman asks me a question and I have no idea what he's talking about. I really need to keep my mind on my work, but with so much drama circulating, it's hard to care about things that won't matter in a year.

When I finally escape into the fresh air, I continue the message to Travis, then decide to call him while I walk back to my room. He answers on the second ring.

"Dornan. How are you, man?"

"How are you, more importantly?"

He huffs out a long breath, rasping like static in my ear. "Fucked, Dornan. I'm fucked."

"What's going on?"

"Lina's a complete nightmare. She's vomiting all the time and then raging at how this baby is ruining her life…and then she blames me for ruining her life because, of course, I got her pregnant on purpose."

"Fuck, Trav, that's hardcore."

"Tell me about it. I met a few friends from my old company last night just to get out of the house."

"Doesn't she still work there?"

"Yeah. Andrea, who works for her, tried convincing me to return to the US."

"How come?"

"She said she overheard Lina telling someone that the baby's father doesn't want to have anything to do with her."

"When was this?"

"The day before she came to tell me about the pregnancy."

"Fuck." I shake my head, narrowly avoiding a girl holding a stack of books and running in the opposite direction. "So, that can't have been you?"

"I guess she might have said I didn't want anything to do with her."

"Did she say it that way, or did she say it as though he knew about the baby?"

He pauses, thinking. "She said she thought he knew about the baby."

"Travis. What the fuck are you still doing there? She's using you, man. She got dumped by the father of the child, and now she's using you as a stand-in. Just come back."

"I can't," he says, his voice turning quiet.

"What's the name of the guy she cheated with?"

"Why?"

"You can try to find him. That way, you'll know for sure. If Lina told him first, he must be the father, and you'll be free to come home."

"Maybe." He sounds defeated. "How's Celine?"

Travis doesn't know about Eddie and the video. We've kept it from him so far, but maybe now's the time to let him know. Celine's distress could be enough to tip the balance.

"She's been better, Trav." I explain to him what happened and he's furious with Eddie. "We were in the hospital yesterday with Elias's…his mom is sick…and I think that has taken her focus off what Eddie did."

"She's sick?"

"It's bigger than that, but it's Elias's story."

Travis makes an understanding grunt. "I feel terrible being here when there is so much shit going down."

"Don't worry about it. Celine just wants you to come back. We all do."

Travis is silent for a few seconds, which feels much longer as the rasp of the international line fills the silence. The wind whips around me, tugging at the hood of my sweatshirt and rustling the trees so that they sway in heaving arcs.

"I'll try to find him," Travis says eventually. "It's the

only way I'm going to feel okay to leave." He clears his throat. "Well, I'll still be thinking about the kid. I mean, whether it's mine or not, Lina is so fucked up. That baby deserves better."

"It does," I agree, "but it isn't something you'll have any power to do anything about other than maybe suggesting the actual father takes his responsibilities seriously."

"Yeah. Good idea."

"Let me know how it goes."

"And you will let me know how Celine and Elias are?"

"I will."

We hang up just as Ellie appears through the doors to the building I'm passing. "Dornan." She sounds out of breath.

I hug her as I always do, feeling a deep sense of relief to be in her presence. We've been friends for so long, she's become part of me.

"How's Celine? She hasn't returned any of my calls."

"She's with Elias reporting what Eddie did. She's going to call when she's done."

Ellie swipes her hair back from her face. Her cheeks are pink from rushing, and she has something white on the shoulder of her jacket that she probably doesn't know about—toddler mess! "Thank goodness. I was worried she might refuse. I know she likes to handle her own shit."

"Yeah, well, there's no way of handling this that doesn't involve the law or violence. I wasn't about to let her do anything that would jeopardize her future."

"I've been hoping to run into that filthy jizz sock all day so I can give him a piece of my mind."

"Jesus," I laugh, "If you do, you should definitely call him that."

"I will." Ellie grins and rummages around in her purse, pulling out a water bottle. She downs what's left in three big glugs.

"Hey...slow down."

She smiles as she stuffs the empty bottle back. "I still find it weird to be by myself and not have Noah needing me every second. I'm used to doing everything super-fast before he has a chance to demand my attention again."

"Time to slow down. I need to get around to see that little guy."

"Not so little anymore," she smiles, pulling out her phone to show me the latest cute toddler pic.

"So, I just spoke to Travis. I think there's a chance he might come back. I really hope he does."

"You do?" Her eyebrow quirks high and she peers at me with her dark eyes that always make me feel like I have to tell her everything. It's her superpower.

"I do."

"Does that mean there's something serious going on between you guys? I mean, when Celine came up with her revenge games idea, I thought it was doomed to end in disaster."

"Your relationship started with seven minutes in heaven. That's a game"

"It did. So is it heaven for you guys?"

I raise my eyes skyward, finding soft white clouds passing overhead. It's hard to know what to say when I haven't processed the idea myself. "It's good," I admit. "Better than I imagined, and not just because I have a thing for Celine."

"You've always had a thing for Celine," she corrects. We haven't discussed it, but her woman's intuition identified it anyway.

Shrugging, I continue. "It's having friends who care for the same woman, knowing that we're a group against the world, not just a couple. There's something really supportive about it."

"And you have that with Elias?"

"Yeah, and Travis."

"Travis, I can see. He's easygoing, but Elias is a hot head."

"He really isn't. I used to think the same, but now... he's a decent guy. A solid person. He's good for Celine, and he's loyal to the rest of us in a way I don't think he expected of himself."

"I always thought of Elias as a lone wolf."

"I think he always thought of himself that way. Funny how circumstances can throw everything up in the air so it falls differently."

"And what about the rest of them? Do you think they feel the same way?"

"I don't know," I admit. "Maybe it seems too crazy for them."

"Well, they know us, and they know Gab. Does it look that crazy from the outside?"

"Surprisingly not."

"Then maybe there's a chance?"

I shift my feet, allowing myself to imagine a time when I could call Celine my girl and keep Travis and Elias in our lives.

"Maybe," I say. "If the universe gives us all a moment between the drama, it keeps tossing in our direction."

She crosses her fingers and holds them high. "Tell Celine I told her to call me when she can and come over soon. The boys would love to see you."

We hug again and I watch my friend disappear into the crowd. She's found her place in the world. I'm still working on finding mine.

Am I close? Only time will tell, I guess.

Or maybe now's the time to put everything on the line.

25

CELINE

As we leave the police station, I slide my hand into Elias's. For a second, he seems to flinch as though the idea of holding hands doesn't fit with his super independent persona, but then he relaxes and squeezes my fingers gently as he leads us back to the car.

It was mostly a wasted morning. The police were sympathetic to both of our circumstances but without clear evidence, there isn't much they can do. Elias's mom could have fallen down the stairs while she was alone in the house. It could have been anyone behind me in the video. They didn't tell us what the next steps would involve, just that they'd be in touch. I couldn't work out if that was a promise or a way to get us out of the building.

"I'm sorry," I say when Elias opens the car door for me. He jerks his head back in surprise.

"You didn't push my mom down the stairs."

I punch his shoulder gently, nudging him away. "I know I didn't. I mean, I'm sorry they're not going to rush out and arrest your dad."

"She'll tell them when she wakes up," he says. "This

time, I'm not taking no for an answer. I swear to God. She's reporting that bastard, or I'm never seeing either of them ever again. And then they'll have to charge him."

"Do you think she will?"

"She could have died."

"I know, but do you think she will?"

He's thoughtful for a moment, then shakes his head. "No. I don't think she will."

"All you can do is try," I say. "Parents don't always live up to expectations. Sometimes, they're an epic fail."

I climb into the car, and Elias shuts the door and rounds the front. When he's seated and fastening his belt, he asks in a quiet voice. "Are your parents messed up, too?"

"They didn't used to be." I stare out the front window, not wanting to meet his eyes. "But after they separated, it's like they divorced Marie and me, too. Now, all we hear about from them is how evil they both are, and how miserable. If we get a phone call at all."

He squeezes my knee, then puts the car into drive. "Dornan's dad is like a fucking saint. He's always coming around with snacks, and not just for Dornan. He's nicer to me than my own fucking sperm donor."

"Gab's mom is a saint, too. I swear, that woman wants to feed the world. She's so caring and nurturing. I hate myself for feeling jealous."

"Don't hate yourself. A starving man craves what's on a rich man's plate. It's natural."

I turn to stare at him. "That's very philosophical."

He quirks a lopsided smile. "I keep telling you I'm not just a pretty face."

I snicker and play with the loose threads on the hole in my jeans. "But you are so pretty."

He really is beautiful. I always thought that, even when

he was being a cocky asshole. Somehow, now I know him, he's become even more attractive. All the things that make him awkward and opinionated, loyal, and kind, and everything in between, makes him shine in my eyes. I think the same about Dornan. He's such a good man, not just to me because he likes me, but also to Elias and Travis and his other friends and family.

And Travis. Well, he's traveled halfway around the world on the off chance he has a baby that might need protecting in five months. Who does that?

Elias laughs out loud at my compliment; it's such a great sound that I feel like crying. In all the years I've known Elias, he rarely laughs.

He takes my hand. "You're pretty too, Celine. Obviously not as pretty as me..."

I struggle against his grip, pretending to be offended. "That's it. No more sex for you."

He fixes me with a pretend enraged stare. "Don't go joking about that."

I purse my lips, remembering the fun we had. "It won't be the same without Travis."

As the words leave my mouth, I fear Elias will be offended. I don't mean that he's not man enough for me. Of course, he is. He rocks my world every time. I just mean that most of our time together has been as a foursome, and I've gotten used to being surrounded by them. I've gotten used to them working together, laughing and joking, vibing off each other. I'll miss that.

Elias doesn't reply either angrily or with understanding. He just focuses on the road to take me back to my dorm, lost in his thoughts.

My phone rings from deep within my purse, and I hunt for it, surprised when I see Dad emblazoned across the screen. He's seriously calling me now, after all this time.

Maybe he's found out about the video.

The thought sends my stomach through the floor of the car. "Dad." I don't even say hi. I'm so fucking out of practice at talking to him.

Elias's gaze whips to me before refocusing on the road.

"Celine. I'll be in town tonight. I thought we could have dinner." Tomorrow night, I promised to go with Elias to the hospital. I can tell he's daunted at the idea of going alone, and there's a chance his dad will be there. If he sees that man, he won't be able to hold onto his rage, and that's not something I'm prepared to risk.

"I'm sorry, Dad," I say. "I have other plans."

Elias hisses 'go' at me, but I ignore him. "What do you mean you have other plans?" Dad's voice is angry and weird. "I'm in town for one day, and you can't cancel your plans to spend a few hours with me?"

"I can't. I'm sorry."

"You know what, Celine. You've been using my credit card like it's crack. I know you're failing. I've been considering withdrawing my funding for next semester on the basis that it's a bad investment."

"A bad investment?"

Elias can hear the conversation, and he turns again to send my phone a look of withering disgust. "You're obviously focusing on other things and not your work. Why should I go out of my way to facilitate you wasting more of your time."

"You know what, Dad? You do whatever you want. You always do." I hang up and throw my phone back into my purse.

"Jesus, Celine."

"It's nothing. Don't worry about it."

"You should go. Call him back and tell him."

"No way. I'm coming to the hospital with you. That's my priority. My dad's flying surprise visit when he's basically been ignoring me is not."

He's quiet for a while, but I can practically hear his brain turning. He's wondering how I can turn down seeing my dad and risk my financial support for him. He doesn't realize that I know he'd do the same for me if the situations were reversed.

Elias is more important to me than my dad, and it's nothing I'm going to be embarrassed or sorry about. People do what they want, and my dad has proved he doesn't care about being a father to me. Elias proves over and over that he's a good person who cares about me.

He's worth any sacrifice.

When we arrive, he leans over to kiss my lips softly. "I can't believe you did that," he says.

"You'd do the same, wouldn't you?"

We're so close that I can feel his breath on my lips and see the little scar he has on his eyebrow. He rests his hand against my cheek so tenderly that a knot of emotions ties tightly in my throat. "Don't worry about Eddie," he tells me. "He'll pay for what he did, one way or another."

"I don't want you to do anything. I mean it." I especially don't want him to think he owes me something now because I turned down one ridiculous dinner offer.

He blinks his long, dark lashes, and I can tell he hasn't heard me. I'd rather leave Eddie to remain unpunished so that Elias doesn't get into trouble. My desire for revenge has withered behind my care for this man.

"Please. Don't do anything."

He kisses me again and reaches across me to open the door. He's telling me to get out without saying the words. "I'll see you later."

"Okay. Call me."

As soon as I'm out of the car, I miss him. I watch him drive away in his rust bucket that makes a strange noise and belches out a cloud of toxic fumes, wondering what we're doing. I don't think either of us knows.

Dornan is waiting on the steps to my building with his earbuds in and his eyes closed. He's pretty in the same crazily masculine way Elias is. He's the light to Elias's dark. The easy to Elias's tough. I'm glad he's here.

When I get close enough that he senses me, he opens his gorgeous blue eyes and stands, tugging his earbuds and dropping them into his shirt pocket. "How did it go?" he asks, bending to press a soft kiss to the corner of my mouth.

"They were vague about everything."

"So they're not investigating?" He sounds annoyed, and I shrug because none of this feels important to me now. Eddie's my past. If I keep looking back all the time, I'll never move forward.

All I want is for the video to be taken down and for Dornan, Elias, and Travis to be in my life. I want us to be happy, not bogged down by drama and issues. I want to be able to focus on them because they deserve that.

They deserve love, and I do, too.

My heart swells but then contracts because what I want and can have are two very different things.

"They're looking into it but without evidence…"

"Isn't evidence gathering part of police work? I mean, what the fuck do they want you to do? Turn up with the case wrapped up and present it to them like a Christmas gift? What are they getting paid to do?"

"I think they mean that without witnesses, it will be hard to prove."

"FFS."

"You wanna come up. I have beer."

"I can't. I have classes. I just stopped by on my break on the off chance you might be done."

I rest my hand on his arm, touched that he cared enough to go out of his way for me. "Thanks."

"It's nothing." He waves away my appreciation and then shoves his hands into his pockets. "I spoke to Travis. He's even less sure that he's the father."

"So he's coming home?" I blush at the hopefulness in my voice but make a mental note to message Travis. I can't tell him to come home for me, but I can be supportive like Dornan is. I can be a friend if nothing else.

"I don't know. Maybe. He's going to call after he does some investigating. I'll keep checking in with him."

"You're such a good man," I tell him, resting my hand at the center of his chest where I can feel his kind heartbeat. "Always looking out for other people."

Dornan waves me off again, then leans in to kiss me again. It's sweet and soft, then deep and searching. Butterflies take flight in my belly, and skittering excitement rushes up my spine. I grip his warm shirt, not wanting him to go, but when he pulls away and says goodbye, I let him leave.

I've lost one of them. I need to get accustomed to losing them all because they'll never all want what I want.

I can't expect three men who were never friends to suddenly want to merge their lives to be a part of mine.

No. This will be over soon, whether I like it or not.

Dornan will go back to being my friend. Travis will come back and slip into his new life, the way he was supposed to. Elias will go back to hiding behind the shield he built to protect him from the world.

I could never choose between them, so I'll have to lose them all.

I have to keep this knowledge in mind and in my heart so that it doesn't burn the way it did when Eddie betrayed me, and I was left all alone.

26

ELIAS

When I park outside my building, all I can think about is how easily Celine chose her commitment to me over her father. She risked a whole lot so that she can keep her promise to come to the hospital with me later. I don't remember when anyone has ever done anything like that for me. Her kindness and loyalty only make the rage inside me swell.

Eddie has to pay for what he did. There is no way I can leave him walking around this campus without a care in the world while people whisper about Celine behind her back. Knowing that so many people are watching her private moment disgusts me.

Her pleasure is something I want to own. Or share, but only with Travis and Dornan, other men who value her as much as I do.

One of Eddie's douchebag friends walks past my car. He glances over his shoulder at me, and before he turns back, his face slips into a sly smile.

My hand flies to the handle but Celine's voice whispers in my ear. *Please don't do anything.* That's what she said. This asshole isn't the target of my fury. If anyone is going to get a beating, it'll be Eddie.

Instead of chasing his smug asshole friend down the road, I pick up my phone and call Dornan. He answers on the first ring.

"Hey."

"We need to fuck up Eddie."

He meets my angry sentence with a sharp exhale of breath.

"Celine won't like it." Of course, he'd be the voice of reason. That's why this thing between us all works so well. Dornan's calm and moderate. I'm an angry hothead. And Travis is mature and funny. Between us, we bring out the best and moderate the worst.

"Celine got into this whole thing with us because she wanted revenge. She went to the police because she wants him to pay."

"Not at our expense, Elias."

"So, come with me. Make sure I don't pulverize him."

"You think I could stop you?"

We both laugh. We're evenly sized and weighted, but every man knows that a crazy, angry man somehow finds the strength of two. "If you're there, I'll stick to the agenda."

"Which is?"

"Getting the proof from his phone."

"Shouldn't we leave this to the police?"

"They have way more pressing things to deal with. This is never going to be a priority. You didn't see how they looked at Celine like she brought this all on herself by being promiscuous."

Dornan's quiet for a while, and I think I can hear him rubbing his stubbly chin, the way he does when he's thinking. "Okay. I have class now, but can we get him before practice?"

"Yeah. I'm not going to practice, but I can be there before."

"Have you told Coach?"

"Not yet. It's next on my list."

"Okay. I'll see you there."

We hang up and I grab my bag and head to my class. It's a relief to have something to think about that isn't worrying about my mom, worrying about Celine, or wanting to tear off Eddie's balls and feed them to him piece by piece.

My fingers move over my keyboard like lightning, and I get lost in the lecturer's words and the subject he's immersing us in. By the end, I have pages of notes and a plan for how to complete the assignment that's due next week.

I wonder how Celine's getting on with the course I've tutored her in. Her dad was saying she's failing and he's going to withdraw financial support for her. I don't want her to drop out. She needs to stay on track and make the most of this opportunity. I need to get her to see that education is the key to being self-reliant. For the first time in a long time, I find myself grateful that my fucked-up home life has given me the inspiration I need to improve my life. There is no way I'm going back to the kind of existence I had in my childhood. I'm ready for bigger and better things. I will make my way in the world, however hard I have to struggle to do it.

I get a few minutes to eat the sandwich in my bag and glug down a large bottle of water before it's time to meet Dornan. I haven't planned what I'm going to do to Eddie or even what I'm going to say. I just know I have to make him admit that he's the one who released the video to get the proof I need. I'll take his phone and hand it to the police with the passcode if I have to.

Dornan's standing outside the locker room with his

hands in his pockets. He nods a greeting to me.

"Have you seen him?"

He shakes his head. "He's always late."

"Maybe we should stand over there." I nod to the wall away from the door. At least then, Eddie won't see us when he's approaching, and we can step into view when it's too late for him to get away.

We wander in the direction I pointed to and wait. It's weird that I now feel more comfortable around Dornan than I ever have with another man. There's no competition between us even though we obviously care for the same woman. I used to feel jealousy towards him, but that emotion has disappeared and been replaced by respect.

I know he's got my back, and that's something I'll never take for granted.

"There he is." Dornan's off before I have a chance to react. "Hey, Eddie," he yells.

Eddie's rushing to the locker room when he jerks in reaction to his name. His eyes widen when he sees us both barreling in his direction. He grabs the handle to the building as though he hopes he can get inside to safety, but Dornan grabs his shirt and yanks him back. He's not a small guy, but he's about fifty pounds lighter than me and Dornan. "What the fuck?"

He sounds indignant, as though we have no good reason to drag him around the back and kick the ever-loving shit out of him. If he pretends that he's not the one who circulated the video, I don't think I'll be able to restrain myself.

Eddie struggles against Dornan's grip but only to free himself, not to land any punches. He knows that against the two of us, he doesn't stand a chance.

"You can come with us willingly, or we'll drag you. You choose." Dornan's growl is surprisingly menacing for such a nice guy.

"I didn't do anything."

I jab him in the chest to silence him. "We know what you did. Don't humiliate yourself by pretending to be a good guy."

"But..."

"Shut the fuck up, Eddie."

As Dornan shoves him forward by the neck, I lead them around the back of the building. This doesn't require an audience. It's better for all of us that what's spoken about and done next remains between us.

Eddie ends up with his back pressed against the rough brick wall. He's panting and sweating, and his face has gone a weird mix of red and gray.

"Give me your phone." He looks like I've slapped him, and he makes no move to get it. It's stuffed into the front of his jeans. "Get it, or I'll get it, and I don't think you want me grabbing at things that are around your filthy junk."

"My filthy junk fucked your girl," he says, and I jolt forward, making him recoil before I start to laugh.

"Seriously, dude. You think words are going to mess with my head. I'm not that weak. Just give me the fucking phone."

Reluctantly, he pushes his hand into his pocket and holds it out. I press the screen and ask him for the passcode. He tries to get away, but Dornan slams his hand next to his head on the wall.

"PASSCODE..." The volume of his voice makes Eddie jump.

"Twenty-twenty." He hangs his head as I tap the numbers on the screen. It opens, and I start to tap through his messages and emails. There are whole message threads of people laughing about the video and metaphorically slapping him on the back for getting Celine back. Back for what? For fucks sake. He was the one who did her wrong.

I run a search for the porn site the video was posted to, and I find his account. He watches some seriously fucked up shit. Old women with young guys. Extreme BDSM. I don't even want to look at it. But then I discover his one upload.

I take screenshots of everything and send them to my phone. I want to delete the video, but I have to leave it where it is for the police to review the evidence. "You're a fucking small dick asshole." I shake my head and shove his phone in my back pocket. "You think you won by doing this shit. All you've done is tell the world that you're bitter and fucked up. All the girls at this university are going to know what you've done. You think any of them will ever want to let your pathetic dick near them?"

His face is blank, but I don't give a shit. He obviously has zero empathy or moral standards. I know it's impossible to teach people like this. He reminds me of my dad in a lot of ways. Just out for himself. Prepared to use other people in horrible ways to satisfy his twisted urges. Willing to destroy others to make himself feel better or to get what he wants.

"Expect a call from the police."

I jerk my head so Dornan knows we're leaving. He gives Eddie such a disgusted look; it's a miracle he doesn't turn into dust. Then, we leave him behind, hopefully shitting his pants.

Dornan keeps pace with me for a while until we're out of earshot. "Do you want me to blow off training, because I can?"

"Nah. I'm good. I'll deal with this, but thanks for helping."

"You didn't need my help, but it's all good. I was worried you would lose your cool, but you seem to have calmed right down."

He's right. I have. The burning, rumbling energy that I

used to carry isn't there anymore. It feels good to be without it.

"I'll let you know what happens," I say.

His mouth twitches with a smile. "Let me know how you get on at the hospital. If you need anything, I'm around."

I want to give the guy one of those manly bro hugs I've seen on TV but never done myself, but although I feel different in many ways, I'm not there yet.

"I can't wait to see that guy get punished."

"Me, either." Dornan looks over his shoulder, and we watch Eddie make his way into the locker room with hunched shoulders. "Training is going to be interesting today."

"Maybe you should tell Coach. It'd be just like Eddie to try to get you into trouble."

"If I have to, I will."

A phone rings and vibrates against my ass, but I resist answering it. Let them wait. Eddie can explain why he doesn't have access to his phone anymore.

"I'll see you later." It's one of those flippant things people say, but I mean it. It would be cool if we could hook up with Celine. Maybe get a takeaway and hang out at Travis's. Maybe do some other stuff, too.

"Yeah. Call me when you and Celine are done if you want to meet up."

It's like he read my mind.

"Okay. We will."

As I walk away with Eddie's phone still buzzing and Celine waiting for me, I feel more settled than I have in years.

The police took the phone. They ask me how I got it, and I reply, 'no comment.' The officer presses his lips together but bags the device up anyway. When I give him the password, he cocks an eyebrow but still doesn't ask. I guess he's happy that he has the chance to easily clear a case from his workload.

At the hospital, Celine holds my hand as we make our way to the ward. Mom has been moved now that she's conscious. When I'm asked if Celine is family, I tell them she's my fiancé, so she can come inside with me. The blush that spreads up her cheeks at the suggestion makes me want to kiss her hard.

Mom blinks up at me, surprised to see us. It's been a while since I visited her at home. The risk of running into my dad is too great, so I've stayed away for months.

"Elias." She stretches her hand out, and I take it. It's weird that I don't really feel anything when I touch her. As a kid, I was desperate for her love and protection. When Dad would beat me, I'd look at her and plead with my eyes, but she'd never stop him. She'd look away or go into another room. I know it's because she feared he'd turn his fists on her. He did it often enough, but I was her kid, and she should have done whatever it took to defend me. Her weakness isn't forgivable, even if it is understandable.

"How are you feeling, Mom?"

"Like I got run over." She laughs lightly and then winces.

"I went to the police," I tell her. "I told them it was Dad."

"Why did you do that?" Her horror makes my skin crawl. Celine, who's still holding my other hand, gives it a squeeze.

"Because he needs to be stopped. He's not going to change. Maybe next time he'll kill you."

"No," she says, but it sounds weak.

I'm not going to argue with her about this. I decided when I went to the station that things would be different. She has to take a stand, or I'll cut them both off entirely. There's no middle ground anymore.

"Either you tell the police that he assaulted you, or I'm not gonna see you anymore, Mom. You have to decide now. I can't watch this happen to you over and over anymore. It's gone on for too long."

Her face twists like she's in pain.

"He showed up at my game the other day and started throwing his weight around. I don't want to see him anymore. I'm done. And you should be too."

"But Elias…"

I hold my hand up, and she shrinks against the pillow, worried I'll hurt her like he does. That stings worse than anything. Her hair is matted, and her face is a patchwork of green, blue, and purple. She looks old before her time and so damned tired.

"There are no buts anymore, Mom. This is it."

Her lips thin as she presses them tightly together, and I know I was right. She's not going to say anything. Nothing's going to change. She can't live without him, and that's the disturbing truth. In my heart, I knew. It's why I went to the police first, so that she'd feel some extra pressure. I hoped it would be enough, but it's not.

"I'm happy you're awake. You're obviously recovering, and that's a good thing. But I'm not going to come and see you again. Not until he's out of your life for good."

I turn to Celine, and her pretty, green eyes are so soft when they focus on me; it's like she's stroking my face tenderly just by looking.

"Let's go," I say, and we do.

When we get to the car, Celine wraps her arms around me and holds me tightly. I encircle her with my arms, and we embrace for the longest time. "You're doing the right thing," she murmurs against my chest.

"I know."

"It's hard, and you have to stay strong. She'll come around."

"If he doesn't end her first."

She squeezes me tighter and then tips her face to mine. I don't even think about what it means to kiss her. I don't ask if it's okay. We're still walking this tightrope where neither of us has admitted to feelings or been honest about wanting more. I want her so badly, my palms itch with it. It's the same way I felt when I was a kid, hoping Santa would bring me something good. A yearning hopefulness that I keep praying won't be dashed.

When we part, I think about earlier. "Dornan wants to hang out tonight. Are you up for it?"

"Sure. Shall we go to Travis's?" It's like she read both our minds.

"You call Dornan. I'll drive."

So that's what we do.

And a difficult day turns into a perfect night, but still none of us are brave enough to say what's really in our hearts.

27

TRAVIS

Fake Date Group Chat.

Celine – We're at your apartment but it feels weird without you.

Dornan – Yeah, dude. It's not the same without you.

Elias – Celine's out of control. We need you to come back and show her who's boss.

Celine – You all know who's boss. She's tight and wet and warm and greedy.

Dornan – Jesus, Celine. Are you trying to give us all heart attacks?

Elias – She's not wrong, though. Pussy power's a thing.

Celine – We miss you…what's happening with the investigation?

Travis – I have news…

When the plane lands, I feel such a sense of relief. I love Germany as a country - the culture, the beautiful landscapes, the friendly people - but Lina made my stay there unbearable.

Returning home a second time is even more emotional because I know there's no reason to go back.

I only have a small suitcase with me so there's no need to wait for luggage. In the arrival hall, I expect to walk straight through to search for a cab. Instead, I find Celine waiting for me, flanked by Dornan and Elias.

She runs to me, throwing her arms around my body tightly and pressing her face into my neck. I breathe in her soft floral scent, and it's like I've shed a concrete overcoat to run across a sunny field barefoot. The relief to be back and in her embrace winds me.

Dornan and Elias wait for our reunion with smiles on their faces. When Celine eventually lets me go, I press a kiss to her lips and then greet the boys, shaking hands. "We thought you might appreciate a ride?" Dornan says.

"I definitely appreciate it."

"And we have your keys." Celine pulls them out of her pocket and dangles them in front of me. "We might have christened your bed just a little."

"That's good. I wish I'd been there."

"You were in spirit." She smiles and takes my hand. "Maybe you can be later?"

Hell yeah! I want to scream it from the rooftop, but instead, I smile and kiss her. "I wouldn't miss it for the world."

"So, what happened?" Elias takes the handle of my suitcase and wheels it behind him. As we start walking, I tell them everything that happened.

"Dornan was right. I managed to find Lina's ex, and he

told me he's the child's father. At least, Lina had told him he was two weeks before she told me. It seems she got on a plane out of desperation, hunting for a man to be a father to her baby. I guess she knew I was loyal and wouldn't desert her. Leaving the baby behind was tough, even knowing it's not mine. That poor kid has got to grow up with Lina as its only parent. Maybe one day, she'll find another sucker to step in. In fact, I'm sure she will because that's the kind of person she is. I'm just glad it's not me."

In the car, Dornan leaves me to sort out the playlist, and I select something I know Celine will like. As soon as the first bars play, she immediately squeals. The journey to my place becomes a singalong, and even Elias joins in.

When we're getting close, Dornan signals in the wrong direction. "Where are you going?" I ask.

"We need food. My belly is growling."

He pulls up to a fast-food drive-thru; not exactly a healthy meal I should eat but fuck it. The plane served gross slop, and I'm hungry as a wolf. Unless they've been grocery shopping, my cupboards are going to be bare. We order a mixture of burgers, wings, and fries, with milkshakes and sodas. Dornan drives to the next window to pay.

"I'll get this," I say. I'm not rolling in it, but I've been working for a couple of years, and these guys are all students.

"No way. I'm getting it." Celine pulls out her credit card and attempts to lean through Dornan's window. She manages to tap her card on the reader, and the server pulls the machine back in. He looks up and shakes his head. "It's declined."

Celine looks confused but pulls out another card. "Try this one." She taps the machine again. After a few seconds, the server shakes his head.

"It's declined."

Celine shrinks back, staring at her open purse and the cards.

Dornan hands over his card, and it goes through right away.

We exchange looks as he drives to the collection window.

I turn to find Elias resting his hand on Celine's knee. "Do you think he canceled your cards?"

Celine shrugs. "I'm not sure. It's never happened to me before on one card, let alone two."

"He threatened it, didn't he?"

She purses her lips, still staring at the cards. "He did, but I didn't think he'd go through with it. For what? Because I wouldn't drop my plans for his last-minute invitation after he hadn't called me for weeks. The only thing he does for me is give me money."

"Do you want to call the bank and find out for sure?"

She shakes her head. "It's obvious that he's cut me off financially. What am I going to do?"

"There's a job going at the Daily Grind. I heard they pay okay," Dornan offers.

"Yeah. That could work, but it won't help me with the cost of my accommodation. That's only paid up until the end of the semester."

I don't offer immediately, but now that I'm moving out of home, my room is free. I'm sure Gab and my mom would be cool with Celine moving in with them. I'd offer for her to stay with me, but my apartment is further away from campus, and I don't want to freak her out with gushing offers of serious commitment just yet. Plus, this thing we're in involves two other people. I'd have to consult with Dornan and Elias before offering anything. Treading on toes in such a big way wouldn't exactly maintain great relations.

"We'll sort something out," I offer. "Don't worry about anything. You have three men here. Between us, we'll come up with a plan. Dornan nods and when I turn, Elias raises his head in agreement.

Celine's smile is falsely bright; a straight line of tight lips that doesn't meet her eyes.

Her father's action isn't just about the physical withdrawal of cash. It's more than that. He's emotionally withdrawn from Celine, too. I know what it's like to lose a parent. Worse still, I know what it feels like to think you know someone but find out that they're a different person.

When it's a parent, it shakes you to your core.

My dad projected that he was the perfect family man. It wasn't until he was killed in a car accident, next to a woman we didn't know, that we found out he was living a double life. His betrayal still cuts me despite the years that have passed.

The drive to my place is short. Celine is quiet, and her low mood affects us all. I'm relieved that the music overlays the silence.

It's weird to go into a place that's mine, but I've never lived in. Elias, Dornan, and Celine have spent more time in this apartment than I have. But, as we spread our food out over the table, it starts to feel like home.

"I'm just going to wash up," I tell everyone. I take my suitcase into the bedroom and head to the bathroom. Closing the door, I pull out my phone and dial mom's number.

Her relieved gasp of my name makes me smile.

"Hey Mom, I'm back."

"Are you coming home?"

"Not right now. I'm just hanging out with some friends."

Her happy humming noise makes me grateful she's so

cool.

"Listen, I wanted to ask if you'd be okay with letting Celine move into my old room. She's having some family issues that have become financial. From next semester, she won't have the money to pay for accommodation."

"Of course," Mom says. "She's not only your friend. She's Gabriella's, too."

"She'll probably be at my apartment a lot of the time," I add.

"That will be nice for you both." Mom's unseen smile is obvious. She hasn't asked me what's going on with Celine, but I can tell she's made assumptions and is happy about them.

"Okay. I'll see you tomorrow," I say.

"I'll have dinner ready at seven pm. You can invite your friends if you want."

I love my mom, not only because she's been a rock of stability and love throughout my whole life but also because of how warm she is to all my friends. She loves people, and she loves feeding them even more!

"I will. Thanks, Mom."

Everyone's tucking into their food when I return to the open-plan living space. I take a seat between Elias and Dornan, facing Celine, and tell her about the arrangement I've agreed with my mom.

"Are you sure?" she gasps, as though I've offered to give her Buckingham Palace.

"Are you kidding me? My mom is desperate for more people to feed. Just be prepared to start letting your pants out at the waist."

She laughs, and it's the sweetest sound. Everything about Celine is a contrast to Lina. Her loyalty and kindness. Her fierce desire to support the people she cares about. Her sense of fun and warmth.

"That's great," Dornan says, touching her arm.

"And you can crash at mine anytime you want," Elias says.

I can tell they'd both invite her to stay if they could, but dorm rules are strict about sharing.

"Is it okay to ask what's happened about the video?" I take a bite of my burger and then a long swig of soda, enjoying the familiar tastes.

"The police have Eddie's phone. They arrested him last night, but we haven't heard anything else."

"That's good. Is the video still up?"

Celine shakes her head. "It's been taken down from the site he uploaded it to. I checked last night. But who knows how many times it's been downloaded and shared."

"Hopefully, it wasn't up long enough for that to happen."

"And it's impossible to keep track of without immersing myself in gross content twenty-four-seven."

"Exactly." Elias offers her one of his hot wings, and when she doesn't take one, he offers one to me, too.

"Thanks, man," I say.

"So, what's the plan with you?" he asks. "Do you think you'll still be able to start that job?"

"I called them from Germany to explain what happened and tell them I'm coming back. They haven't filled the role, so they're happy for me to start. I get the feeling that they're a little worried I'll let them down again. I guess the only way I can prove I'm reliable is by being reliable."

"So, Lina didn't fuck things up for you?"

"I'm out of pocket for two flights. I can handle that. It was the right thing to do. I had to be sure."

Celine nods. She goes to say something but then brings her lips together.

"What?" I cock my head to the side.

"I just..." She looks around at each of us in turn and her cheeks warm. "I just wanted to say that I really enjoyed playing revenge games with you, but now Eddie's well and truly out of the picture, I release you from your commitment."

"Release us?" Elias's nose wrinkles like he smells something gross.

"I just mean, I don't have any expectations for what this is, so if you don't want to do this anymore, all you have to do is let me know."

"Errr." Elias looks like Celine just said she wants to hack off his testicles.

Dornan lowers his burger solemnly. "You're joking, right?"

"I just...well, we haven't exactly talked about what this is..." She waves her hands around to encompass us all.

"I thought it would be obvious by now," Dornan says. His eyes search mine and then Elias's, checking to see if we're all on the same page. We both nod.

"Obvious?"

"Yeah. It's what you said you were doing at the Red Devil."

"What?" Celine's confusion is too cute, and it makes me want to kiss her on the tip of her nose and then shackle her to my bed.

"Gathering your own harem!"

Her smile is brilliant and bright. She drops her burger and leaps up, taking Dornan's surprised face between her hands and kissing his lips. She does the same to Elias, who's reluctant to let her go, and slaps her ass when she tries to pull away. Then she rounds the table to me.

When I left for Germany, I thought this thing between us was going to be over before it even started. The way I missed her felt stronger than it should. I tried to tell myself that I was being an idiot for even thinking she'd want more than what we started. Dornan's one of her best friends, and she's known Elias intimately since before we started playing as a group. If she was going to choose to solidify a relationship with any of us, it was going to be one of them. But as she kisses my lips tenderly and lets me pull her into my lap, I feel the truth.

She wants us all, and it's not in a greedy way. She sees each of us individually and how we work as a unit. What should be impossible feels infinitely possible with Celine at our center.

"I missed you," she whispers. "I'm glad you're home."

Home.

This apartment I've never lived in feels warm and inviting because of the three other people here with me.

I feed Celine chips, and we laugh at a stupid story Dornan tells us about yesterday's locker room antics. And when we're done eating and the conversation slows, Celine stands and leads me by the hand into the bedroom, encouraging the others to follow.

28

CELINE

We're back together, and it doesn't seem real.

Now I know they want the same thing as me, I'm practically trembling as I lead Travis by the hand to his bedroom. A few days ago, I didn't think he'd be coming back. I imagined him with a new life in Germany, wheeling a baby in a stroller down a Berlin Street with that bitch, Lina, by his side. In my grim fantasy, his face was drawn and gray, and I wanted to pull him back to where he'd be happy. I wanted a chance to make that happen for him.

And now he's here, and I can hardly believe it.

And Dornan and Elias are here.

They want us to be together, not just to play games, but for real.

It shouldn't be possible, but they say it is. We have a second chance.

I was scared to hope, but I'm not anymore. The fluttering in my chest morphs into something different, my heart unfurling like the wings of a resting butterfly before it takes flight.

In the bedroom, Travis, Dornan, and Elias surround

me. I start to unbutton my shirt to give my trembling hands something to do, but Travis takes hold of my wrists and lowers them until they hang by my sides. Our eyes meet, and the emotion that passes between us is an ocean swell that almost knocks me over. He touches my face, and my throat constricts and shifts at his tenderness. "Let me do it." His voice is gruff as his fingers find the first button. I forgot how much he likes to be in charge, but this feels different. He's taking care of me, and even though it's a simple act, the part of me that's always on edge, always ready for a flight, settles with the soft stillness of midnight snow. Travis is slow to remove my shirt like the slide of every button through its corresponding buttonhole builds his arousal the way it's building mine.

Knowing that Elias and Dornan are watching and waiting makes everything so much sweeter.

Underneath my shirt is a simple black satin bra, but the response from the men when they see it is far from simple. Three gruff moans cut the silence, and those moans only increase in volume when Dornan and Elias take a strap each and slide them from my shoulders, tugging to reveal my breasts.

Elias's dark eyes hold desire but also something reverential, his fingers grazing my skin with a tenderness that makes me ache. Dornan's crystal-clear gaze is as intense as blue fire, but his lips form a soft half-smile that mirrors my contentment.

Everything between us feels as sweet as candied apple and as bright as the first peek of the sun over the horizon.

We are four, but somehow, together in this moment, we are one.

Travis's hands are the first to touch me there, kneading and then pinching my nipples until I'm moaning, and my legs feel as though they might go out from under me. His deep blue eyes linger on my face, drifting to my lips as I dart my tongue out to wet them. I want him to kiss me. I need to feel his mouth, his passion, his tenderness. He gives me everything I need as Elias begins to unbutton my jeans. Dornan cups my cheek, turning my face to his so that he can kiss me slowly, too. Every nerve in my body feels alive with sensation and anticipation as I'm passed from man to man.

I'm liquid, slipping between their fingers, seeping between their lips, molding to them as they work together to explore all that I am and all that they make me want to be.

My fingers tingle with the urge to undress these men who are responsible for changing my life and filling me with the kind of love that I never thought I'd find.

I try to search beneath the hem of Dornan's shirt, making contact with the undulation of his abs, but Travis removes my hand again. This time, as Elias strips my jeans and panties from my legs and taps my calves so that I'll step free, Travis takes my hands and binds them behind my back with my bra. He tugs his shirt over his head, revealing the lean, muscular body I've missed so much. My mouth dries, my tongue feeling papery and dusty as he smiles cockily like he's aware of just how much I want to taste his skin.

"No touching," he says, undoing his thick brown leather belt before he tears it from the loops of his jeans. The sound it makes reverberates between my legs. He flicks open his fly and reaches for his thick cock, palming it a few times. "On your knees, Celine."

His order isn't harsh, but my body reacts like kneeling in front of him is a life-or-death action. I stare up at the full expanse of his body as my mouth fills with saliva at how gorgeous he is. Blue eyes gaze down at me with a softness that shouldn't match his dominance but somehow does. This dynamic is as much for me as it is for him. I love my submission as much as he loves to control.

He gestures to Dornan and Elias in turn, and they

begin to strip, too. When their cocks are also free, he touches my cheek. "You're going to suck us now, Celine. You're going to suck us deep, and when we're good and ready, we're going to fuck your sweet pussy until you can't take anymore."

When he uses his cock to stroke my bottom lip, I flick out my tongue to taste him. "Put your tongue out," he says, and then he rests his cock on it, easing back and forth. Tapping the side of my face, he tells me to "open up." And then it's on.

I forgot how thick and long he is. Remembering was too painful when he was so far away with a wall of promises to another woman between us. But now, all that he is is mine. It's a struggle to balance with no hands to steady myself, and the position I'm in somehow makes the process feel more like he's using my mouth for his pleasure. The cool air in the room chills the wetness between my legs. My clit swells, anticipating a touch that doesn't come. Instead, Travis pulls back and turns my face to take Elias's cock. "That's it," Travis says. "Suck him like a good girl."

Elias stares down at me with eyes as black as coal but somehow as soft as a cloud. He threads his fingers into the hair at my nape and rests them there, never urging or demanding. I suck him like a form of worship because I know the hardships he's lived through, and I'm proud of the man he is despite them. He groans when I swirl my tongue around the head and flick the sensitive underside.

Travis, who's watching everything, strokes his cock with slow but mean-looking pulls.

"Dornan, now!" he orders.

Elias's dick slips from between my lips with an audible pop, and he releases his grip. I turn to find Dornan's thick cock ready and waiting for my attention.

I've seen porn just like this with one woman on her knees, taking man after man into her mouth. It always seemed degrading to me, but as I suck Dornan deep into my throat, I marvel that it doesn't feel anything like that in real life. I might be servicing them, but the way they're looking at me and touching me is with care and awe.

Dornan tastes salty-sweet, and his hand on my cheek is warm and rough. The more I take him, the more I crave to be filled. When I push my legs together, squeezing rhythmically for some release, Travis takes pity on me.

"Let's get her onto the bed."

I'm suddenly lifted by three men and placed so I'm kneeling on the bed. Elias lies next to me and urges my leg over him until I'm straddling his chest. "Sit on my face, baby," he says, cupping my ass with his big hands and nudging me forward. When my pussy is spread over his mouth, he tugs me down.

With my hands restrained behind my back, I'm forced to allow him to maneuver me in short, tight thrusts over his tongue. Dornan climbs onto the bed, cupping my right breast and then sucking the tightly beaded nipple.

Travis leans in to kiss my mouth, not caring where it's just been. His fingers trail the length of my spine from my neck to my ass so slowly that I tremble from the rippling sensation of awakening nerve endings. When his fingers trail lower, stroking over my taint, and Elias flicks my clit with the very tip of his tongue, my body seizes, vibrating with an orgasm so strong that I almost fall.

"That's it," Travis says, his face so close to mine I can see the yellow halo that surrounds his pupil. "That's it, baby. Come all over Elias. Let him taste you."

"Fuck," I rasp as Elias slaps my ass once, triggering another mini-spasm between my legs. I'm lifted from Elias, who turns as Dornan shifts so he's behind me.

I blink slowly, still dazed from pleasure. When Travis sits in front of me, with his legs splayed on either side of my knees, I don't immediately understand what he wants.

Dornan's cock at my entrance wakes me a little. The first inch goes in smoothly, but I'm familiar with his girth now and anticipate the burn of full penetration before it happens.

"Holy fuck."

Elias laughs at my gasp in a way that sounds giddy. I know how he feels. None of this feels real because it's too good…too perfect. Travis strokes my face and pushes two fingers into my mouth, which I take, feeling the sweet violation, wanting to give him everything that I am. His knees come up, and he eases me forward until my upper body rests on his bent legs. Dornan holds my wrists as he pumps deeper, and Travis eases his cock between my lips.

I can't move. I'm captive.

Fingers probe between my legs, finding my clit at the same time they tweak my nipple. An unholy link of nerve endings and submission trips my switch again. I groan around Travis's cock as Dornan speeds his thrusts. "Fuck, she's coming again," he gasps. "Fuck. Ohhhh fuck."

The pulsing grasp of my pussy is met with the expansive swelling of Dornan's cock as he fills me with warm pleasure. Travis pulls back, letting me dwell in the dark place behind my eyelids where bursts of light break through.

Emotion tightens my throat, but I don't let it take hold as I'm eased onto my front, so my breasts are pressed into the comforter, and my head is turned to the side against the pillows. A shiver racks my whole body as Elias presses soft kisses down my spine.

Dornan slumps somewhere at the end of the bed as he struggles to get his breath. Travis's fingers ease the binds from my wrists, and he eventually rolls me until I'm on my back.

"Ready for more?" he asks.

I don't know if I am. My brain is shattered, and my

body is weak. Then again, Travis likes me immobile, and I love it when he does whatever he wants to me and doesn't give me any choice in the matter. I flex my fingers and stretch my arms over my head.

"Hold her." Travis nods to Elias, who clambers behind me, taking my writs in his huge hand and clamping them together. He leans over me, kissing my mouth in an upside-down position as Travis eases his cock inside me. With my legs over one shoulder, Travis folds me so the penetration is deep. His eyes are glazed as he looks down at me through fair eyelashes that are lowered with arousal. "You're perfect," he says, trailing his hand over my breast. "Totally fucking perfect."

His words touch a place inside me that was damaged at Eddie's rejection. When he discarded me, everything I'd given him felt worthless. I didn't love him, not truly, madly, or deeply. We just had fun, and I thought he respected me. What a joke that had been. Now Travis, Dornan, and Elias fill me with happiness and warmth. I didn't need revenge sex to get over what Eddie did to me. I needed this; the connection with these men, their kindness and care, their willingness to work together to be what I need. In the beginning, they weren't even friends. Now, they're prepared to commit to me and each other. Our union isn't simple. It feels momentous.

The slide of Travis's cock in and out is perfect. The undulation of his hips, which ripple his abs and clench his thighs, is heavenly. I don't know what I did in a previous life to deserve these three men, but it must have ended in heroics or martyrdom.

"Oh god," I gasp as he looms over me to get deeper. I tug at Elias's grip, struggling as the sensation between my legs becomes too much. I'm too sensitive, and I can't take it anymore.

"Easy," Elias soothes. With his free hand, he glides over my ribs, slowly up and down, avoiding my breast and ignoring my impossibly tight nipple until I want to scream at him to just touch me where it counts. Instead, I groan frustratedly, and he laughs.

"Is this what you want?"

The slight twist of my nipple is like fire between my legs. "Oh fuck. Yes. Yes. Yes…" It's slurred and garbled, but I can't manage any better because I'm coming just as Travis pulls out and fists himself until he finishes. My feet drop to the bed, and I get a front-row seat to his release. With his head thrown back, thick throat bared, biceps clenched, and cock leaking all over his tight fingers, he's an erotic masterpiece. "Fuck, Celine. Fuuuuuuuuck."

Behind me, Elias laughs again, so high on what we're doing that it no longer sounds like him.

Travis releases his cock, which is still ridiculously hard. He uses his cum to paint circles around my nipples like he's claiming ownership of me in the most primal way.

Only Elias is left now, but I don't know how I'll deal with more. Who knew too much pleasure could be a thing? He lets my wrists go and shifts until he's next to me. Then suddenly, he rolls me, and I'm on top.

My hands are free, and I run them over his broad chest and rounded pecs. I slide my slit up and down his cock, coating him with my arousal and whatever mess Dornan and Travis have left behind. He groans, gripping my hips and thrusting upward, the power in his body making me feel as insubstantial as a rag doll.

Just looking at him gets me hot.

"Are you going to ride him, Celine?" Travis asks.

"Yeah, she is." Elias's dark eyes focus where our bodies are almost joined. All it will take is a slightly different angle, and he'll be deep inside me. "Take what you need," he says, tugging me in for a deep kiss. He pulls on my hair to separate us and whispers against my lips. "Use me."

I gasp, "Okay."

There's no resistance when I slide down onto his waiting erection. I'm so slick and open that I can take him easily despite his huge size. I rest my hand on his chest, giving a few testing rolls of my hips. The depth is crazy, but if I lean forward just a little, I can handle it. We move together like the calm ocean lapping against the hull of a ship. I lose myself in his eyes, his mouth, the press of his fingers into my flesh. I'm overwhelmed with feelings that tumble over and over in my chest, threatening to escape at any moment.

"That's it, baby," he says. "That's it. That's fucking it."

His eyes are scrunched tightly, his face twisted, and his neck strained. So close to release, he's even more beautiful.

The sense of unshackled power that rushes through me spins my mind as my body spasms.

"Oh fuck." His hips lose control, and then he's pumping up, releasing so deep that I almost fall off him. Only Travis and Dornan's steadying hands keep me where I need to be.

I don't stay upright for long, though. Somehow, I end up on my side with my head on Elias's chest and Dornan at my back. Their bodies are so warm and huge that I can't move at all.

There's no room for Travis to embrace me, but he doesn't seem bothered. He kneels over me with my legs between his, slicks his finger over his tongue, and runs it between my labia, landing on my clit.

"I can't," I groan, but he only laughs like my denial is the funniest joke he's ever heard. I understand why. With only a few tight circles, I'm already close again. "Use your fingers, Elias," Travis says.

Even though Elias is groggy as fuck, he pushes two thick fingers into my ravaged pussy and moves them in and out with a twist in easy strokes. Dornan kisses my neck and tells me I'm beautiful, and I come all over again, surrounded by loving words and persistent, gorgeous men.

The words "I love you" spill out of my mouth like a plea. It's said to no one in particular, and as soon as those three little words leave my lips, I'm stunned. I've never spoken them before. Eddie was never in my love zone, and it seems that I was never in his. In all the time we were together, I never felt the kind of connection I feel with these men.

"She's sex drunk," Elias says, but he peers down at me as though he isn't sure if that's the only reason I said the four-letter word that he probably fears as much as I do.

"I love you, too," Dornan says without hesitation. "I've felt it for the longest time, but I thought we'd just always be friends."

Travis bends to kiss the outside of my thigh. "I love you, too, baby," he says, threading his fingers through mine. Dornan kisses my neck, and I close my eyes, slipping into the bliss that is love and being loved.

A hand cups my face, and I open my eyes to find Elias gazing down at me. There's so much uncertainty in his expression. He hesitates, opening his mouth and pressing his lips together as though he's at war with himself. "It's okay," I whisper because it is. This isn't a race to the finish line. I know he cares about me. It's in every look and every touch and every protective act. I don't need words to feel treasured.

I touch his chest, and his heart beats at a rapid pace against my palm.

He kisses my lips so softly that tears spring to my eyes. These last weeks have been so fraught with emotion and so packed with craziness that I don't know whether I'm coming or going. When he pulls back and sees my tears, his swallow is audible.

"Don't cry," he says. "Don't cry because I'm an emotionally crippled asshole who can't express his feelings." He laughs dryly, using his rough thumb to brush away the single tear that escapes to run down my cheek.

"I'm not crying because I'm sad," I admit. "I'm crying because I never thought I could be this happy."

He blinks, surprised. I turn to kiss Dornan's lips, languishing in our first love kiss that is sweet and light and perfect. I scramble to sit so that I can wrap my arms around Travis and kiss him, too. His body is warm, and his touch is so gentle that another tear leaks from my eye.

Before I can return to Elias, he's there to ease me from Travis's embrace and pull me against his chest. His arms hold me so tightly I can hardly breathe. "I love you, Celine," he says. "It terrifies the fuck out of me, but there's nothing I can do about it."

Laughter bursts out of me the way it does when happiness is so large it has to overflow. This is it. Everything that I want is here. Everything that I'll ever need is wrapped up in these men.

No more games.

What we have is real, and I'm never going to let it go.

EPILOGUE

CELINE

It's moving-in day.

Travis, Elias, and Dornan arrive bright and early to help me shift my boxes and bags down the stairs into their waiting cars. I'm embarrassed about how much stuff I have, but they don't complain. Maybe it's because there are three of them, and they all want to be manly in front of each other. Or maybe I really have just hit the jackpot and found three perfect men.

I think it's the latter.

Since Travis returned, and we all admitted wanting the same thing, my life has transformed.

I'm not the Celine I was when Eddie was constantly forcing himself into my life. I'm not the Celine who wanted to take revenge on my ex and used three men to play ridiculous games.

I'm the real Celine, and they make me feel like a goddess every single day.

"Last one." Elias lifts the big box of books like it contains a feather pillow. His biceps bulge, and it takes every ounce of my self-control not to cross the room and lick him.

He lumbers through the door, and I'm left alone in the space that's been mine since the beginning of the year. It's seen some changes, that's for sure. Eddie helped me move in. Three different men have helped me move out. I felt trapped at the beginning of the year. I now feel freer than I ever have in my life.

It took Dad cutting me off to realize that it wasn't good for me to rely on him for money when he wasn't prepared to give me the love and affection that he should. It was an empty link with him, impacting my attitude toward money and my sense of self-worth. Now I'm working and earning for myself, I see everything differently. I don't spend out of anger. I spend it out of necessity.

I have love to fill the empty parts of me.

I look in the mirror and touch my dark hair. It's grown out at the top, and I have to use a brown spray to touch it in so my red roots aren't visible.

It's the last thing left over from a time when I wanted to be a different person.

Now, I want to be true to who I really am. I want my little niece Lonie to touch my curls that are just like hers and tell me how pretty they are. I twist my hair into a bun and decide it's time, then I take one last look at the place I used to call home and leave it behind, ready for a new start.

Gabriella throws open the front door before any of us gets a chance to ring the bell and jogs down the front path before enveloping me in a fierce hug. "I can't believe we're going to be roomies. This is so exciting."

She's been saying the same thing since her mom told her I'm moving in. She doesn't know yet, but I bought us some sheet face masks and hand treatments so we can do them together later. It's been a while since I had Marie to do those kinds of girly things with.

Travis walks past us, smiling at his sister's excitement.

Last week, he asked me to move in with him rather than here. We've been hanging out so much since he returned from Germany. We all spend at least three nights a week at his place, thanks to the extra giant bed he added to his bedroom. It's the only place we can all get a good night's sleep together after our shenanigans.

And I need all the sleep I can get.

I turned Travis down, though.

Moving in is a big step, and if we're going to do it, I want it to be something we all do together. Travis's place isn't big enough for us all, and when we're together, our priorities aren't in the right place. Exams are looming. We need space to get through this chapter of our lives, and then we can focus on our relationship and not risk our futures because we can't keep our hands off each other.

I can't wait for the next chapter.

"Let her go," Travis tells his sister. "We need to get these boxes inside."

"Bossy."

Gabriella tosses her hair over her shoulder, grabs my hand, and marches us into the house. "I hope he doesn't boss you around like that," she hisses.

I snicker because she has no idea just how much I love his bossiness. I'm grateful that she's never asked me if Travis's kinky porn mags are reflected in our sex life! It's probably because she'd find her brother's sex life a gross topic to broach.

It takes thirty minutes for all my stuff to be taken upstairs. My men won't let me lift a finger, so I sit in the kitchen, eating chocolate muffins and strawberries while Darleen tells me about the trip she's planning with her boyfriend, Lucas.

HUGE GAMES

When Elias and Dornan leave for practice, I make my excuses and head to the mall.

The same hairdresser who dyed my hair chestnut leads me to a chair. "What am I doing today? Touching up your roots?"

I shake my head, grinning at her in the mirror. "I want to go back to my natural color."

She smooths her hands over my hair and grins back. "I knew you'd regret losing those beautiful red curls." She fluffs my chestnut curls. "It's going to take some work."

"That's fine," I say. "I enjoyed being a sassy brunette. It was fun. But I like the real me better."

It does take serious work and a lot of hours, but when she's done, my hair is almost the same as it was before. The color is slightly darker than my natural shade, but it's fine. It'll probably fade a little over time, anyway.

"My boyfriends are going to have a heart attack when they see me."

"Boyfriends?" She frowns, but then her face splits into a broad grin. "Boyfriends plural...those sexy boys you showed me last time?"

I laugh and scrunch my curls, so happy to have them back, already anticipating how Elias, Travis, and Dornan are going to react. "Yes. All those sexy boys."

"Good for you." She rests her hands on her wide hips. "If I was a few years younger..."

"I don't think there's an upper age limit to harem living," I say. "You just need to find men who like to share."

"It's not easy to find one man at my age who doesn't snore. Forget about men who want to share."

We both laugh, but I tell her not to give up on the idea. I never thought I'd find the kind of love I have.

I use my new key to open the door at Travis's family home—my home now. Inside, the TV is on at full volume, and a sportscaster is roaring out a play-by-play commentary. Men's voices rumble, and the sound of the extractor in the kitchen builds it into a cacophony of sound.

I make my way down the hall, finding Gabriella and Ellie in the kitchen with Darleen and Dalton. There is food everywhere. Dalton has his sleeves rolled up, revealing the intricate tattoos that his brother has inked for him over the years. He lifts a large tray of food from the oven and the steam is so intense, he has to hold it far away from his body.

Gabriella's the first one to notice my transformation.

"Your hair!" she gasps, leaving the salad she was dressing to look at me. "I'm so happy you're red again."

"Me, too," I smile, already feeling more like myself.

Travis, hearing the commotion, looks up from the game, his mouth falling open in shock. Ignoring the screen, he rises to look at me, followed closely by Dornan and Elias. "You went back."

"Celine's back," Elias whoops.

"She was only gone for three hours," Darleen laughs. "You guys are too needy."

"Not back back." Travis laughs. "Her hair." He fluffs my curls, making them even crazier than they were when I left the salon.

Dornan touches them, too. It's like they're discovering a rare plant or marveling over an alien from outer space.

"Okay, guys," I laugh, swiping their hands away. "It's just hair."

"No, it isn't," Dornan says. "It's a sign."

He gets it. They all get it, and I kiss them tenderly, one

by one, despite the audience.

"Food's ready," Dalton says, and there's a rumble from all the football-watching men. They fill the kitchen one by one, hovering around the table, waiting for a plate.

Colby, Seb, and Micky ensure Ellie puts her food first, then follow her around the buffet, heaping all the delicious options onto their plates. Kain and Blake compliment Dalton and Darleen for their efforts. The doorbell rings, and it's Lucas, Darleen's boyfriend, coming to join in the fun.

Travis is quick to hand me a plate and urge me closer. He slaps my ass and tells me to eat well, or I'll make his momma sad. He urges Elias forward, too. He knows how much he loves Darleen's cooking and is more than happy to share his mom's culinary skills with the two men he's joined with to love me.

I look around at the happy groups that have come together through love.

Our brand of relationships might not be considered normal, but I don't care what anyone else thinks.

We're not playing games. We're making a future filled with friendship, commitment, hope, and love.

I can't wait to see what happens next because I know I have Dornan, Elias, and Travis by my side through thick and thin.

No more games.

We're playing for keeps.

ABOUT THE AUTHOR

International bestselling author Stephanie Brother writes high heat love stories with a hint of the forbidden. Since 2015, she's been bringing to life handsome, flawed heroes who know how to treat their women. If you enjoy stories involving multiple lovers, including twins, triplets, stepbrothers, and their friends, you're in the right place. When it comes to books and men, Stephanie truly believes it's the more, the merrier.

She spends most of her day typing, drinking coffee, and interacting with readers.

Her books have been translated into German, French, and Spanish, and she has hit the Amazon bestseller list in seven countries.

Printed in Dunstable, United Kingdom